STAY WITH ME

A LAST FRONTIER LODGE NOVEL

J.H. CROIX

*E*li Brooks leaned his head back and swallowed a sigh. "It's fine, Mom. I'll swing by the bank later this afternoon," he said into his phone.

"I'm sorry to ask again so soon," his mother said, probably for the fifth time in the last five minutes.

"No need to apologize, Mom. How's Ryan?" he asked, biting back the frustration rising inside and trying to shift gears in the conversation.

"He's fine," she said quickly.

A horn honked nearby and Eli glanced over to see a car backing out of a parking space, the driver clearly not bothering to notice another car passing by. He bit back a laugh when he saw the other car simply veer around and keep going. The minor distraction helped him get through this call without his annoyance showing. He genuinely didn't mind giving his mother money to make ends meet, but he'd been getting suspicious lately that his father had moved back in due to the frequency of her requests for help. After a few more minutes of stilted conversation, he managed to get off the phone.

With a shake of his head, he started his truck and put it in gear. He glanced over to the passenger seat to make sure he hadn't left the bolts in the hardware store. His mother's call had come in while he was in line, distracting him. He rolled slowly through the parking lot. It was summer in Diamond Creek, Alaska, which meant the town was swarmed with tourists, and RV's and campers crowded the roads and parking lots, limiting visibility and generally contributing to plenty of driving mishaps. He stopped to wait for a giant camper as the driver backed up. After several failed attempts of the camper to successfully back out, Eli put his truck in park and climbed out with a sigh. He'd have to serve as the back up guide for the driver, or he'd be here all day.

* * *

JESSA HAMILTON STARED at the photo in her hand and swallowed against the tightness in her throat. She kept pulling this photo out and looking at it, as if she looked enough, something would be different. Yet, nothing changed. Walls blackened with smoke, charred furniture and nothing else recognizable. Only she knew what had been contained within its walls. Hot tears pressed against the back of her eyes, and she took a gulp of air. Her name was called, and she quickly slipped the photo in her purse and stood. She walked up to the small pick-up counter and grabbed the coffee with her name on it. Once she sat back down at her table, she took a sip and glanced out the windows. The view here was simply breathtaking—a picturesque bay sparkled under the sun with mountains rising tall on the far side. A glacier lay in a valley between two peaks, glowing translucent blue and almost mesmerizing her. The sheer beauty took her mind off the ashes of her life she'd left behind.

After a few more minutes of coffee and soaking in the

view, Jessa felt able to drive the last leg of her journey. She slung her purse over her shoulder and walked outside into the parking lot, her coffee cup warm in her hand. It was early summer in Diamond Creek, Alaska and the air had a definite chill to it. Her small blue truck was waiting for her. She climbed in and sighed. Right now, this truck was the closest thing she had to home. It held everything she owned, which at this point was the clothes she wore, a small bag of clothing, and a toolbox that contained her beloved paintbrushes and art supplies. She ran her good hand over the dashboard and gave it a loving pat. "Okay Blue, we've got a few errands, a short drive up the mountain and then you can take a break for a while."

She started the engine and put the truck in gear. She had to maneuver carefully with her left hand, which had been injured in the same fire that burned up the apartment she left behind. With a quick glance behind her, she started to back up when she felt a thump. She whipped her head further back and saw a black truck to the far corner of her line of sight. "Oh hell. Really? Did I really just back into someone?" she wondered aloud. "Sorry Blue, just gave you a little bump there. Here's hoping we didn't hurt the other truck." She laughed to herself, realizing she talked to Blue more than just about anyone. She took a deep breath and rolled the truck forward before putting it back in park. Another deep breath and she climbed out, prepared to face the music of an irate driver. She prayed she'd left nothing more than a small dent in the other truck.

When she walked to the back of her truck, she saw a man leaning against the corner of the black truck and immediately lost the ability to breathe. The man in question had dark brown hair and green eyes that locked onto her the moment she looked up at him. He wore a denim jacket over a navy blue t-shirt and faded jeans that were so worn, the soft fabric molded over his muscled thighs. A pair of scuffed brown leather boots completed the ensemble. His shoulders filled out his jacket, and she caught a glimpse of his muscled chest and abs in the gap where his jacket hung open. His thumb was hooked in a pocket. Her brain fuzzed and her pulse galloped. Desperate for air, she managed to force her lungs into gear and take a few gulps.

"Hi, um, I think I backed into you. I'm really sorry. I thought I looked, but I obviously didn't look enough. Is there any damage? Let me get my insurance card and..."

The man pushed away from the truck, shaking his head. "No need. Your bumper took the hit," he said, gesturing to Blue's rear bumper. "My bumper's so beat up, I probably wouldn't have noticed anyway."

Her eyes seemed stuck. She just stood there and stared at him. When he arched a brow in question, she finally managed to tear her eyes away and look at her bumper. The corner of Blue's rear bumper bore a round dent. The knot of tension in her chest loosened slightly. She'd been carrying the little ball of tension for so many weeks now, she was used to it. Any easing of it was a pleasant surprise. She took a breath and looked back at the man, her pulse rocketing again when she met his green gaze.

"Well, that's not too bad. Blue can live with it," she said, gently patting the bumper.

"Blue?"

"My truck. Her name is Blue," she offered in explanation.

"If that's how you name trucks, I guess you'd call mine Dusty," he said with a chuckle.

His eyes bounced from her truck to her. "You from Washington?"

"Good guess."

"Not a guess. Your license plate," he said, gesturing to it.

"Oh, right." She couldn't seem to think of what else to say, not when this way-too-sexy man had her tongue-tied and her thoughts fuzzy.

"If you're planning to get that dent banged out, my friend has a mechanic shop just down the street."

Normally, she would want to get the dent taken care of, but normally she wasn't flat broke. She shrugged. "I'm not sure when I'll have a chance to do that."

He nodded slowly. "Well, if you decide to get it fixed, Dan does good work. Can't miss it. It's the shop down the road, says Auto Shop outside."

"Just Auto Shop?"

"Yup. Dan keeps it simple. What brings you to Diamond Creek? Long drive from Washington. Well, long drive from just about anywhere outside of Alaska."

Jessa was doing her damnedest to get her pulse under control, but her pulse appeared to have a mind of its own. Aside from the fact that she couldn't seem to think clearly around this man, the last thing she wanted was to think about what brought her to Alaska. She took an unsteady breath and called upon her manners.

"I'm here visiting family for a bit."

"You have family here?"

"My brother, Gage Hamilton, runs Last Frontier Lodge. My other brother, Garrett, moved up here last year. He's married to Delia. I think her maiden name was Peters."

"Delia Peters is right. I've known her for a while. I do some business with Gage and met Garrett once or twice. Everyone in Diamond Creek is damn happy about the lodge being open again. I've been up there a few times to ski myself." His green eyes crinkled at the corners. "Suppose I could introduce myself. I'm Eli Brooks." He held a hand out.

Her arm moved of its own accord, lifting and placing her hand in his. His palm engulfed hers, the calloused surface and warmth sending shivers followed by heat rushing through her. Once her hand was in his, she froze again. After a long moment, too long to be polite, he slowly loosened his grip and released her palm. Another few beats passed before he spoke again.

"Don't suppose you'll tell me your name?"

Her cheeks heated. "Oh, oh, right. Jessa Hamilton." Right about now, she wouldn't have minded if a hole opened up in the ground to swallow her. Cliché or not, she would have liked somewhere to fall in and hide. Eli was doing nothing other than being polite, and she could barely hold a conversation with him.

"Nice to meet you, Jessa," Eli replied with a slow smile. "If you're here for a bit, I'll probably see you around. Diamond Creek's pretty small."

Her belly fluttered and her heart gave a little kick. What the hell was going on with her? She'd backed into Eli's truck, and now she was all but drooling on him. She realized she was about to enter into another long moment where she should say something. That's how conversation worked. One person said something, the other person listened and formulated a reply. If this were a game of tennis, she would have definitely lost because she couldn't manage to swing her racquet. She gathered her scrambled thoughts and forced herself to speak.

"Nice to meet you too. I'm sorry about bumping into your truck. It's been a long few days of driving. I'm glad your truck's okay."

Eli grinned. "No problem. Like I said, I probably wouldn't have noticed if you had." He stepped away and opened his truck door. "See you around," he said with a quick wave.

She watched while he drove away. A gust of wind blasted from the direction of the bay, blowing her hair wild.

$\mathcal{E}$li glanced in his rear view mirror and saw Jessa Hamilton standing in the parking lot. Her brown hair blew in a swirl around her face. He stopped where the parking lot met Main Street and watched as she brushed her hair back with one hand and turned to hurry back into her truck. She cradled one arm against her waist, and he wondered why. He turned out and headed toward his shop. He was looking at the road in front of him, but all he could see in his mind's eye were Jessa's eyes. He'd never seen eyes like hers before—smoky gray with glimpses of silver.

When he was driving by and saw her start to back up, he didn't have enough time to stop. For a flash, he was irritated as hell. Between the call from his mother, helping a hapless camper driver back up, and dealing with the general madness of his summer schedule, he'd had to bite back his frustration. Summer was the busiest time of year for him. Owning his own business was great, except for the fact that sometimes he only had himself to count on. He owned Game to Fish, a retail store and guiding business for the hordes of wilderness travelers that descended on Diamond

Creek once the snow melted. He'd been up since way too early this morning and didn't have time to deal with a fender bender. For a split second, he considered driving on past the little blue truck that bumped into him. He'd meant it when he said he wasn't worried about his bumper, but it seemed a tad rude to keep driving when she pulled forward and started to climb out of her truck.

One look at her chocolate brown hair, those silvery gray eyes, and her lush, curvy body, and his frustration evaporated. He could have cared less if she'd completely bashed his bumper. He forgot that he only had a few minutes to get back to his store. Now, he had to make up the minutes he lost and gunned his truck. Within moments, he came to a jerking stop in front of his store and grabbed the small bag from the hardware store. The doorbell jingled when he walked in, and Cliff Gibson glanced up from behind the counter.

"Hey Eli, did they have the bolts we need?" Cliff asked.

Eli tossed the small bag from the hardware store to Cliff. Cliff caught it and immediately dumped the bolts on the counter. Without a word, he stepped from behind the counter and strode to the front windows to climb on the ladder there.

"Need a hand?" Eli asked, slightly bemused by Cliff. Aside from himself, Cliff was Eli's primary employee. He had a few other employees, but Cliff was the only one involved in every aspect of his business from the retail store to fishing charters to guided hunts. Like Eli, Cliff had been born and raised in Alaska. He knew just about everything there was to know about fishing and hunting in the area. Sometimes, Eli was amazed at how responsible Cliff was given that he'd only graduated from college a year ago.

Cliff glanced down from the ladder. "I left the bolts on the counter," he said with a grin.

Eli stepped to the counter and snagged the two bolts.

After he handed them over, he watched while Cliff carefully adjusted the display rack hanging from the ceiling and replaced the two broken bolts on one side. Once he was done, Cliff returned the ladder to its storage spot in the back room and immediately got back to work on ordering supplies and gear for several upcoming trips.

Eli walked into his office and looked around. His office was small and crowded. A small desk and chair were tucked into the corner with two chairs on the other side of the desk. The rest of the office was filled with a jumble of fishing and hunting gear, everything from fishing rods and hunting knives to high-end outerwear. He kicked a box out of the way and sat down at his desk, quickly opening his laptop and starting to plow through emails for reservations on guided hunts. As usual, he simultaneously tapped the speaker button on his office phone and started listening to his voice mails. The first two were from customers and the third was his mother.

"Hey Eli, haven't heard from you in a while. I wanted to see how you were doing. If you get a chance, give me a call." There was a long pause. He could hear his mother take a deep breath. *"I'm doing okay, just so you know. Love you."* The recording held another deep breath from his mother before she hung up. She must have called here before she tried his cell phone.

Eli tried to keep reading his emails, but nothing was registering in his brain. He leaned back in his chair and ran a hand through his hair. His mind circled back to his mother's call earlier. He'd taken purposeful steps to cut his ties with his family, almost solely due to his father. He hadn't spoken to his father in over a decade when he moved to Diamond Creek from Juneau. Alaska was such a part of him, he couldn't imagine living anywhere else, so he moved far enough away to get some distance—literally and figuratively.

The only time his mother called was when she needed money. She only needed money when his father went on a drinking binge and blew through what little she had to get by. Eli wished she would call more, but he knew she didn't because she felt guilty. Even though he'd done his damnedest to keep his father boxed out of his mother's life, his father still had access to her bank accounts and she didn't have it in her to cut him off. Eli kept in touch with his mother and tried to keep tabs on his younger brother Ryan, but he could only do so much from a distance. He was in a much better place than he had been when he moved away, but one thing that helped bring him peace was steering clear of the wrecking ball that was his father. The thorn in that peace was the guilt he felt leaving his mother and Ryan behind.

Eli shook his head sharply and forced himself to focus on work. He confirmed a few reservations and made it through the rest of his emails before walking back out front. Cliff was talking to a few early tourists and issuing temporary fishing permits for them. He glanced to Eli when he rounded the back counter.

"I'm headed to the bank and maybe a coffee run. Need anything?" Eli asked.

"Thought you were getting coffee earlier," Cliff replied with a grin.

Eli shrugged. "Forgot. How about now?"

"Sure thing. Just get me whatever the house coffee is at Misty Mountain today."

"You got it. Be back in a bit."

Eli swung through the bank and transferred enough money into his mother's bank account that she could get by for a few months. Shortly thereafter, he walked out of Misty Mountain Café, took a welcome gulp of coffee and climbed back into his truck, tucking Cliff's coffee in the holder while he kept his in hand. As he drove down Main Street, he saw

Jessa's bright blue truck at the grocery store. He found himself pulling into the parking lot and walking into the store, compelled solely by the possibility he might see Jessa again.

Grabbing a cart, he started tossing groceries in as he passed through the aisles. He couldn't quite believe he was meandering through a store, hoping for an incidental encounter with a woman he'd met for a total of maybe three minutes, five tops. Yet, here he was. He was jittery with restless energy between the jolt of coffee, his call with his mother, and this out of the blue attraction to a woman he barely knew. He practically careened around the end of an aisle, swinging his cart into the next aisle when he bumped into something, or rather someone.

"Ooomph!"

At the muffled comment, he glanced up to find Jessa standing in front of the pasta section. His cart rolled back into him. He took in a few more details this time. She wore a denim skirt over blue leggings with a fitted white t-shirt and a gray fleece jacket tied around her waist. A pair of black cowboy boots that looked beyond worn completed her attire. As his gaze traveled to her face, her amazing silver gray eyes met his. Her hair was tied in a loose knot atop her head with wispy brown curls framing her heart-shaped face.

"I'm sorry! I wasn't even paying attention. Are you okay?"

She cradled her left hand against her, the same one he'd noticed earlier. "I'm fine," she said quickly. "Just a little bump. My hip can take it." Her mouth hooked in a rueful smile at that.

"You sure?" he asked with a nod toward her hand.

She glanced down and then up again. "Oh, you didn't hit my hand. I, uh, injured this a few weeks ago." She held it out, and he saw her hand was sporting a gauze wrap. "It's healing fine, but it seems like I'm always walking around with it pinned to my side. I don't even think about it."

All kinds of questions tumbled through his mind. He didn't know what it was about Jessa, but she made him want to know everything about her. He didn't think it was prudent to bombard her with questions, so he merely nodded. "Well, I'm glad you're okay."

She laughed softly. "You didn't hit me nearly as hard as I hit you with Blue."

He chuckled. "Yeah, but that was my truck. This was you."

One shoulder lifted in a slow shrug. "I'm fine. No need to worry." Her eyes canted down into his grocery cart. "Wow, that's a lot of frozen pizza."

He looked into his cart and saw he'd tossed probably ten frozen pizzas in there, along with an array of snacks. He shook his head and met her eyes again. "Not the best cook. Once I've got some fish stocked up, I'll be eating a bit better. Then comes hunting season in the fall. Usually, I've got enough to make it through to summer, but my back up freezer died a few weeks ago, so I lost my stock," he offered with a rueful smile.

Jessa's eyes widened, alarmingly so. "You fish? And hunt?"

He nodded slowly. "I do. Hard to find anyone in Alaska who doesn't."

Jessa was quiet for a long moment. "Oh." She fiddled with the sleeve of her fleece jacket, twining it around her good hand. "I guess you don't get many vegetarians here, huh?"

Eli couldn't help but laugh as he shrugged. "Maybe a few. We get plenty of people visiting just because they like to fish and hunt though."

Jessa bit her lip, her teeth denting its plump softness and

sending a jolt of awareness through him. "Oh. Well, I'm a vegetarian." She offered this with a slight smile.

"There's plenty to do here that doesn't involve hunting and fishing, but I'd suggest you steer clear of the harbor when the boats are coming in."

"How come?"

"Because once fishing season starts, when the boats roll in, that means fish," he offered with a grin.

CHAPTER 3

Jessa came awake with a start. She pushed herself up and leaned back against the head-board. Her heart was pounding and her skin was damp with sweat. She gulped in air and shoved away the flames flickering in her sleepy brain. It had been over three weeks since the fire, but she could only manage to sleep through roughly every other night. The nights in between found her jolted awake, fear choking her as she felt trapped again in her apartment with flames climbing the walls. She didn't remember much from the fire other than waking up with it all around her, struggling to breathe through the smoke and scrambling to get out. She vaguely remembered gulping in the cool air once she crashed through the window, but that was it.

She forced herself to breathe slowly and kicked the covers back. A few minutes later and she stood in the shower, cool water cascading over her. She'd never in her life considered anything other than a hot shower until she woke from these fire dreams. Several moments of cool water washed away the fear and then she turned up the heat and savored the hot water. Once her mind was clear, she stepped out and toweled off, snagging the luxurious terry cloth robe hanging on the back of the door.

She'd visited Gage and Marley here a few times now, but she still marveled at what Gage had done. He'd come up here on his own to restore Last Frontier Lodge to its former glory after its closure over two decades ago. He'd pulled that off and then some. He was headed into the ski lodge's third season, and it was already fully booked for next winter. It was also mostly booked up for the summer with Gage focusing on pulling in business from the tourists that poured into Alaska every summer, seeking a glimpse of its wilderness and breathtaking scenery.

As she padded out of the bathroom, her breath caught in her throat. Even though it wasn't quite five in the morning, the sun was already cresting behind the mountains. Jessa had heard summers in Alaska meant long days and short nights, but it was still strange to wake at this hour and find the sun rising. Her suite, along with every suite at the lodge, had a clear view of the ski slopes behind it and the mountain range stretching beyond. To one side of the view lay Kachemak Bay, its water glimmering in the soft light of dawn. Jessa cast her eyes up to the horizon where faint rays of light angled skyward behind the mountains mingled with streaks of pink and lavender.

After a few moments, she turned away and climbed back in bed. She propped herself up on the pillows and pulled a book out of the nightstand drawer. She was an avid reader, but her books and her digital reader had been destroyed in the apartment fire. Marley had given her free rein to borrow from her own collection of books and a rotating pool of books for guests at the lodge. Knowing she likely wouldn't fall asleep again, Jessa settled in to read. She was faintly surprised when she woke later, the book tumbled to the side of her on the bed and bright sun splashing through the windows. She was squished down into the pillows, so she slowly pushed them out of the way and sat up again. A glance at the clock told her it was past nine in the morning. She swung her legs off the bed and stood, straightening her robe as she did.

A little while later, Jessa walked into the lodge kitchen, the scent of freshly baked bread assailing her immediately. The large kitchen was a whir of activity with two line cooks standing side by side at a grill, quickly preparing orders, and waitresses spinning in and out of the kitchen. The swinging door that led into the restaurant was in motion constantly. Jessa glanced around, wondering what she should do. Marley had insisted she make herself at home at the lodge, but she didn't know quite what that meant. She'd yet to meet all of the staff, so she wasn't sure if they even knew who she was. She heard her name and looked in the direction of the voice to find her sister-in-law Delia standing by a doorway.

"Hey Delia!" Jessa called out as she made her way across the kitchen to Delia's side.

Delia immediately pulled her into a warm hug. When she stepped back, she started to slide her hands down Jessa's arms, but paused when her hand bumped into the bend of Jessa's elbow. Her eyes canted down and back up. "I didn't know you got hurt in the fire," she said, her voice soft.

Jessa shrugged. "Nothing major. I got a few burns on my hand and arm when I climbed out the window."

Delia turned and gently tugged Jessa through the door into an office. Jessa glanced around, her eyes taking in the space. A fern hanging in the window and a multicolored rug in front of the desk gave the office a warm, lively feeling. Delia's desk held a laptop and papers scattered over its surface. Delia sat on a small couch across from her desk and patted the cushions, indicating for Jessa to join her.

"So, how was your trip? I still can't believe you did the drive all the way from Washington by yourself."

Jessa sat down on the edge of the couch and looked over at Delia. If someone had told her Garrett would fall for Delia, she'd never have guessed it. Yet, once she saw them together, there was absolutely no question Delia was perfect for Garrett. Her honey gold hair was pulled back into a loose ponytail, wispy curls framing her face. Her blue eyes were warm, and she carried a soft energy that soothed the sharp edges of Garrett. Garrett was Jessa's second oldest brother and Becca's twin. Like Becca, he was a brilliant attorney. His brains, sharp wit, and strategic thinking had catapulted him into being one of the most sought after corporate attorneys in Seattle. Jessa had watched while he chased success madly, yet even when he was wealthy and at the top of his game, he'd brimmed with restlessness and dissatisfaction. Delia came into his life and he fell so hard for her that he said goodbye to his corporate career and moved to Diamond Creek. Jessa was beyond happy to see how well he was doing now.

She looked into Delia's gaze and fiddled with the silver chain that hung around her neck. "The drive was long, but it was beautiful. Have you ever driven the Alcan Highway?" She was referring to the Alaska-Canadian Highway, abbreviated for so many years, it was known simply as the Alcan. The lone highway through the Yukon into Alaska stretched 1382 miles through pristine lands, following along glacial rivers, winding through mountains, dipping into valleys, and hugging the shorelines of massive lakes. Portions of the highway were so remote, even today sections of it remained gravel.

Delia shook her head. "Nope. I was born and raised in

Diamond Creek, but I haven't traveled too much around Alaska beyond between here and Anchorage."

"Well, just getting from the border of Alaska to here is over three days of driving," Jessa commented wryly.

Delia laughed softly before her gaze sobered. "So, how are you? Garrett's been worried ever since you called a few weeks ago. We've all been worried, but you know how Garrett gets."

Jessa felt a little twinge in her heart. Garrett held his cards close, but he was a protective older brother. He'd sent a few potential customers her way over the years. Seeing as her income relied on people willing to pay pretty high prices for her individually designed and painted furniture, he'd helped her maintain her business. That thought sent a knot of fear and anxiety spiraling through her. What little of her artsy furniture she'd stocked up had been burned to ashes in the apartment fire. She'd used the second bedroom in her small two-bedroom apartment for storage and her living room to paint. Everything there was gone, gone, gone. Her thoughts must have shown on her face because Delia reached over and squeezed her hand.

Jessa glanced over and took a breath. "I'm okay. It's just been a long few weeks." She lifted her injured hand. "This really isn't much, but it hurt like hell at first. The doctor told me I need to keep putting the burn cream on and changing the bandage every day until the skin heals over. It's almost there."

Delia nodded. "How are *you* though?"

Jessa slumped against the couch cushions. "I don't know. I lost everything in that fire. Everything. I didn't have any money saved up, so I pretty much have to start all over. I didn't know where to go, so here I am." She lifted her good hand and let it fall against the armrest.

Delia's eyes coasted over her, and Jessa felt like she could see right through her. Delia couldn't know this because it wasn't something Jessa talked about to anyone, but she'd always felt like the bumbling sibling in her family. She was the youngest and had never quite felt as if she was put together as well as the rest. Gage was, well, Gage. He was a Navy SEAL with all of the qualities associated with being a SEAL naturally part of his personality. On top of that, he was warm, kind and the rock of their family. Then came Garrett and Becca, twins who were so different and so alike. Both were brilliant attorneys and fearless. The only time Jessa had seen Becca vulnerable was when she saw a look between her and Aidan. Aidan seemed to be the only person who got behind Becca's guard. Next came Sawyer who'd followed Gage's footsteps into the Navy SEAL's and was now traveling the world on one classified mission after another.

Then, there was Jessa. She'd always been a step out of tune. She'd done perfectly fine in school, but she'd chafed at the structure. Once she got to college, she found her calling in painting classes. Even though she loved designing and painting furniture, she always felt like she should have tried to make herself conform to something more traditional. A stint as a paralegal and then in banking had made her miserable. It didn't help that she tended to barely scrape by even when she had good months. In the last few weeks, she'd spent hours and hours beating herself up for not having some kind of long term plan. An apartment fire started by the neighbor down the hall who fell asleep with a lit cigarette had burned up her life and illuminated just how flimsy its foundation was. Broke with nothing to fall back on, Jessa couldn't bring herself to move back in with her parents, so she'd called her brothers and spent what little money she had left on the gas to get herself here. A knock on Delia's office door broke through Jessa's train of thought.

"Yes?" Delia called out.

The door opened and Garrett stepped through. Jessa

forgot how depressed she was about the shambles of her life and leapt up. "Garrett!"

He caught her in a swift hug before stepping back. "Hey sis. Gage told me you got in late yesterday afternoon. I'm sorry I couldn't make it for dinner last night. We had to go to Nick's school concert. I thought about asking if you wanted to come, but I figured after a drive like that, you probably weren't up for a school concert. They're a special kind of music and you never know what to expect," Garrett said with a grin.

"It might have been fun, but I was exhausted. What're you up to today?"

"Breakfast with you." He looked past her to Delia who stood up from the couch. "You have time to join us for a bit?"

Delia glanced at her watch quickly. "Enough time for a coffee. I'll meet you two out there in a few minutes. I have to check on the soufflé I left in the oven."

Jessa followed Garrett through the kitchen out into the lodge's restaurant while Delia veered over to the massive baking oven on the back wall in the kitchen. Once Garrett pushed through the swinging door into the restaurant, he immediately sat down in a booth in the closest corner.

Jessa looked around and saw the cluster of customers waiting in the reception area. "Shouldn't we wait?" she asked, gesturing in that direction.

"Nope. Gage and Marley keep this booth for family. Don't go feeling bad about it. Look around. This is the only booth that doesn't have the nice new leather upholstery. It's also way back here in the corner and doesn't have the view like most of the tables do."

Jessa scanned the room and saw he was correct, not that she doubted it. She sat down across from him. When she looked over at his sharp blue eyes and his ever-present half-grin, the knot of tension inside eased a little more. Even if she often felt like the oddball of her family, she loved her siblings and felt more comfortable with them than anyone in the world.

"So, how was the drive?" Garrett asked.

"Long and beautiful. You and Delia should take a trip sometime with Nick on the Alcan. I bet he'd have a blast."

"Oh, I'm sure he would. Maybe someday we will." Garrett scanned her face and looked down at her bandaged hand, his eyes narrowing at that. "You said you didn't get hurt in the fire," he said, his words brusque.

Jessa felt a flash of frustration. Having three protective older brothers was sometimes annoying. She shoved the feelings away because she knew Garrett was only asking because he cared. "It's nothing to worry about. I burned my hand when I was trying to get out. It's almost healed up."

Garrett didn't look convinced, but he let it drop, unfortunately moving on to a more uncomfortable topic. "What's your plan now?"

Jessa shrugged. "I dunno. I lost everything in the fire. I'm not sure what to do now. I figured it was the perfect time to come to Alaska. Isn't this the place people go when they need a fresh start and to get back in touch with, well, life or something?"

Garrett smiled, a hint of rue in his eyes. "Maybe. I suppose that's what I did and it turned out to be the best decision I've ever made."

At that moment, the swinging door opened from the kitchen and Delia came through. She held a tray with three large mugs on it. She quickly set the tray in the center of the table and slipped into the booth beside Garrett. "Fresh coffee from my amazing new espresso machine!" she announced as she handed a mug to Jessa and then Garrett.

Garrett dipped his head and dropped a kiss on the side of Delia's neck. "I was just telling Jessa coming to Alaska last year was the best decision I ever made. Actually, that's not right. It wasn't Alaska, it was you."

Delia's cheeks flushed. She kept her eyes on Jessa. "Try the coffee. Let me know what you think. I wasn't sure what your preference was, so I made a triple shot Americano. Seems like everyone in your family likes their coffee strong and dark."

Garrett lifted his mug and took a long swallow, leaning his head back with a sigh. "It's perfect." His eyes caught Jessa's again. "She even makes the best coffee."

Jessa giggled, enjoying how relaxed and easygoing Garrett was with Delia. She took a sip of her own coffee. "Oh, this is amazing! You guessed right by the way. I like my coffee dark and strong."

Delia laughed softly. "Good to know. So what's on the schedule for today?" she asked generally.

Seeing as Jessa had absolutely no plans whatsoever, she was relieved when Garrett immediately answered.

"After breakfast, I'm headed to the office. I've got some work to do on that zoning case."

Delia nodded and started to reply when her name was called from the front of the restaurant. "I'd better go. Harry's up to his ears out front since our breakfast hostess called out sick. Natalie apparently got a fishhook caught in the back of her head yesterday. She said they had to shave her hair to stitch it up. She doesn't know when she can work again." Delia shook her head and sighed. "My guess is she won't be in for weeks. Natalie likes to look good, and her partial buzz cut probably won't meet her standards. That means I've got to figure out how to cover her shifts."

Garrett rolled his eyes. "It's not like you have to hold her job for her forever."

Delia's eyes widened. "If I let her go over this, no one would want to work here. Diamond Creek's not much bigger than a thimble. Everyone would know and I'd look like a bitch."

"I can help," Jessa said, suddenly energized at the idea of being useful somehow.

Delia and Garrett looked to her in unison. Delia's eyes immediately glanced down at Jessa's bandaged hand. "I don't know if…"

"My hand is fine! I just have to be a little careful. I waited tables all through college. If the hostess part is mostly seating customers and helping out to fill waters and coffees, I can do that with one hand. In another week or so, I could even help waiting tables. Please let me help."

Delia took a sip of coffee, her eyes considering, before she nodded. "Okay, but not today. I'll check with Harry about Natalie's schedule and you can start covering her next shift. This way, I can do a run through with you later tonight." A slow grin spread across her face. "This is awesome!"

Jessa felt a little bubble of joy inside and returned Delia's grin. She liked to help and was craving something to help her feel grounded and useful again. Helping Delia when she needed it gave her a little boost inside and right now, she could use every boost she could get.

Delia slipped out of the booth. "Okay, make sure to help yourself to the buffet. We have some amazing smoked salmon to go with the bagels and cream cheese."

Garrett caught her hand as she started to turn away. He leaned over and dropped a kiss on the inside of her wrist. "See you tonight."

After Delia rushed off, Garrett looked across to Jessa. "Well, you'll be busy if that's what you were hoping."

"I love being busy. Maybe I wasn't sure what I planned to do when I got here, but I don't want to just sit around."

Garrett grinned. "No worries there. This place is

hopping all day up through about midnight. Just promise me you'll take it easy on your hand if you need to."

Jessa rolled her eyes. "Oh my god. Don't worry about me. My hand is healing up just fine. I can certainly handle managing a waitlist and walking customers to their tables. Right now I'm starving though, so let's get some food." She slid out of the booth and headed over to the buffet.

A splash of seawater hit Eli right in the face. He wiped his face on his sleeve and held on to the fishing line. "Keep reeling it in!" he called out, glancing over his shoulder at the man standing a few feet behind him on the boat.

Eli and Cliff were running a fishing charter today. Two brothers, Ed and Jack Rogers, and their two sons, Lee and Toby, were handling the semi-rough seas well today. Kachemak Bay was stirred up with a steady wind cutting across it. Cliff was holding the wheel of the charter boat, keeping the boat at a slow pace through the water. They were fishing for silver salmon. So far, their customers had caught one each and were all hoping for one more, the daily limit at two apiece. Silver salmon were considered some of the most fun fish to catch for anglers. They were strong, aggressive and acrobatic. Eli had been relieved to discover the four men with them today were fairly experienced. At the moment, he was standing by the rail, ready to net the fish, as Ed was close to bringing in another salmon. The wily salmon had been playing the line for close to an hour now. Ed was tiring, as he should've been, so Eli wanted to make sure he didn't lose the fish at the last minute.

Another small wave crested just in front of them, splashing the side of the boat and Eli's face. He chuckled as the silver salmon gave a twisting flip just a few feet away. "You've almost got it," he called over his shoulder.

Seconds later and the salmon was right by his hand. He grabbed the net and dipped it in to bring the fish up and over. Ed came to his side. "Damn, I know that's a good sized silver, but hard to believe a fish that size nearly wore me out."

"Silvers make you work for it," Eli replied and handed over the fish whacker as he stood and got out of the way.

Cliff tossed him a towel from his station by the wheel. Eli immediately wiped his face with it and turned to check if Ed needed any help. He was already carrying the fish to the back of the boat where a large cooler waited. He set the fish carefully inside and closed the cooler. Eli stepped past Cliff and walked down the short set of stairs into the tiny, utilitarian boat cabin. He opened the small freezer and tugged out another bag of ice, the only thing they kept in there. Returning to the deck, he carted the ice to the cooler and carefully poured it over the fish, sifting it with his fingers to ensure the fish were fully covered.

A while later, Eli did a last check on the boat deck to make sure everything was tidied up before he locked the cabin and left the harbor. Cliff had left with the customers to deliver their fish to the Fish Factory, a local business down the road from the harbor that catered to locals and tourists by filleting and flash freezing fish. They ran such a brisk business in the summer that they were open until midnight every day. The long days of Alaskan summers lent themselves to long days on the water. Eli strode down the harbor dock and paused when he reached the top. Turning to face the bay, he savored the salty, briny scent of the ocean air. Today's trip had been fairly short, so it was only late afternoon. The sun was just beginning its slide down the sky, glinting off the surface of the bay. The mountains across were dark against the brightness. Mount Augustine, one of several volcanoes nearby, stood sentry beyond the bay in Cook Inlet, rising tall out of the waters. An eagle flew low over the water, snatching a fish out as it swooped up swiftly. He tracked the fierce bird as it flew to land on the rocky beach and immediately tore into the fish.

Eli turned and walked toward the harbor parking lot. His eyes were on the ground as he headed toward his truck parked in the far corner. He heard a voice that sent a ping through his center. He lifted his eyes and almost laughed aloud when he realized he'd unconsciously recognized Jessa's voice. Ever since he'd seen her yesterday, he'd had a hard time not thinking about her. She was walking along a path that led from the beach to the parking lot. As he watched, he realized she was talking to a crow who was hopping along the edge of the tall grasses flanking the path. She leaned over and held her hand out. The crow paused and looked up at her and then continued hopping.

He couldn't keep his eyes off of Jessa as she walked the remaining short distance to the parking lot. Her chocolate brown hair was loose today, falling around her shoulders. As she got closer, he realized she had gold streaks in her hair, which shone in the sunlight. She wore leggings again and his eyes automatically traced up her legs and over the curve of her lush hips. Her flannel shirt was unbuttoned, revealing a fitted tank top that hugged her ample breasts. A pair of bright red rubber boots completed her attire and brought a smile to his face. Given that his body had gone tight with lust the moment he laid eyes on her, anything to snap him out of it was a good thing. He forgot he was staring when he realized she'd noticed him.

Jessa turned toward him and stopped a few feet away. "Hi," she said simply.

He took in her silvery-gray eyes and saw something flash in their depths. After several beats, he realized he hadn't replied. "Hey there. Taking a walk on the beach?"

She nodded. "It's so beautiful here. How are you?"

"Good. Just in from running a charter trip."

"Oh, you mean like when you take people out on guided fishing trips?"

"Exactly. That's what I do. Well, not just that, although fishing charters make up at least half my business in the summer." He recalled she was a vegetarian and had a moment where he didn't know if it was a good idea for her to know what he did. Then, he realized it was downright ridiculous to try to hide that from her just because she was the sexiest woman he'd ever met. Because if there was one thing he was sure of, it was that he didn't do relationships. Watching the toxic stew of his parents' marriage had made it easy to avoid entanglements. He continued. "I own a wilderness guiding and retail business. My life is fishing, hunting and selling the gear for it."

"Oh. Well, I guess you make good money around here, huh?"

"I stay busy if that's what you mean."

He found it hard to stay focused when a loose curl blew wild over her face. She tried to catch it and missed. Before he realized what he was doing, he'd stepped right in front of her and lifted a hand to brush the errant lock of hair out of her eyes. When he tucked it behind her ear, he felt the hitch of her breath. His hand seemed to have a mind of its own. The second he felt the soft skin behind her ear, his thumb stroked down, savoring the silky feel. He lifted his eyes to find hers had gone dark and smoky. He stood close enough that he could feel the rise and fall of her breath. He ached to pull her into his arms and feel the soft, lush curves of her against him. Under normal circumstances, he'd never have found himself in this situation, inches away from a woman he barely knew with lust coursing through him so fast, he could barely think. Jessa had upended any sense of normal and knocked him sideways into this burning attraction.

Oddly, though he'd only encountered Jessa a total of three times now if he counted this one, he somehow felt as if he knew her much better than he possibly could. He felt comfortable with her, albeit the disconcerting attraction. The air around them felt charged, alive with the connection between them. As he stood in front of her, his hand slipped down along the downy skin of her neck and laced into the hair at her nape. With not a single thought passing through his brain, he moved on instinct and dipped his head. Her lips were bow-shaped and full, so tempting, all he wanted was to know how they felt under his.

JESSA STOOD THERE with Eli inches away, the feel of his hand in her hair sending a current of electricity down her spine. All she wanted was to twine herself against him and lose herself. She was rattled by the depth of her pull toward him, but her body seemed to be running the show, kicking any doubts to the curb temporarily. Eli's lips caught hers. He moved slowly, almost a question at first. The sensation of his warm mouth against hers sent a shock of heat through her. She gasped and his tongue swept inside, and she all but went up into flames. His kiss was confident and strong, his tongue stroking against hers in between tracing her lips. Within seconds, she was drenched, inside and out. She arched into his kiss, wanting more. His hand loosened in her hair and slid down her back, creating a path of shivering heat. She hadn't realized it, but she'd plastered herself against him. When his hand slid over her bottom, she pressed closer and sighed when she felt the heat of his hard shaft against her.

Suddenly, he tore his lips away and swore roughly. He didn't move away, but his hand stroked up over her bottom, coming to rest in the dip of her waist. Reality filtered into Jessa's awareness and she tucked her head into Eli's shoulder, not quite believing that she'd been so out of her mind with need, she'd wanted much more than a kiss from this man she barely knew while they stood in a public parking lot. Embarrassment flooded through her, notching up the heat already burning inside of her. The sound of distant voices reached her. She forced herself to lift her head and found his mossy green eyes looking down at her. Her belly fluttered at the desire reflected there.

"I, um, I..." she started and stopped, unable to articulate anything.

"Well. I'm not sure what happened there. I'm, uh, sorry about that. I let things get away from me there," Eli said, his voice husky.

A giggle slipped out, and she blushed. She was embarrassed, and she wasn't. It was all just so unexpected and... hot. Sweet hell. Eli made her want him like she'd never wanted anyone. She bit her lip and took a breath. All the while, his eyes were on her. Hot and bothered didn't even begin to capture how she felt. She marshaled herself inside. "Do you usually just walk up and kiss women like this?" she asked archly, teasing him.

His sun-burnished cheeks reddened slightly. He shook his head slowly. "No, never actually."

She giggled again and slipped her hand up around his neck, tugging him down for another taste of him. She meant to be bold, but the second his tongue stroked against hers again, she almost lost herself again. She broke away, flushed and hot to her core. "Well, we're even now," she managed to say.

His low laugh sent another wave of need coursing through her. He slowly moved away, and she instantly missed the feel of his hard body against hers. When he stood a few feet away, a gust of wind came off the water. The air was brisk and cool, knocking her out of her semi-trance. When she looked back over at Eli, her breath caught. Dear God, the man was a danger to her sanity. He was all kinds of sexy and rugged. He wore a long-sleeved t-shirt that somehow managed to outline every inch of his fit body. His chest was all muscle. Faded jeans hugged his muscled legs. Given what it sounded like he did for a living, he wasn't in shape because he worked out, he was in shape because he lived a life that meant using his body to its fullest. She'd never thought she'd be turned on by a man like him. She'd imagined herself somehow finding another artist who would appreciate her whimsical furniture and her commitment to finding a way to make a living that didn't mean she had to take a job she hated just to pay the bills.

While she couldn't have said she had a clear idea what that man would be to her, Eli was just...all man, pure masculinity. Even now being several feet away, it was as if a current encircled them. As she stood there, unable to figure out what to say next, a crow's call came nearby, sharp and clear. She turned to see the crow in question sitting atop the small sign labeled "Otter Cove Harbor" near the entrance to the path with an arrow pointing toward the boat harbor. The crow called again, staring right at her as it did.

"Well, hello," she replied, only to blush furiously when she heard Eli's low chuckle.

She swung to him and shrugged sheepishly. "Sometimes I talk to birds and animals."

His warm grin sent another wash of heat through her. Dear God this man had one hell of an effect on her.

Someone called Eli's name from across the parking lot, and he turned. "Yeah?" he called out in reply.

A truck was coming in their direction and slowed to a stop beside where they stood. A young man with blondish-brown hair and brown eyes glanced between them before he spoke. "Just checking to see what time you wanted to head out tomorrow."

"Let's aim for seven. That's early, but not so early our customers will end up being late." He paused, his eyes flicking between the young man and Jessa. "Cliff, this is Jessa Hamilton. She's the person I met in the parking lot yesterday. Her brother owns Last Frontier Lodge. And Jessa, this is Cliff. He's my main employee and basically helps me keep my sanity when things get crazy in the summer."

Eli's roguish grin sent her stomach in a slow flip. She managed not to throw herself at him, although he made her want to do just that. Instead, she smiled politely and looked at Cliff. "Nice to meet you."

Cliff nodded and winked. "So you must be the woman who backed into Eli yesterday?"

Jessa blushed. Again. Maybe it wasn't precisely because Eli flustered her beyond recognition, but it would be nice if she could do something other than blush around him. "That's me, but I didn't hurt his truck, just got a little dent in mine."

Cliff grinned. "Even if you had dented his truck, it would've been hard to find."

Eli laughed and shook his head. "No need to give my truck a hard time, or Jessa."

Cliff put his truck in gear and grinned again. "All in fun," he replied. "See you a few minutes before seven tomorrow."

Eli waved as Cliff drove off. He turned back to Jessa, pulling a set of keys out of his pocket. "I should get going." He paused for a long moment. "Any idea how long you'll be in Diamond Creek?"

His question zoomed right into the center of her uncertainty about the shambles of her life. She mentally shook herself and aimed for a casual shrug. "I'm not sure right now. At least for a month or two."

A month or two? You have no idea what you're doing or where you're going next. You can't even afford to drive back to Seattle. Unless a miracle happens, you're stuck for now.

Unaware of her mental machinations, Eli nodded, his eyes considering. "Don't suppose you'd want to try a trip out in the bay?"

"You mean like on a boat?" The moment the question left her mouth, Jessa mentally kicked herself. *As if there's another way to get out there.*

He smiled slowly. "Exactly. If you can handle the fishing part of it, you might like it."

"Would I have to fish myself?"

"Oh no. Just thought I'd give you an open invite to come out sometime with us. We run trips almost every other day, so if you'd like a chance to see the far side of the bay, let me know."

Before she realized it, she was nodding. The truth was, she was a vegetarian, but she'd never been too dedicated. It was more for health reasons and due to her concerns about mass meat production, not because she was queasy about eating animals. Outside of places such as Alaska, it was near impossible to routinely eat animal products that weren't part of the chain of mass production. The other truth was she'd give just about anything for more time in Eli's company. She'd also love to see the far side of the bay where a glacier shimmered translucent blue under the sun.

Eli graced her with another of his roguish grins, his green eyes locking onto hers. She was surprised sparks didn't fly up in the air around her when he smiled. Her body hummed with need.

"How about you let me know when you want to come with us?" He pulled out his phone, tapping the screen. "Give me your number and I'll text you our schedule."

She quickly recited his number and fumbled for her phone. "Let me get your number…"

"Just texted you. You'll see it," he replied quickly.

They stood there for several more beats, simply looking at each other. Just when Jessa was beginning to think she needed to get some kind of grip and behave normally, Eli took a step back and started to turn. "I guess I'll see you when you're ready for that boat ride."

CHAPTER 5

Eli pulled up in front of Game to Fish. It was going on midnight, but his store's alarm system had sent him an alert that there was motion outside the store. When he first got the alert, he'd surmised the motion sensors had been tripped due to wildlife walking by, likely a moose or a porcupine, the most frequent visitors in the downtown area at night. After a few minutes, the alert repeated itself several more times. As of yet, none of the sensors for the windows or doors had gone off, leading Eli to assume no one had broken in yet. He'd dragged himself off of his couch to come down and check because he didn't want to risk someone actually breaking in. His retail store held a number of high value items. Beyond the pricey outdoor gear he stocked, he sold guns and fishing equipment, items that cost plenty of money and were in high demand in tourist rich Southcentral Alaska.

He turned his truck off and glanced around. Nothing appeared amiss. The outside lights were on, keeping the parking lot bright in the darkness. He stepped out of his truck and quietly closed the door. He let himself inside and did a quick tour, finding nothing out of the ordinary. As he walked from his office back toward the front of the store, he heard motion outside. He moved swiftly, stepping through the door and moving around the building to the source of the sound. When he came around the rear corner of the building, he stopped when he saw a tent tucked into the trees. His store was on a downtown street where a small cliff rose up behind it. Spruce trees were scattered on the level portion of the ground behind his store. Whoever had set up the tent appeared oblivious to his presence as a flashlight beam bounced erratically around inside the tent. Eli figured it was the flashlight that kept setting off the motion sensor on the back corner of the building. He waited a moment to see if the person would come out before striding over to the tent and pausing outside its entrance.

"Hello?"

"Oh shit!"

The return greeting, if that's what it could be called, didn't engender a friendly welcome from Eli. Alaska was filled with campers, so it wasn't a complete shock someone threw up a tent, but the back of his store was a rather odd place to select. Eli listened while whoever was in the tent rustled around. The sound of a zipper came as the opening was slowly unzipped. A young teen poked his head out. "Eli?"

Eli tilted his head to the side, a strange sensation rolling through him. This kid felt familiar, but he didn't know why —until the kid scrambled out through the tent opening and stood up. Eli found himself staring into a pair of green eyes almost precisely like his. A queasy feeling coiled in his stomach.

"Ryan?"

The boy nodded, his messy brown hair falling over his eyes. He brushed it back quickly. "It's me," Ryan replied.

Eli's mouth fell open, and he took a step back. Ryan was

his little brother who he hadn't seen since he left Juneau ten years ago when Ryan was four years old. He'd done what he could to make sure Ryan didn't share the same fate he had under his father's roof by pretty much bribing his father to move out and leave his mother and Ryan in peace. Thoughts tumbled rapidly through his mind as he considered why the hell Ryan was here. The old guilt that he couldn't quite shake rose inside.

Ryan was all arms and legs at fourteen. He stood in front of Eli in the light cast from the back corner light on the store building, his eyes uncertain and almost pleading. Eli forced himself to take a breath and eyed Ryan. All this time he'd been gone, he'd tried to manage his guilt and worry about Ryan, telling himself he'd done the best he could to give Ryan a shot at a life that didn't involve the misery of their father.

Norm Brooks was a run of the mill jerk on a good day. On a bad day, he was verbally, emotionally and physically abusive to those in his orbit. His favorite target was their mother, Beverly, although he didn't shy away from taking his frustrations out on Eli once Eli was old enough to talk back. Norm's physical explosions were few and far between, but he constantly emitted a simmering anger and frustration, lashing out verbally over every little thing. When Eli could, he mostly stayed in his room, but the small apartment made it hard to avoid his father. When Eli realized he was close to giving his father a dose of his own medicine, he'd made the only decision he could and left Juneau. He was determined never to become like the man his father was—constantly angry and swinging that anger around like a wrecking ball to smash into anyone within his radius. Eli had known for years his father stayed with his mother mostly because she could pay the bills with her job as a manager at the local grocery store. Meanwhile his father could barely hold a job down, getting fired again and again after being insolent and a generally crappy employee. Eli had made a deal: his father moved out into an apartment Eli paid for and left his mother and Ryan alone.

Norm, being the loser he was, had sworn up and down, but he went along with it. Eli knew the offer would be appealing because Norm often left for days at a time anyway. His returns led to explosive fights with their mother. To this day, Eli didn't understand why she would be hurt that his father was gallivanting from bar to bar and picking up other women, but she was. Eli figured paying for his father to stay away was the only way Eli could leave. He still felt guilty, but he had to leave. He'd been worried he'd end up turning on his father with the same kind of violence his father had doled out for years.

Eli's mind rolled through these thoughts as he stared at Ryan, wondering why the hell his little brother was here in Diamond Creek by himself in the middle of the night. "What are you doing here?" Eli finally asked.

Ryan shuffled on his feet, shifting his weight from one foot to the other, and tucked his hands in his jean pockets. "I, uh, was hoping I could visit for a little bit."

Eli nodded slowly. He knew without a doubt there was a lot more to the story than that, but now wasn't the time. Ryan's eyes held that same guarded quality Eli knew so well, and it scared the hell out of him. He forced himself to keep his mind right here, right now. "Okay then. If you'd called ahead, you wouldn't have to set up your tent here in the dark," he said with a wry grin, aiming for a light tone to ease the tension emanating from Ryan.

Ryan smiled nervously. "It's okay?"

"Of course. Grab your stuff and let's get to the house."

A while later, Eli watched Ryan practically inhale a heated up frozen pizza. Ryan probably wouldn't admit it, but Eli was willing to bet he hadn't eaten all day. He opened the freezer and grabbed another pizza to throw in the oven.

By the time Ryan had eaten a pizza and a half by himself, he finally leaned back and looked around. Eli lived in a spacious home about ten minutes away from downtown Diamond Creek. He was on the East side of town up a winding hill that offered a spectacular view of Kachemak Bay when it was daylight. He'd hesitated to purchase this home, in part due to its size, but he'd always been a sucker for a good deal and the home had been for sale at a crazy good price since its owners had run out of money and hadn't quite finished it. Eli had purchased it and finished most of the work on the home, including the siding, most of the plumbing and installing a boiler. He had an amazing view, privacy and four bedrooms, only one of which he needed and ever planned to use.

The main living area had a cathedral ceiling with windows stretching from floor to ceiling. The kitchen sat against the back wall with an island dividing it from the living room area, which was sparsely furnished with a sectional and a coffee table and not much else beyond a few lamps. A television was mounted on a side wall. Ryan's gaze scanned the room and landed back on Eli who was seated on a stool at the kitchen island, nursing a beer while Ryan ate.

"Do you own this house?" Ryan asked, his eyes wide.

Eli nodded and took a swallow of his beer. "Yup. Bought it for a killer deal and finished it."

Ryan fiddled with his unused fork and looked down at the table. "Is it okay if I stay for a little bit?"

"Sure. Mind telling me if Mom knows you're here?"

Ryan's eyes whipped up, fear flashing in them. "Um, no. I kinda just left."

Eli's stomach turned. "You left?"

Ryan nodded, his hair falling in his eyes when he did.

"Have you called Mom at all since you left?"

Ryan nodded again. "I don't have a cell phone, but I used

my friend's phone and told her I was with him. I didn't tell her I was coming here though."

"How come?"

Ryan's eyes flicked to Eli and back down at the table. He was clearly nervous. "Because she would have asked me not to. Can we talk more about this tomorrow?"

Eli thought for a moment and finally nodded. Much as he wanted to know what was going on, it was the middle of the night. They wouldn't be able to resolve anything at this hour. He moved on. "How'd you get from Juneau to here?"

"I hitched a ride with my friend and his parents all the way to Whittier. They were going fishing there for a week or so."

"And?" Eli prompted, circling his hand.

Ryan looked down, flipping the fork back and forth between his fingers. He mumbled something.

"What did you say?"

Eli could see Ryan take a deep breath, his skinny shoulders rising and falling along with it. "I hitchhiked from Whittier the rest of the way here," he finally said. He lifted his eyes to meet Eli's, a hint of defiance glimmering within the worry held there.

A rush of anger, born out of concern, rose inside of Eli. He started to say something and then snapped his mouth shut. It wouldn't help to swear at Ryan when he'd made it here all in one piece. Eli drained his beer and ran a hand through his hair. "Not the safest plan, but I suppose you're here, so it's not worth giving you a hard time about it now."

Ryan slumped in his chair and sighed, a wobbly smile stretching across his face. As they sat there, it occurred to Eli that while he'd thought about Ryan with frequency over the years, he barely knew him. Ten years was a long time in the life of a child. The little boy Eli had known before he moved away was on his way to being a man. He had enough grit to find his way to Diamond Creek all on his own. Eli had so many questions about why Ryan left, he didn't even know where to begin. Another glance at Ryan, and he realized his questions would need to wait. Ryan was barely keeping his eyes open.

Eli pushed his stool back and stood. "Let me show you the bedroom."

Ryan stood quickly and snagged the battered backpack he'd brought with him. Eli led him up the stairs, which graced one wall and led to a balcony hallway. Over the railing, one could share the same view as from downstairs while four doors flanked the hallway, three leading to bedrooms and the fourth to a shared bathroom. Eli used the master bedroom, which was downstairs and had its own bathroom.

He gestured to the only room up here he'd actually put a bedroom set in. He'd questioned the point, but since the room would have remained empty otherwise, he'd figured it made sense. "Here you go. It's all yours. The bathroom's right beside you. I'm downstairs, so you've got the space up here to yourself."

He flipped the light switch on while Ryan dropped his backpack on the floor and looked around the room. His jeans were dirty and his t-shirt was faded and worn. Eli's heart clenched looking at him. Eli doubted Ryan had much more than the clothes he wore. "Do yourself a favor and shower before you go to bed."

Ryan's head whipped up again, a mottled flush crawling up his neck.

Eli chuckled. "Hey, I'm as bad as you after a day on the water. I sleep better when I'm clean."

At that, he turned away and headed back downstairs, calling out as he did. "I have to head out early for a fishing charter. If you want to come along, be up by six. There's an alarm clock by the bed."

* * *

ELI STOOD at the kitchen counter and grabbed a granola bar out of one of the cabinets. He glanced at the clock above the stove, wondering if Ryan would try to get up in time to go fishing with him. He wasn't too comfortable leaving Ryan to his own devices the first day he was here. As he was stuffing his backpack with water bottles, he heard movement upstairs and then water running. A few minutes later, Ryan came walking downstairs. Even after a short night's sleep, he looked worlds better than he had last night. His hair was damp from his shower and dripping onto the shoulders of the same t-shirt he'd been wearing last night.

"Morning," Eli said with a grin. It was good to see Ryan, so good it was disconcerting for Eli. His almost-stranger brother carried himself with a friendly awkwardness.

Ryan nodded. "Morning. Thought I'd try to make it in time to go fishing if that's okay."

"Of course. Glad to have you. Hang on, let me grab a few things."

Eli walked past the kitchen into the small alcove that led to his bedroom suite. He walked immediately into his closet and snagged a clean t-shirt and a windbreaker. His jeans would be too big for Ryan, but he hated to see Ryan starting the day in what was probably his only ratty t-shirt. When he returned to the kitchen and tossed the t-shirt to Ryan, Ryan flushed.

"I don't need…"

Eli waved a hand and cut him off. "Sure, you can start the day in that t-shirt, but you'll feel better if you don't. I could care less how you look, but you'll smell like fish by the end of the day, so you might as well start off right. I've got t-shirts coming out of my ears, so don't worry about it."

Ryan's nodded quickly and ran back upstairs. In seconds, he returned with the clean t-shirt on. Eli's stomach felt hollow. Seeing his little brother after all these years made him feel strange. He wanted to skip fishing and take Ryan shopping for whatever else he might need. He mentally shook himself. Now was not the time. He had customers on their way and needed to get to the harbor on time.

Not much later, he swung his truck into the small parking lot by Red Truck Coffee, aptly named for the old red square truck in which it was housed. Red Truck Coffee was situated just before the turn onto the road leading to Otter Cove Harbor. As such, Eli stopped here almost every day he came to the harbor in the summer. He and the other regulars kept this place hopping, while the tourists pushed it to overflowing at times. Even now, at a mere six-fifteen in the morning, there was a line.

"Coffee?" he asked, glancing to Ryan before he hesitated. "Wait a minute. Do fourteen-year olds drink coffee?"

Ryan laughed and shrugged. "I dunno. I don't drink it, but do you think they have anything to eat?" His question came out, and then his face fell. "Never mind. I don't have any money left," he mumbled before looking away to stare out the window.

"Ryan, look at me," Eli said, fighting the anger rising inside. Not anger with Ryan, but anger with his mother. He wasn't going to pump Ryan for information today, but it was becoming more and more clear that Ryan's needs, however minimal, had been kicked to the curb. He'd gone in circles with it in his mind last night, considering that Ryan could have runaway for no good reason, but Eli's gut told him otherwise. Given that Eli had rarely had decent clothes and almost never had any spending money when he was a kid, Ryan's circumstances were painfully familiar. Eli had hoped the money he deposited for his mother went to help take care of Ryan, but it was looking more likely that was not the case.

Ryan turned away from the window, his eyes guarded.

After a quick second of eye contact, his gaze landed on what seemed to be Eli's shoulder. A ruddy flush covered his face. "Yeah?"

"You don't need to worry about food or anything like that while you're here. If you're hungry, just assume I'll buy whatever you need. I'm not sure how long you'll be around, but maybe we can take a run to Kenai for shopping and get you some clothes. I'm thinking you haven't got much in that little backpack of yours." He paused to see if Ryan would say anything. When he didn't, Eli continued. "So, if you want something to eat now, come on."

Eli didn't wait for Ryan's answer and climbed out of the car. As he strode toward the coffee truck, he heard Ryan running behind him to catch up. When they reached the back of the line, Ryan stood with his hands stuffed in his pockets and looked around. "Wow, it's busy here. Is it usually like this?" he asked as his eyes followed the line of vehicles turning from the highway onto the road and then scanned the cluster of people in line here.

Eli chuckled. "All summer long. Once everyone gets out on the water, the traffic will ease up a little."

The line moved quickly and within a few minutes, they stood at the counter. "Morning, Cammi," Eli said to the woman who looked up with a warm smile.

"Hey Eli!" Cammi replied, her blue eyes lighting up when she saw him. Cammi owned Red Truck Coffee and was here almost every day all summer long. She had a ready smile for anyone who came along and remembered the favorites for her regular customers. "Triple shot in the dark?" she asked Eli, tucking a pen behind her ear and brushing her light brown hair out of her eyes. She kept her hair short in a pixie cut, so she reminded Eli of an elf with her warm smile.

"As usual."

Cammi's eyes bounced to Ryan and back to Eli with a question in them. "This is Ryan, my little brother," Eli said.

Cammi's eyes widened, along with her smile. "Ryan! So nice to meet you. I'm Cammi." She reached across the narrow counter and offered her hand to Ryan.

He nodded and gave it a hard shake, perhaps too hard, because he dropped her hand quickly. "Sorry."

Cammi's smile didn't waver. "You've got a good, strong handshake. No need to apologize. Now what can I get for you?"

"Um, I don't know. Do you have a muffin or something?"

"I certainly do! Today you can pick from blueberry or raspberry muffins. Do you want something to drink?"

Ryan chewed the inside of his cheek for a moment before he answered. "Um, I'll take blueberry. I don't drink coffee though, so I don't know what else you have."

"I have some sodas and even hot chocolate if you want."

"Hot chocolate?" Ryan asked.

"Of course! It'll be chilly for another few hours. Trust me, I sell plenty of hot chocolate."

Ryan looked to Eli as if he was unsure.

"Go for it. Get whatever you want," Eli said with a nod.

"Okay, I'll take the hot chocolate then."

Cammi grinned. "Coming right up. Give me a sec."

She whirled around, working the espresso machine with one hand and prepping the hot chocolate with the other. Within moments, she handed the two drinks over and put the blueberry muffin in a bag for Ryan.

"Have fun on the water today!" she called out as they headed back to Eli's truck.

Hours later, Eli steered the boat through choppy waves and glanced over his shoulder. Ryan had shown himself to be fairly experienced with fishing. Through bits and pieces of conversation throughout the day, he'd learned Ryan often went fishing with a friend's family. Ryan was also a hard worker. Once he was on the boat, he simply did whatever was asked and offered to help with everything. Eli watched him now as Ryan helped one of the customers work a fish-hook out carefully and then carry the salmon in question over to the cooler. The awkwardness he carried dissolved once he was busy working. Cliff had been warm and welcoming, which also helped Ryan get comfortable.

Eli turned to face forward and savored the salty breeze gusting across the bay. It was early afternoon, and they were headed back into the harbor. A good day fishing was about the ideal way to spend a day with his little brother.

CHAPTER 6

Jessa adjusted her stretchy black skirt over her leggings. "Are you sure I look okay?" she asked Marley.

Marley, her sister-in-law and adored wife of Gage, brushed her auburn hair out of her eyes and adjusted her six-month old daughter in her arms. Holly wiggled mightily and tried to grab ahold of Marley's hair. "Here, play with this," Marley said as she snagged a small rubber loop off the kitchen counter and handed it to Holly. Holly immediately began chewing on it. Marley looked up at Jessa and smiled ruefully. "Sorry about that. I've only been a mom for six months and I've discovered conversation is mostly a series of interruptions."

Jessa smiled softly and stepped to Marley's side, looking down at Holly and stroking a finger through her soft brown hair. "She's so darn cute."

Marley laughed. "I think so." She adjusted Holly again and walked over to the couch where she sat down and set Holly inside a small cushioned seat on the couch. Holly kept gnawing away on her toy while Marley leaned back with a sigh and looked over at Jessa. "You look great! What are you so worried about?"

Jessa looked down at her worn cowboy boots, her eyes traveling over her black leggings and skirt and fiddled with the collar on the flowy blue blouse Marley had given her today. She insisted she never wore it, so Jessa should have it. "I don't know. How do hostesses dress around here? Is this nice enough?"

Marley grinned. "Hon, you could wear rubber boots and jeans, and no one would care. Delia tries to keep the lodge restaurant a step above, but she wouldn't care if you had to make do. People would think it gave the place added character."

Jessa sighed and plunked down in the opposite corner of the couch. "I know, but I'm trying to do this right."

Marley's expression sobered. "You don't need to be worried. Delia could use the help more than she'll ever admit. You look great, and it'll be fine. Plus, Gage told me you used to wait tables. All you need to do is smile and keep track of who goes where."

Jessa wasn't quite sure why she was so nervous. She supposed it was because she wanted to help. She needed to find a way to feel useful since she'd been at loose ends for the last few weeks and facing the reality of cobbling her life back together with next to nothing as a foundation. She scraped by for years on the income from her whimsical furniture, but it had never been enough for her to save. The fire was making her pay a price for that. The owner of her former apartment building had told her she may eventually qualify for an insurance payout to cover costs for relocation, but it would be months before that came through. Not to mention, she hadn't bothered to obtain renter's insurance, so the total loss of her belongings wasn't covered. She needed to have something to latch onto and helping Delia in the restaurant gave her that.

Jessa fiddled with the simple silver chain she wore around her neck and looked over at Marley. "You're right. I don't need to worry. As long as you think I look okay, I'm good to go."

"You look great! What time are you heading downstairs?"

Jessa glanced at the clock on the wall above the windows. "Delia said five was good, so I'll walk down in a few minutes." Her eyes fell to the view through the windows. Marley and Gage lived in an expansive private apartment in the ski lodge with windows stretching across the living room and kitchen, affording a wide open view of the ski slopes, the mountains rising tall behind them and an opening in the corner where Kachemak Bay winked under the sun. Jessa had vague memories of coming to visit their grandparents here, but that was it. Her family had moved away months after she was born, so she didn't share the childhood memories Gage had of Diamond Creek. She recalled coming to visit, warm hugs from their grandmother and running around through the woods as she tried to keep up with her older siblings.

The sun fell through the spruce trees lining the ski slopes, casting lacy shadows on the grassy slopes. With the snow absent in the summer, the slopes were still busy since Gage had set up marked hiking and mountain biking trails. At the moment, two bike riders were zooming down the grassy ski slope, dodging boulders and, as far as Jessa could tell, risking their lives with a wild ride down the mountain. "It's so beautiful here. Do you ever stop being amazed by the view?" she asked on a sigh, glancing to Marley.

Marley shook her head, her green eyes crinkling at the corners with her smile. "Never. Diamond Creek is amazing, but it took moving away for a decade for me to realize how much I didn't appreciate it when I was here before. I've been back going on two years now, and if I'm having a rough day, all I have to do is look outside. It doesn't hurt to have one of the best views in town."

"I'd say," Jessa replied as she scanned the view again, its beauty both energizing and soothing. "Do you mind living here at the lodge?"

"I wondered if I would, but I love it. This apartment is so private, it feels like our own home. Here and there we've talked about maybe building a separate home on the property, but I'm in no hurry. It's nice to be right here when things come up. If there's one thing I've learned running a lodge like this, something always comes up."

Jessa's heart warmed to see Marley like this. When she'd first met Marley, she'd known Marley was the woman for Gage. She was the first woman he'd ever introduced to the family. Gage was the best kind of brother—kind, protective, strong and helpful—but he was guarded when it came to his own heart. Until he met Marley, Jessa had worried he'd never let down his guard. Since he'd moved back to Diamond Creek, fulfilling his childhood dream, and met Marley, Jessa felt good about where he was with his life. As if on cue, the door to the apartment opened and Gage stepped inside. He walked immediately to the couch to drop a kiss on Holly's forehead and another in the curve of Marley's neck. He whispered something in her ear, and two spots of bright color crested on Marley's cheekbones.

Gage stretched before plopping down in a rocking chair adjacent to the couch, his eyes landing on Jessa. "Did you get settled in today?"

"Of course. There wasn't much to settle because I don't have much. The suite is lovely. Thanks for letting my stay for a bit."

Gage angled his head to the side, his gray eyes assessing. "No thanks necessary. You can stay as long as you like. Move in if you want. I'm just glad you made it out of that fire and you're here."

"I'm not going to move in," Jessa replied, swallowing at the defensiveness that rose inside. She didn't like needing help like this. "I just need somewhere to land for a bit until I figure out what to do next."

"Our home is your home," Marley said firmly. "Don't you dare try to think you're in the way. We're thrilled to have you."

Jessa felt that knot of tension she'd been carrying ease just a little but more. She took a breath and let it out. She'd do anything for her family, so she needed to realize it might be okay to accept help in return. "Thank you. It's been a long few weeks. It's good to be here," she finally said. At that moment, the clock on the wall chirped like a bird. She glanced up at it and then between Marley and Gage.

Gage chuckled. "Garrett brought that over after he saw how much Holly likes this little toy she has that makes bird sounds."

Jessa grinned. "It's awesome! Time for me to go. Are you two coming down for dinner?"

Marley nodded. "Oh yeah. I've pretty much given up cooking dinner since we had Holly. We'll be down for a little bit even if it's just to grab something from the buffet."

Jessa made her way downstairs and within an hour, she'd completely forgotten why she'd ever been nervous. She loved talking with people and found the customers at the lodge restaurant to be a varied bunch, a mix of locals and tourists from all over the world. Since the restaurant was crazy busy, Jessa found herself constantly manning the waitlist and chatting with the customers while they waited. Harry Lawson, Delia's front manager, ran Jessa through the paces of what she needed to know and then left her to her own devices. He breezed by occasionally and threw encouraging smiles at her, even swinging by to deliver a glass of wine.

"I can drink when I'm working?" Jessa asked, amused by

the idea.

Harry winked as he set the glass down with a flourish on the reception desk. "A glass a night is fine. Plus, you're taste testing. This is a gooseberry wine from Diamond Creek Brewery. They mostly do beer, but they've been expanding into wines lately. You can let me know what you think and maybe we'll serve it here."

"Oh, sign me up! I love wine, but I've never even heard of gooseberry wine." She lifted the glass and sniffed it. "It smells delicious," she said as she glanced into Harry's dark eyes. Harry was dark and angular—dark brown hair with eyes to match and a thin frame. He appeared to love his job and thrived on the restaurant running at full speed. He nodded at Jessa's comment. "It does smell good, doesn't it? Tell me what you think."

She took a sip, the flavor rich and warm. "Wow! That's really good."

Harry grinned. "I thought so too. Delia wants to make sure enough people like it before she buys it. I'm leaving this bottle here," he paused and lifted the bottle in his hand. "You can offer small glasses while people wait if they want to try it. I figure that might give us a good sample."

"Perfect! Hand it over." She carefully took the bottle from him and set in on the desk. She'd noticed the desk was stocked with small wineglasses earlier, so she opened the cabinet doors, pulled out some glasses and lined them in a semi-circle around the bottle of wine.

Harry smiled approvingly and gave a wave as he dashed off. He seemed to mostly spin about the restaurant, always in motion, always doing something. Customers loved him with his light and easy humor and engaging manner that made it feel as if you'd somehow known him forever. Jessa appreciated how welcoming he'd been of her. After he dashed off, she offered the gooseberry wine to the customers already waiting.

Hours later, the last of the customers wandered out into the falling darkness, and she locked the front door behind them. She quickly tidied up the reception area and carried the many wineglasses used for the taste testing into the kitchen on a tray, along with four empty bottles. To say the gooseberry wine was a hit was an understatement. She'd blown through it. When she pushed through the swinging door into the kitchen, she walked to the back corner to set the dishes in the massive rack to run through the commercial dishwasher and washed her hands in the sink. She glanced around and smiled. Delia was putting a tray of pastries in the refrigerator, ready for the oven first thing tomorrow morning, Harry was in the far corner entering something in the register there, and one of the line cooks was wiping down the prep counters. The space was calm and quiet.

Delia closed the refrigerator and leaned her hips against the stainless steel table that ran down the center of the kitchen. She reached her hands up to loosen her hair from the haphazard knot atop her head. It fell in honey gold waves around her shoulders. She sighed and glanced over to Jessa, patting the table beside her as she slid up to sit on it. "Have a seat. We can ask Harry to bring us some hard cider."

Jessa walked to her side and slipped onto the cool table. "I forgot all about your amazing cider. It's the perfect way to end a busy night." She glanced around to see Harry had shut off the register and was already headed over to where the cider was kept in the corner. "Hot or cold, ladies?"

"Cold," Delia called out, arching a brow in question at Jessa.

"Me too!" Jessa added.

"Coming right up," Harry said, as he snagged two mugs from the hooks above the cider.

Delia leaned back on her hands. "Thanks for helping out tonight. Harry said you did great. I can't tell you what a relief it was to have you here. Without you, I'd have been running around trying to do ten things at once."

Harry approached them and handed over the two mugs of cider. "You're always running around doing ten things at once," he offered with a grin. "With Jessa here, everything ran smoothly, while it would have been a madhouse without her." He threw his grin in Jessa's direction. "You were awesome. The customers loved you, and I'd say we have a definitive vote on the gooseberry wine. What do you think?"

"Well, I blew through four bottles if that's what you mean."

Harry chuckled. "Exactly. Even when things are free, if people don't like it, they take a sip and move on. Once people got seated, they wanted to buy bottles, but we don't have enough to sell yet."

Delia took a swallow of her cider. "I'll call down to the brewery tomorrow and ask how much we can order. Since they just started making it, I'm not sure how much stock they have."

Jessa swung her feet from the table while Delia and Harry chatted about the menu for the rest of the week. They had a regular menu, but they had a range of daily specials, which were dependent on seasonal products. As the conversation continued, her ears perked up while they discussed which salmon would be running when. Thinking about salmon brought Eli to mind, and she flushed straight through when she recalled their kiss. She didn't quite know what to think about her attraction to him. All she knew was that kiss with him yesterday had been about the best kiss she'd ever experienced, and she wanted more.

In an effort to distract herself, she started asking questions. "How many kinds of salmon are there up here? I'm a little familiar with it because they sell tons of seafood at markets in Seattle, but I never paid much attention. Just from listening to the customers out front, it seems like there are some opinions about what salmon's the best."

"King salmon," Delia and Harry said at exactly the same moment.

Jessa burst out laughing. "Wow! That was fast. How come people even eat other salmon then if king salmon is so good?"

"It's all good, well except for pinks. They're good for smoking and canning, but they can't compete with the rest. The others are silvers and a few different types of red salmon. You'll even hear preferences about the same kinds of salmon from different rivers. Like the red salmon that run in China Poot across the bay are much smaller than the reds that run in the Kenai River. The reds that run in the Kasilof River are somewhere in between. You'll find anyone to argue any of those are the best. King is king, but the rest are awesome too."

The door to the kitchen swung open and Garrett walked through. He immediately went to Delia's side and dipped his head to catch her lips in a kiss. When he looked up, his eyes were relaxed and warm. Until he'd moved up here and found Delia, Garrett had almost always been high-strung. He was still high-energy and sharp-witted, but the tightness he carried had eased. Jessa grinned at him. "Hey big brother! Didn't expect to see you here."

"I'm the taxi tonight. I dropped Delia off on the way to Nick's baseball game," Garrett said with a grin. "I see you're enjoying some of the best hard cider in the world."

Jessa took another swallow, savoring the bite of the cider. She didn't know how Delia did it, but she managed to turn apple cider into a magic nectar with a touch of alcohol, just enough to burn. "Yup. We had a busy night."

Delia glanced up at Garrett who'd stepped away to lounge against the counter opposite them. "How's the game go?"

"We won. Again."

Delia pumped her fist in the air. "Woohoo!" She glanced to Jessa and Harry. "Nick's team is awesome this year. He's having a blast."

Jessa leaned back on a hand and sighed. "Didn't you say you were helping coach this year?" she asked Garrett.

Garrett nodded. "Oh yeah. It's been fun, although I can't believe the schedule they have. We practice five days a week and have three games every week. It wears me out, but Nick loves it."

Delia finished off her cider and slipped off the table. "Okay. Let's skedaddle. I'm worn out."

A few minutes later, Jessa walked up the main stairs that curved along the front entrance wall and made her way down the hallway to her suite. When she reached her room, she left the lights off, walked straight to the windows and looked out into the dark sky. It was past midnight. She'd left a window open and cool summer air sifted through the screen. The wind rustled in the trees outside. An owl hooted softly in the distance. After several beats, another owl answered. Jessa leaned on the windowsill and looked into the sky. A half-moon hung above the mountains, its light casting a silvery mist over the trees. Stars stretched across the sky, bright against the velvet canopy.

She finally turned away and flicked a lamp on, her thoughts giving in to the temptation to think about Eli... and that kiss. She remembered suddenly that she'd hastily texted him earlier. She'd gotten so busy with work, she forgot to worry about the fact he hadn't texted back yet. She glanced around for her phone and snagged it off the counter where she'd left it hours and hours ago. His name blinked brightly at her when she tapped the screen on. She swiped the message open. He was short and to the point. *Would love to take you out on the water. Meet us at six tomorrow at the harbor.*

CHAPTER 7

Eli leaned his elbows on the kitchen island and looked over at Ryan. Ryan was gobbling up a piece of pizza. Eli had stopped by and picked up takeout from Glacier Pizza on the way home from the harbor. Ryan's brown hair was damp from the shower he'd just taken. When he finally paused in his speed eating and sat up on the stool, Eli chuckled. "Don't forget to breathe."

Ryan flushed and took a gulp of water. "Thanks for the pizza. I was starving!"

Eli glanced over at the pizza box, which had one lonely piece of pizza left. He'd already eaten by the time Ryan made his way downstairs after showering and changing into another one of Eli's t-shirts and a pair of his sweatpants, which nearly swallowed him. Eli made a mental note to plan to take Ryan shopping soon. He would have done it tomorrow, but he couldn't resist offering to take Jessa out for a charter when she'd texted him earlier. His mind immediately flashed to the feel of her soft curves against him. He'd never thought about a woman as much as he'd been thinking about Jessa the last few days. Kissing her had been completely out of character for him, but he didn't regret it for a minute. He shook his thoughts off of her and focused on Ryan. He was determined to sort out what brought Ryan to Diamond Creek in the middle of the night.

"So, how about you tell me why you're here?" Eli asked, electing to tackle his questions directly.

Ryan took another gulp of water and fiddled with his napkin. He looked across at Eli, his eyes uncertain. He chewed on the inside of his cheek and finally spoke. "Dad moved back in about six months ago. Mom didn't want him there, but you know how she is with him. She can't stand up to him. I tried, but it got ugly. I mostly tried to stay out of way, but..." Ryan shrugged and shook his head. "I don't know what he was like when you were there, but he's a fuckin' asshole now. I don't know if it's worse when he's drunk or sober. At least when he's drinking, I just have to wait long enough for him to pass out."

Anger flashed through Eli. He closed his eyes and clenched a fist, waiting for it to pass. He'd spent most of his life determined not to let anger rule him the way it did his father. After a moment, he opened his eyes and looked over at Ryan. "Doesn't sound like he's changed much. Mom ever tell you why Dad wasn't staying with you guys?"

Ryan nodded. "A few years back, she told me you made Dad leave. She didn't say much about it, but I could guess why. Even though I didn't see him much, I knew he was a jerk. He was always showing up and demanding money from her. I don't think I knew how bad he was until he moved in."

Eli was furious with his father, but he was also angry with his mother. If she'd told him his father had moved back in, he would've gone down there to do something about it. He knew she was cowed by his father, but it didn't change his frustration with her inability to walk away from him. They didn't talk often, but when they did, she'd definitely omitted the significant detail about his father moving back in. He hooked his foot on the rung of a stool nearby and tugged it over, plunking down on it and running a hand through his hair. He felt suddenly weary. Ryan watched him, his eyes guarded and wary.

Eli mentally shook himself. Ryan didn't need to know how much Eli had wished he could have protected him from ever seeing this side of their father. "I'm sorry to hear that. Dammit. I should've known he'd eventually find a way back in."

Still twisting the napkin in his hands, Ryan shrugged again. "Once he finds out I took off and came to see you, he's gonna flip. I wasn't thinking about that when I came here. I just wanted to get the hell away from him."

Eli rubbed his hand over his face and sighed. He wished Ryan was wrong, but he knew their father wouldn't take kindly to Ryan running away to stay with Eli. "Right. Yeah, to say he and I weren't on good terms when I left is an understatement. We have to call Mom though. When did you leave with your friend?"

"Four days before I got here. His parents took us on the ferry to Whittier. It took me another day to get here."

Eli glanced at the clock over the stove. "If she doesn't hear from you soon, she's going to start worrying. You wanna call tonight? Get it over with?"

Ryan's eyes widened. He started to shake his head and then stopped, his shoulders sagging. "I don't want to call at all, but I guess I can only blow it off so long." He paused and took a deep breath. "What do we do if Mom says I have to go back?"

The same question had been tumbling through his mind since Ryan had shown up here. Eli couldn't stomach sending Ryan back to Juneau with their father living in the same house now. Yet, it wasn't like he had a leg to stand on legally. He knew his father well. In all the years of being abusive to his mother, once in a while, she'd actually pressed charges. Each time, their father threw his energy into refuting it. Any challenge to his rights as a husband and father was like waving a red flag in front of him. He ran at it with all his might. It didn't matter that he couldn't be bothered to actually care about how he functioned in those roles. All that mattered was someone was daring to question his right to do so. Eli mentally sighed. He'd hoped he'd left tangling with his father in his past when he left Juneau. Much as he didn't want to, he couldn't stand by and let Ryan return. Not as long as his father was back in his mother's home.

Eli met Ryan's gaze, his gut churning when he saw the worry held there. "What do you wanna do?"

Ryan's eyes flicked to his hands twisting the napkin and back to Eli. "Do you think maybe I could stay with you? I won't be a problem. I'll stay out of your way and work whenever you need some help."

Eli's heart clenched. He knew just how Ryan felt. When he used to work on the docks in Juneau, he tried to work the hardest, so he could earn the option to work late—anything to keep him out of the house longer. Here Ryan sat in front of him promising to stay out of the way and more. It hurt to see him like this.

"You can stay. If Dad's there, I don't want you there. But we'll have to have a few ground rules."

Ryan's mouth went slack. "Really? You're not gonna make me go back?"

Eli shook his head. "I need to talk to Mom first. If she won't agree, I'll take it to court. First though, those ground rules." At Ryan's nod, he continued. "You know, the basics: a reasonable curfew, letting me know where you are, asking if you want someone to come over, stuff like that. Think you can handle that?"

Ryan nodded emphatically, his hair falling over his eyes as he did. "But what if Dad flips out?"

Eli laughed bitterly. "There's no 'what if' on that. He will definitely flip out, but I'll deal with him. Don't worry about it."

Ryan breathed a noisy sigh and kept twisting that napkin. "Did Dad hit you?" he asked, his question soft.

Eli considered what to say and then mentally shrugged. If he tried to hide things from Ryan, he'd figure it out eventually. He nodded. "Yup. It got worse the older I got. When I was little, like you were when I moved away, he just yelled and avoided me mostly. Once I got old enough to talk back, that was it. We had a huge blow out one day, and I decided I had to go. All my life, I promised myself I wouldn't become like him —a violent asshole. Not once, even in that big argument, did I ever lay a hand on him. But it was coming if I didn't get out of his orbit. I took some of the money I saved up from working my tail off on the docks and charter boats in Juneau and gave him a choice. Either he moved out on my dime and stayed away, or I started going to the police no matter whether Mom wanted me to or not. He already had enough of a petty record, he knew he'd be cycling in and out of jail if I did that, so he moved into the apartment I rented for him. Mom couldn't stand up to him, so I did. Just so you know, I don't hold that against her. He beat her down for so long, it's a damn miracle she wakes up everyday. I think she was relieved when I forced him out. To be honest, I'm surprised it took as long as it did for him to show up again. I've been paying his rent all along, so I'm curious to know where that went these last six months."

"He got evicted because he trashed the place one too many times. I didn't hear that from him, but I heard Mom talking to him about it one night."

Eli closed his eyes and shook his head before pushing off his stool and stepping to the refrigerator to grab a beer. He took a swallow as he returned to his seat at the counter and eyed Ryan. "So, what was your plan when you left?"

"I didn't really have one. My friend invited me to go fishing with them, which I do all the time anyway. When we got to Whittier, they were planning to stay for two weeks, so I told them I wanted to come see you. They have no idea I hitchhiked down here. I figured if things didn't work out with you, I'd find my way back to Whittier before they left."

"So how come you didn't just tell Mom you'd be gone for a few weeks?"

"Because I didn't have a plan," Ryan said with a roll of his eyes, his uneasiness fading. "I came home from school and Dad lit into me over something about the TV. I told him to fuck off and left. I called Mom on the way over to meet my friend."

Eli twirled his beer bottle on the counter before taking another swig. "Okay then. Whaddya say we call Mom?"

CHAPTER 8

Eli drove away from the harbor after dropping Ryan off with Cliff to get the boat ready for today's charter. Jessa would be joining them with a couple and their young son. Eli wanted to grab a few coffees and some bakery items from Misty Mountain Café for the morning. Red Truck Coffee was great for a quick stop, but if one wanted more than a snack, Misty Mountain was the place to go. As he drove over, he considered the call last night between Ryan and their mother. It hadn't been terrible, but it hadn't been great either. Needless to say, their mother's response wasn't a surprise. She wanted Ryan to return home right away. When Eli confronted her about their father moving back in, she'd gone quiet. He felt like he'd entered a time warp. He couldn't count how many times he'd begged his mother to leave his father. Yet again, he found himself doing the same thing—this time on behalf of his little brother. The call ended in a stalemate.

He turned into the parking lot for the cluster of stores where Misty Mountain was. It happened to be the same parking lot where Jessa had backed into him. He couldn't help but smile at her concern over the potential harm she'd done to his truck. As Eli thought about last night and looking forward to seeing Jessa again, he was a muddle inside. In the decade since he'd removed himself from the toxic world of his father, he'd found it easy to steer clear of any hint of relationships. Oh, he hadn't been celibate, but he kept things light and casual. Yet, he'd never met anyone like Jessa. One kiss with her and any time he thought of her, lust jolted through him. He parked in front of Misty Mountain and jogged inside. Moments later, he headed out with a carrier filled with coffees and a bag of fresh pastries. Against all expectations, the anticipation of seeing Jessa overrode his instinct to avoid entanglements. His mood was light as he drove back to the harbor.

When he reached Otter Cove Harbor again, he parked where he usually did in the back of the lot by a cluster of spruce trees. He kicked his door shut, juggling the coffees and pastries. As he began to walk across the lot, Jessa's distinctive little blue truck came into sight at the entrance. His smile was reflexive. She waved when she saw him and pulled into the spot beside his truck.

She bounced out of her truck wearing a red parka over black leggings and red rubber boots. He definitely would not lose sight of her on the water. While her outfit was entirely practical, her vivid colors stood out among the typical boots worn in Alaska. The common brown and black boots were nothing against her bright red pair.

"Good morning! I'm not late, am I?" Jessa said as she walked to his side. Her chocolate brown hair was pulled into a ponytail high on her head. A blonde streak ran down the center of her swinging hair. Her eyes were silvery in the morning light. Her radiant smile sent a score of heat through him.

You're going fishing, dude. That's it. Just because she makes you half crazy doesn't mean you can't get a grip. You've got other things to focus on right now, like maybe your little brother who ran away from home. He mentally shook himself. "Nope. You're early. How's it going?" He forced his tone to be light and casual and was relieved his hands were full because he itched to pull her into his arms find out if kissing her was as phenomenal as he remembered.

"Great! I can't wait to get out on the water. How close will we get to the other side of the bay?"

They started walking, the gravel crunching under their feet. "If you want, we can plan to stop for lunch over there," he replied.

Jessa glanced sideways to him, a gust of wind blowing a loose lock of hair across her face. She tucked it behind her ear. "Really?"

"Over in Halibut Cove and Seldovia, there're a few restaurants. Depending on where we find the fish, we can stop for lunch. Customers usually love it."

Jessa's sensual, full lips stretched in a wide smile, sending another jolt of heat through him. "Oh! This is so awesome!" She clapped her hands together and skipped a few steps.

A wash of joy rolled through Eli, a feeling somewhat foreign to him. His childhood hadn't offered him much time for simple pleasures. While he loved the outdoors on a pure, visceral level, he sought them out as an escape, almost a meditation of sorts. He savored the affinity with nature and the calm he found there. Jessa's excitement was contagious. He grinned at her.

"Well, sounds like today will be fun for you. Have you ever been fishing?"

She nodded quickly. "Yup. I mostly grew up in Bellingham, Washington. It might not be Alaska, but there's plenty of fishing there. My dad took us out fishing when we were kids. I won't pretend I've had tons of experience, but I had a little. I knew enough to know I'd better wear rubber boots." Her grin flashed again when she held a booted foot aloft.

He chuckled as they reached the top of the docks. Jessa paused at his side and took a deep breath. Her hand held to her chest, she stared out over Kachemak Bay. Eli followed her gaze. At just before six in the morning, the sun had started its rise roughly an hour before. It had yet to crest the mountains, although its rays stretched skyward—pink and gold streaking above the backdrop of the jagged peaks.

Light glimmered on the water as it rolled softly in the dawn. The tide was coming into shore in rhythmic waves. A gust came off the water, carrying the briny scent of the ocean with it. The peace Eli sought whenever he was near the ocean came with the breeze. He settled inside, even with Jessa's effervescent presence beside him. He glanced over to see a look of wonder on her face. Her silvery-gray eyes were wide. She took another audible breath and turned to him, her eyes catching his.

"It's so beautiful here," she said softly. "Morning is the best time for a place like this."

He nodded wordlessly, unable to look away from her. Her eyes held his for several beats before her hand fell from her chest. "I suppose we should go, huh?"

Eli could have stood there all day with her, but her question snapped him back to reality. He scanned over the docks and saw their customers were already on the boat. He could see Ryan and Cliff helping load gear into the boat. The moment with Jessa had felt so peaceful, he hadn't even heard the usual summer commotion on the docks. Otter Cove Harbor was a bustle of activity all summer long with boats following the tide in and out. At the moment, many charter companies were readying for their daily run, while a few larger commercial fishing vessels were also busy with activity. Voices carried over the water, mingling with the calls of seagulls. He glanced back to Jessa and nodded. "Yup. If we don't get to the boat soon, Ryan and Cliff might take off without us."

They started walking again. Once they stepped off the stairs, the industrial floating docks rocked softly in the waves under their feet.

"Cliff's the guy I met the other day, right?" Jessa asked.

"Yup. He works for me. Ryan's my little brother. He's here for a visit." Eli had considered how to explain Ryan before and figured the basic truth was the simplest explanation. He wasn't ready to go into more details with Jessa just yet. Since Cliff had known him for a few years and Ryan had never visited in that time, Eli had offered him a little more detail, but he wasn't too fond of talking much about his family. All these years, he'd hoped geographic distance would allow him to keep a barrier between his childhood and his adulthood. With Ryan showing up, he was struggling to come to terms with what that might mean for that barrier.

Minutes later, they were at the boat. Ryan quickly jumped onto the dock and took the coffees and pastries from Eli. "Anything for me?" he asked with a grin.

"Something for everyone. There're two hot chocolates in that tray of drinks. One for you and," he paused and turned to the couple with a smile "and an extra in case your son wanted one."

The woman in the couple smiled broadly and held her hand out. "Donna Canton. You must be Eli." Donna had an athletic, outdoorsy quality to her and was dressed for the day in a yellow windbreaker and jeans paired with black rubber boots. She had short dark hair and bright brown eyes.

Eli shook her hand. "You got it. If the hot chocolate is a no, don't worry about it. Otherwise, I trust these guys have taken care of everything you need?"

Donna grinned. "You've just made Aaron's day! He loves hot chocolate, and it's definitely a bit chilly this morning." She rubbed her hands together quickly and gestured to the man standing beside her. "This is my husband George."

George reached over to shake Eli's hand. "Great to meet you. We're looking forward to catching some halibut today." George was essentially a male version of Donna with short dark hair and eyes and in matching jacket, jeans and boots. He had a laidback, easy quality to him. He lifted his chin in the direction of their son. Ryan had climbed back into the boat and was patiently helping the boy set his fishing rod in the row of holders along the back of the cabin in the boat. "That's our son Aaron. He's beside himself about this fishing trip, so be prepared for tons of questions." Aaron shared his parents' hair, eyes and outfit, although he had a fluorescent orange life jacket on over his yellow windbreaker.

Eli relaxed slightly. He was accustomed to taking completely inexperienced people out to fish, however it was always a relief when they came sensibly dressed and appeared to have an idea of what the day would entail. He glanced to Jessa who stood quietly at his side. "This is my friend Jessa. She's never been out for a charter trip in Alaska either, so she's joining us for the day." Eli hadn't thought ahead about how to introduce her, but he settled on 'friend.'

Jessa quickly struck up a conversation with Donna and George, while Eli went into action with Cliff and Ryan to get the boat ready to leave the harbor. He continued to be impressed with Ryan, mostly because he didn't hesitate to work, asked for help if he wasn't sure how to do something and then carried on. Within a few minutes, they were motoring out of the harbor, one of many boats in a slow parade out into Kachemak Bay.

* * *

"HEY, STOP IT!" Jessa demanded as she wrestled with the halibut she'd just reeled in. The halibut was rather docile, so she supposed she was talking to the fishhook, which she couldn't seem to get out. She heard a low laugh and glanced up to find Eli kneeling down by her side.

"Need some help with that?"

She brushed her hair out of her face and sighed. "Is there a trick to this?"

Eli shrugged and reached over. With a quick twist, he eased the hook out. "A little practice helps."

The subtle brush of his hand against hers sent a wash of heat through her. When she glanced over at him, his green eyes were inches from hers. With his sun-burnished skin, chiseled features and just all around rugged sexiness, she wanted to kiss him so badly it almost physically pained her to hold back. For a few seconds, the air around them came to life. Eli's eyes darkened, and she heard him take a sharp breath. A loud thump nearby snapped the moment. Jessa turned to see Ryan laughing as he helped George with the halibut he'd just dropped when he brought it over the side of the boat.

She stood up with Eli following. His eyes caught hers again, and her breath hitched at the bare desire she saw there. With a subtle shake of his head, he turned away and strode to Ryan's side, quickly engaging in an easy banter with Ryan and George. The rest of the day passed with many similar moments. Not that she needed much to amp up her attraction to Eli, but watching him work did just that. He was clearly in his element—moving through the day with an easy, rugged confidence. He was friendly and funny with the charter customers and patient with their young son who had so many questions, he could have easily annoyed a less patient man.

As the day wound down, Jessa leaned against the railing and watched the boat's wake ruffle in the water behind them. She glanced down at her hand and flexed it. She'd finally felt okay to remove the bandage covering the last of her burns yesterday. The skin was pink, but all healed up in the area along the outside of her wrist and on the back of her hand. With the heavy-duty rubber gloves Eli insisted she wear, she hadn't even worried about it today.

A gust of wind blew and she looked out over the water again. It was early evening and they were headed back to Otter Cove Harbor. The sun had started to dip down in the sky, its light softening. The day had been beyond fun. Between the actual fishing—she'd managed to catch two halibut—the company and the breathtaking view, she'd had a banner day. At the moment, she was watching the mountains on the far side of Kachemak Bay recede. As Eli had suggested, they'd had a quick lunch in Seldovia, a quaint, small and charming village that could only be reached by boat or small plane. The mountains were dark against the sky, their hulking forms casting long shadows on the water. She scanned the horizon, pausing on the volcano in Cook Inlet, just outside the mouth of Kachemak Bay. Mount Augustine sat by itself in the water, a small cluster of clouds circling its peak. She took a deep breath and turned to face forward.

The second her eyes landed on Eli, her breath hitched and flutters twirled in her low belly. Dear God, that man was just...flat sexy...and nice and smart and funny and all kinds of much too good. Jessa had never been much for dating. She couldn't say she'd had her heartbroken or anything like that. She'd just yet to meet a man who ever made her feel anything even remotely like this.

She couldn't say why, but he appeared slightly uncertain at moments in his interactions with Ryan, almost as if they didn't know each other that well. That was the other thing about Eli—he made her curious. She wanted to know all about him. She had gleaned a bit today. Namely, that he'd been born and raised in Juneau and moved to Diamond Creek about ten years ago to start his business here.

She'd savored every second of incidental contact with him—when he reached his arm around to steady her while she held her fishing rod to reel in a halibut, when his hands brushed hers as he helped her unhook the halibut. She smiled to herself when it occurred to her she was ridiculously turned on while they were surrounded by others and dealing with fish all day.

Not much later, Jessa leaned her hips against the boat railing and watched while Ryan and Cliff helped the Canton's carry their cooler and other gear down the docks. Ryan and Cliff were heading out for burgers afterwards with Cliff's promise he'd drop Ryan off at Eli's house later. That left Jessa and Eli on the boat at the dock. Eli had stepped down into the boat cabin to put a few things away. She couldn't help the curl of anticipation that rolled through her to realize she might have a few minutes alone with Eli.

Within seconds, he was climbing the stairs out of the cabin and stepping onto the deck. He'd removed his fishing gear and changed into another pair of faded jeans and t-shirt, both of soft, worn fabric that molded to his muscled body. She'd already had her turn in the tiny bathroom where she stripped out of her fishy clothes and changed into a clean pair of clothes, which were essentially her uniform—leggings and a t-shirt with the only variation in color. For now, she had on a pair of charcoal gray leggings and a red long-sleeved t-shirt that fit snugly.

Eli stepped to the railing and leaned against it beside her. His brown hair was tousled from the wind. His green gaze caught hers, his mouth hooking at one corner. "So, what do you think now that you've had a day of fishing in Alaska?"

"It was perfect! I see why so many tourists come here. You can't beat the view and it's a blast out on the water. Thanks for taking me." She left unsaid that the best part of the day was being with him. While she might not know quite what to do with the strength of her attraction to Eli, she knew she enjoyed just about every minute in his company.

He shrugged. "Anytime. We run charters almost every day some weeks, so if you ever want to go again, just let me know."

"You're out almost every day? Really?" She couldn't help but ask because it seemed like a dream life.

He chuckled. "Really. Fishing's to my business in the summer like skiing is to your brother's in the winter—all day, every day."

"I suppose it would be. Well, it was awesome, so I'll probably take you up on that."

Eli nodded and looked out over the water. She followed his gaze to see the setting sun had created a watercolor in the sky over the mountains with layers of gold, orange and red. A gust of salty wind came off the bay, blowing her hair wild since she'd brushed it loose when she changed. Eli's gaze traveled from the water to her, just as he rested one elbow on the railing and angled toward her. In a flash, the air around them came to life.

Her belly clenched and heat streaked through her. Another breeze came off the water with enough chill to elicit a shiver. His eyes locked with hers, he lifted a hand and brushed a loose lock of hair away from her face, turning fully toward her as he did. He tucked it behind her ear, the subtle touch sending a hot shiver through her. He didn't drop his hand and slid it around her nape. His thumb brushed across the beat of her pulse, sending it skittering wildly.

CHAPTER 9

$\mathcal{E}$li looked down at Jessa. Her windblown brown hair, her flushed cheeks, and her silvery eyes held him transfixed. All day long, he'd been thankful for how busy he had to be on a fishing charter. The constant flow of activity kept him distracted enough that he wasn't fighting a hard-on all day. He'd walked out of the cabin a few minutes ago and just stopped fighting it. Jessa was too damn sexy. She'd also shown herself to be a quick learner when it came to fishing. She seemed undecided about whether she'd be eating the halibut she caught, but she'd called one of her brothers after she reeled it in to announce what she was bringing home for dinner. A fishing charter was fun, but it was also a lot of work. She hadn't shied away for a second, even from some of the less savory tasks involved with cleaning the decks. A stellar day on the water with a woman who seemed imbued with a magic power to make him forget any reservations he ever had meant he couldn't let the chance to kiss her again pass by.

The air felt charged and heavy. Her silvery gaze went smoky. Her pulse beat rapidly under his thumb as he brushed across the soft skin along her neck. His eyes dropped to her lips—so soft and full—right when her tongue darted out to moisten them. He dipped his head and caught her lips. She didn't hesitate and sighed against his mouth, the breathy sound sending a jolt of lust through him. He experienced something with Jessa he'd never experienced before—a need that burned so hot, he could barely contain it, yet the moment he gave in, he could slow down and take all day. Just now, he could kiss her for hours. He traced her lips with his tongue, interspersing kisses in between, until she stepped closer and slipped her hand up around his neck.

He dove into the warm sweetness of her mouth and their kiss took on a life of its own. Her tongue tangled sinuously with his—bold and playful. He stroked through her hair, savoring her low moan when he slid his hand down her spine and cupped her bottom. The soft give of her curves under his palm sent his heart to battering against his ribs. The wind gusted again, and he turned to shelter her from it, bringing his back against the railing and her into his arms against him. He felt drugged between her hands traveling up his chest and feeling the rise and fall of her breasts against him with each breath she took. He tore his lips free, desperate to taste more. He blazed a wet path down her neck, her skin hinted with vanilla and honey.

She slipped a hand up under his shirt. The simple feel of her touch against his skin sent need spinning tighter inside of him. He lifted his head to look down at her. Her hair fell in a loose tangle around her shoulders. Her lips were kiss-swollen and her cheeks flushed. When she opened her eyes and he found her smoky gaze upon him, dark with desire, it was all he could do not to tear her clothes off right then and there. His thoughts a haze of desire, he dipped his head again, unable to consider anything other than needing to taste her again.

This kiss was hotter and deeper, a tangle of lips, teeth and tongue. Jessa flexed against him, and he tugged her closer, one palm cupping her luscious bottom and the other shoving her t-shirt up. He couldn't hold back a groan at the feel of her soft skin as he stroked up her abdomen to cup one of her breasts. Her nipple was a tight bead through the thin silk of her bra. He flicked a thumb at the clasp between her breasts, biting back another moan when her breasts tumbled loose. He tore his lips free and looked down again.

He suddenly became aware of where they were. The bustle of sounds at the harbor, to which he was so accustomed he usually tuned it out, broke through the fog of lust. Yet, the feel of Jessa against him made it hard for reason to cut through. She arched closer. Before awareness knocked sense into him, he had to know if she wanted him as much as he wanted her. With a stroke of his thumb across her taut nipple, he dragged his hand down, straight past the waistband of her leggings, to stroke between her legs. The silk of her panties was wet. Without a thought passing through his mind, driven solely by need, he shoved the silk aside and stroked into her cleft. Hot, wet, silky folds pulsed against his fingers. Her breath came in ragged gasps. He slid one finger into her channel and then another. Even though he knew he wouldn't find his own release now, all he wanted was to make her come. He stroked into her channel, savoring every clench and throb around his fingers.

When she gasped his name, her voice raw with need and reflecting the depth of his, he circled his thumb over her swollen clit. Her head fell against his chest on a soft cry, her body going taut and her channel convulsing around his fingers. When she relaxed against him, he slowly dragged his fingers out and tugged her clothes back into place. Rock hard and desperate for much more, he leaned his head back and took several gulps of the chilly, ocean air. The sound of a boat nearby seemed to nudge Jessa into awareness. She lifted her head from his chest, her eyes widening.

"Oh my. I can't believe I forgot where we were."

Her cheeks flushed deeper, and she bit her lip, which only served to make him want to kiss her again. He kept an iron grip on that impulse and aimed for light.

"I can believe we forgot," he said bluntly.

That elicited a giggle from Jessa. After a moment, her smile faded. He knew she could feel every inch of his cock in the cradle of her hips because he sure as hell knew how hard he was. "This doesn't seem fair," she said. While she didn't state what wasn't fair, he knew precisely what she meant. He might go home unsatisfied, but feeling and watching her find her pleasure was about the best thing he'd ever experienced.

JESSA LEANED against the counter in the corner of the lodge restaurant kitchen. In the short time she'd been here, she'd developed the habit of rising early and helping Delia with the morning baking. They'd just finished prepping cinnamon rolls. Delia had stepped into her office and shooed Jessa over to get some coffee. The espresso machine tucked in the corner where she stood beeped. She turned and poured the two shots of espresso into a mug and added hot water. After a dash of cream, she took a welcome sip and sighed. She pushed away from the counter and through the swinging door into the restaurant. It was still early with only a few customers at tables. She made her way to a small table by the windows and sat down.

It was barely past six and the sun was cresting the mountains. She'd yet to see much darkness since she'd been here. The sun didn't set until after ten at night and the glimmers of dawn broke as early as four in the morning. As she sipped her coffee, Eli strolled into her thoughts. Well, it would be more apt to say he'd been pretty much camped out in her mind since last night. After he'd sent her flying into a shattering orgasm with nothing more than a few strokes of his fingers, she'd somehow pulled herself together and walked down the docks with him like a normal human being. All the while, her body had been reverberating with aftershocks.

Half in a daze, she'd somehow driven herself back to the lodge. She'd fallen asleep with nothing but Eli on her mind. In the span of a few body-melting minutes, Eli had brought her to the most explosive climax of her life. Again and again, the dark desire flickering in his green eyes flashed through her mind. A bolt of heat streaked through her. Beyond that though was how much she simply enjoyed being around him. With her limited experience with liking someone this much, she didn't quite know what to do with it. Complicating matters was the fact she didn't quite know what to do with her life. She took a gulp of coffee, savoring the rich flavor. The sun fully crested the mountain ridge rising up behind the lodge. Its rays instantly brightened the grassy ski slopes and filtered through the spruce trees. Within minutes, a mist rose off the trees and ground, the dew from the chilly night dissipating under the instant heat of the sun.

Jessa took another sip of coffee and leaned back in her chair. Even with Eli sending her body, heart and mind into a tailspin, she was finding that Diamond Creek soothed her soul. She hadn't known she needed this respite before the fire, but she was discovering the slower pace here was doing wonders for her. For the last few years, she'd worked herself to the bone. She loved her art—building furniture and making it fun and whimsical with painting—but she hadn't found a way to make enough money to keep from barely staying afloat. She wasn't naturally competitive by nature, so the marketing and self-promotion she needed to do to make a splash in the art world she inhabited in Seattle wasn't easy. She still struggled with the lingering doubt that what she was doing was silly and pointless.

Before her apartment building burned down, she'd worn herself out in the months prior getting ready for a regional furniture market. The market had been scheduled the weekend following the fire. She'd been smart enough to store some of her stock in a shared storage space, but roughly half of what she'd intended to sell at the market had burned to ash. The fire had wiped out more than her spirit. Reeling, she'd pulled herself together and cut her losses. All she could think was she needed to be with her family and she desperately needed a change of scenery. Her older sister Becca had hugged her close and insisted Diamond Creek would be exactly what Jessa needed. Jessa had packed what little she had left into Blue and taken off for Alaska after a quick stop to see her parents in Bellingham. Once she crossed the border into Alaska, after almost three thousand miles of driving through the wilds of the Canadian Yukon, she'd purchased a tiny Alaskan flag. It was blue to match her truck with its pattern of stars—the Big Dipper and the North Star. Tucked behind her rear view mirror, the little flag lifted her spirits on the rest of her drive to Diamond Creek.

Here she was now with coffee, amazing quiet mornings, friends and family…and an unexpected man who tipped her world sideways. She wished she could be one of those people who knew what she wanted and had a plan to execute. Gage was like that—he always had a plan. Marley was probably the first person in his life who hadn't been part of a plan. Actually, all of her siblings were planners. Becca and Garrett, twins who were so different and so alike at once, were brilliant lawyers. Sawyer had followed Gage into the Navy and onto become a Navy SEAL as well. Then, there was her. Jessa always felt like her hopes and dreams were a tad too, well, dreamy. She loved building and loved making her furniture fun. The combination of practical and whimsical called to her. Yet, she was flying along by the seat of her pants, and she damn well knew it. The fire had illuminated just how shaky her financial position was. Her apartment was home and work to her, and it all burned up together. Her lingering doubts about whether her career choice had been worthwhile came roaring back with a fervor. It was hard not to look at her circumstances and wonder if she'd been a fool.

She shook her head sharply, bringing her mind back to now. She looked outside again to see a stellar jay fly past the windows and land with vigor on a bird feeder mounted on the deck railing. It swung wildly for a moment, the jay entirely unperturbed. Once the feeder slowed its' swinging, the jay began pecking at the bird seed, scattering it on the deck below. The jay's black crown bobbed up and down as it ate, and sun struck sparks off its blue wings.

"Thanks for helping out again."

Jessa glanced up to see Delia pulling out the chair across from her. Delia set her coffee down and sifted her hands through her honey blonde hair, efficiently tying it in a knot.

"No problem. I love getting up early. Seems like Alaska was made for early birds. The mornings here are so beautiful!"

Delia grinned. "I know, right?" She paused and took a sip of her coffee. "So, how was fishing yesterday?"

Jessa felt her cheeks heat and tried to ignore it. "It was great. Eli was an awesome host, and I caught two halibut!" A swell of pride rose inside at that. She hadn't fished in years, so it was fun to actually succeed at it.

"I know. Marley told me they tossed them on ice in the fridge for us to grill tonight. Speaking of fish, did I remember you're a vegetarian?"

"You could say that, but I'm not the best vegetarian around. I'm opposed to mass food production, so that's why I call myself mostly a vegetarian. Most places aren't like Alaska where it's easy to find fresh, local foods. There're some markets in Seattle that are pretty good, but it's practically a fortune. Fresh halibut that I caught myself though? I'll be eating some of that," Jessa replied with a soft laugh.

Delia grinned. "Have you had fresh halibut from here yet?"

Jessa shook her head. "Not yet. When we were up for your wedding, it was a king salmon extravaganza."

"Oh, you're in for a treat!" Delia paused, her gaze thoughtful. "So, tell me what's up with you and Eli?"

Jessa felt the blush race up her neck and cheeks again. She tried and failed to will it away. She took a gulp of coffee, glancing out to the mountains and back again. She shrugged. "Um, I don't know. He invited me to go fishing anytime and I wanted to see what it was like out on the bay, so I went."

Delia nodded slowly, her eyes warm and kind. "Sure. Who wouldn't want to do that? I'm not asking what you did. I already knew that. I was wondering how come you blush whenever his name gets mentioned. Let's be honest, it's not like Eli gets mentioned all that much. I know him, but he's only up here once in a while. He works like crazy. Gage has started getting supplies from Eli for customers. We always need gear for people who forget things when they pack for their trip. But it's funny, you had your little fender bender with him, and it seems like you might like him. That's not a bad thing, you know."

Jessa chewed on her lip. "I know. I might be a little into him," she finally said, blushing even harder. "How in the world do you notice so much?"

Delia chuckled. "I pay attention. You're also one of the most straightforward people I know. I might not have gotten to spend that much time with you, but you just are who you are. It's one of the things I love about you, but it also makes it easy to notice things. You might want me to shut the hell up about now, but should I do some reconnaissance and see what I can find out about Eli?"

"Oh my… why would you think I'd want that?" Jessa finally asked, dying to ask Delia to do just that.

Delia shrugged, a gleam in her eyes. "Because when most people are interested in someone, they're, well, interested."

Jessa threw her hands up. "I can't hide anything around here, can I?"

"It's not too easy. I'm just teasing, you know. I'll steer clear if it makes you feel better."

"Oh no! If I'm going to have to deal with my nosy family, I might as well get something out of it."

Delia threw her head back with a laugh. "It's good to have you here," she finally said when her laugh quieted. "Speaking of you being here, I thought maybe you might want to go with me to Midnight Sun Gallery today."

"I'd love to. If it's an art gallery, I'm there. Any reason you want me to go with you?"

"A friend of mine owns it, Risa Thomas. I thought you might want to talk with her about your furniture. Diamond Creek may be small, but the art galleries here do a brisk business. You might find some opportunities to make a little extra cash here. The tourists spend crazy money."

A sprout of hope unfurled inside of Jessa.

$\mathcal{E}$li stood staring at the phone in his office. It was mid-morning and he'd mentally promised himself he'd call his father this morning. In between ruminations over what to do about Ryan's unexpected presence in his life, Jessa danced through his thoughts. Those few minutes on the boat with her had basically blown his mind. He'd gone home and needed an ice cold shower to get a handle on the raging lust coursing through his body. He'd fallen asleep replaying those heated moments on the boat again and again in his mind. He was rattled at how quickly she'd snuck through what he'd considered his impervious defenses. He didn't do relationships. *Ever.* But Jessa...she made him want more. Beyond the pounding need she elicited, he wanted to just spend time with her. She was light-hearted, funny, curious and damn good at fishing for someone who claimed to have little experience. She had a positive attitude and a spirit to try. The lightness she carried was so intoxicating, all he wanted was to see her again to soak up the way he felt when he was with her.

His office phone rang, snapping him out of his Jessareverie. He stepped to his desk to answer when it stopped ringing. He heard Ryan's voice answering from out front in the retail store. In a few short days, he'd gone from living a private, quiet life to stumbling into the cauldron of his attraction to Jessa and having a tag-along everywhere he went in Ryan. Even with Jessa's forceful burst into his world, his worries about Ryan and how to handle the situation were simmering in the background. Eli had decided this morning that he would find a way to make sure Ryan stayed with him. The problem was how to make that happen without it becoming ugly with their parents.

Eli didn't want Ryan living a life on tenterhooks, wondering when their parents might show up and try to force him home. Eli also wouldn't allow Ryan to return to their mother, knowing that meant a replay of Eli's adolescence. Norm Brooks, their jerk of a father, had reached his worst once Eli was old enough to stand up to him. When Eli was younger, Norm was frightening enough for Eli to steer clear, although he had to stand by and watch the relentless verbal, emotional, and occasional physical abuse of his mother. Once Eli got to be about Ryan's age, he became more of his father's target with his father lashing out verbally, deliberately picking fights over nothing and occasionally swinging his fists. To this day, he wasn't sure he should be proud he'd never responded physically to his father. He'd been determined he wouldn't become the man Norm was. He supposed he should consider it good that Norm hadn't come knocking sooner on his mother's door. Ryan was old enough now to find his own way out.

Eli shook his head sharply and grabbed the phone. He needed to get this over with. He dialed the number for his childhood home, knowing his mother would be at work and his father home.

"Yup." Norm couldn't even be bothered to say hello when he answered the phone.

"Hey Norm, it's Eli." Eli had stopped calling his father anything other than his name years and years ago.

There was a long pause before Norm spoke again. "Eli, huh? Figured you'd be calling sometime soon. Your mother's heartbroken over Ryan. You'd best send him back this way soon."

While Eli should have been startled at his father's matter-of-fact expectation, he wasn't. He knew well that Norm expected others to do whatever he wanted them to do. Why Norm wanted Ryan around was beyond Eli though.

"Right. That's why I'm calling. Ryan's staying with me. You can either make it ugly, or you can let it go. I've already talked to an attorney, and I'm filing for guardianship tomorrow."

"Oh, and you think you'll win?" Norm's question dripped with belligerence.

Eli took a slow breath. He would not be baited into an argument with Norm over this. "I will. Between the police reports over the years, the reports to child welfare when I was little and the fact I'm willing to testify, I've got a solid case. Mom can try to oppose it, but it won't do a bit of good for her relationship with Ryan. If she wants a chance to actually have a relationship with him, she might want to let this go."

Norm was quiet for several beats. Eli could hear the rattle of his breath through the phone line. Norm was probably on his way to emphysema based on his two-pack a day smoking habit. Every memory Eli had of his father involved the labored sound of his breathing, which had only worsened over the years.

"Well, aren't you just the tough guy now?"

Weariness washed over Eli. "Norm, I'm just trying to do right by Ryan. Life with you is hell, so I'm not putting him through that. I don't like knowing you're back with Mom, but she's an adult and she can make her own decisions. Ryan has to wait four more years. All he's had to deal with is six months with you and he ran away. Just let him be."

The line went dead in Eli's ear. He tossed the phone on his desk and sat down in his chair with a thump. Not that he'd expected any talk with his father to go well, but he'd hoped for a little more clarity than that. Norm would either let it go because he genuinely didn't care, but he couldn't admit it; or he'd put up a fight for the sake of it.

"Eli?"

Eli glanced up to find Ryan standing in the doorway. The worry swirling in his eyes told Eli that Ryan had likely heard part of his conversation with their father. Eli cursed himself for forgetting to close the door. He ran a hand through his hair and rolled his shoulders in an attempt to loosen the tension there. "What's up?"

"Was that Dad?"

Eli nodded. "Yup. Didn't mean for you to hear that."

Ryan stepped into Eli's office and leaned against the wall, crossing his arms and staring out the window across from him. It looked out into a cluster of spruce trees behind the building, right about where Ryan had started to set up his tent to camp when Eli found him. "It's okay. It's not like I don't know the deal with Dad. Did you mean what you said?" he asked, his eyes darting from the window to Eli and back again.

Eli cocked his head to the side and arched a brow in question, uncertain what Ryan was asking about.

Ryan's eyes flicked to him and back to the window. "Did you really talk to an attorney?"

Understanding dawned and Eli's heart clenched. He knew Ryan was worried, but he hadn't considered how much it would mean for him to know Eli was going to do his damnedest to make sure Ryan could stay here free and clear. "Sure did. One of Jessa's brothers happens to be an attorney. She gave me his number yesterday, so I called him already. He said I should have a good case if I'm willing to dredge up the past. It's not my preference, but I don't want you going through what I did, so it's no problem. I'm heading over to meet with him at his office in a little bit. Wanna go with me?"

Ryan was quiet for so long, Eli became concerned he'd moved too quickly on this. Ryan's eyes finally bounced to him again, and Eli saw the sheen there. Ryan nodded, his hair falling over his forehead. Without a word, he pushed away from the wall and started to walk through the office door. He paused and glanced over his shoulder, his eyes trained on the corner of Eli's desk. "Thanks."

"No problem," Eli replied, his words mostly for himself because Ryan practically ran into the store after that. He leaned back in his chair and looked out into the cluster of spruce trees, his eyes following a branch that dipped when a gray jay landed. He took a slow breath, trying to ease the tightness in his chest and throat. Ryan brought back so many feelings from his past, it was discombobulating. For a man who'd spent most of his life trying to keep emotional entanglements at a distance, he'd committed himself to doing the right thing for Ryan, and he'd be damned if he let his father get in the way.

Later that afternoon, Ryan walked beside Eli into Garrett Hamilton's office. Eli had driven by Garrett's office almost every day since Garrett had opened it, yet he'd never had a reason to stop. In the short time Garrett had been in Diamond Creek, he'd quickly established himself as *the* go-to attorney in Diamond Creek. Diamond Creek was small enough there weren't too many attorneys to go around. Prior to Garrett's relocation to town, most people headed north to Kenai if they needed legal advice. The only other attorney Eli knew of was mostly retired. Garrett's reputation from Seattle had followed him here.

Garrett's office was on Harborside Road, which ran perpendicular to Main Street and, not surprisingly, was toward the harbor side of town. Harborside Road held a mix of homes and small office businesses. Garrett's office occupied one half of a single-story duplex. When they stepped through the doorway, Garrett waved at them from his desk. He was on the phone and gestured for them to sit at a round table situated by a bay window that offered a view of the boat harbor. He said his goodbyes and strode to the table, reaching over to shake Eli's hand.

"Garrett Hamilton. I think we've met before, but maybe just for a minute," Garrett offered with an easy grin. Garrett was tall and dark with blue eyes. He carried a resemblance to Jessa, but it was subtle. More than anything, he shared her warmth.

Eli nodded. "I believe we met once when I was up skiing. I haven't been up there as much as I'd like. Gage has done an amazing job with the lodge."

Garrett's grin widened. "That he has!" He turned to Ryan. "You must be Ryan," he offered, reaching across the table for another handshake.

Ryan stood quickly, almost knocking his chair over in the process, and shook Garrett's hand vigorously. Once they were all seated, Garrett caught Eli's eyes. "So, I'm guessing you want to review what we discussed yesterday?"

"I'd like to get things rolling. I didn't plan ahead about bringing Ryan with me, but he wanted to come, so here we are. No secrets here. He knows I'd like to file for guardianship and that's what he wants. I guess if I have anything to add other than what we discussed last night, I'm hoping to be able to get this through without Ryan having to be dragged into court..."

Ryan cut in. "It's okay. If I have to be there, I can handle it."

Eli glanced to Ryan whose gaze was resolute. Eli knew

Ryan probably could handle it, but he didn't want to put him in that position with their mother. Eli had already cut his ties. If their mother blamed him for cutting Ryan out of her life, it would be better than her blaming Ryan.

"I'm sure you can, but I don't think it'll be necessary," Garrett said.

Garrett's confidence eased the tension running through Eli. "Alright. Tell me what we need to do."

Garrett leaned back and reached for a folder on the corner of his desk. Once he had it in hand, he opened it on the table, fanning the papers out for them to see. "I've already drawn up the basic guardianship petition. I'd like you to read through this while you're here, so if you have any questions, I can address them right now. Then, I say take it home and sleep on it. It's past four, so we can't file until tomorrow anyway. If you're ready to file tomorrow, drop these off and I'll take care of the rest." He paused and glanced to Ryan, as if considering his next words. "Have you discussed everything with him?" Garrett asked, turning back to Eli.

"Including the no child support part, if that's what you're worried about," Eli replied.

Garrett nodded. "Right then. Anyway, like I said last night, that should make it much easier. From my experience, these cases get messy when people are asking for guardianship and child support. By the way, that would be a reasonable request and I still think you could win if it was contested."

Eli shook his head. "Not worth the mess." He didn't need the child support and couldn't countenance demanding it, knowing it would be coming straight from his mother. It was enough to live with the knowledge she couldn't seem to accept his offer for help and sever her ties with his father. He didn't want to add another burden to her.

"Okay then, let's go over this."

Not much later, Eli stood from the table, Garrett and Ryan standing along with him. "If it's okay with you, I'll sign now and leave these here. No need to wait on it."

Garrett nodded firmly. "Got it. I'll call in the morning to double check before I file them."

Eli snagged the pen on the table and quickly signed the petition. Ryan had gone to stand by a sliding glass door at the back. Garrett caught Eli's eyes and spoke quietly. "You think he's doing okay with all this?"

Eli shrugged. "Think so. Like I told you, last time I saw him was when he was four years old."

Garrett nodded slowly. "A hell of a change for your life. Seems like you're not having any second thoughts."

Eli shook his head sharply. "I might not have expected this, but I don't have a single doubt about it."

Garrett's eyes were sharp and assessing. He angled his head to the side. "You're a damn good brother. I'm glad you called me about this. We'll get it taken care of."

"Do I need to pay you now, or…?"

"No worry. I won't bill until the case is resolved, not in simple cases like this. Plus, you took Jessa out fishing, so you get a discount," Garrett said with a grin.

Eli chuckled, uncertain how Garrett felt that he'd invited his little sister out for a fishing trip. He aimed for nonchalant in his response. "She said she'd never been out on the bay. Seeing as I'm out there almost every day, I told her to call if she wanted to join one of our charters." Eli tried to ignore the vision that flickered in the back of his mind— Jessa's kiss swollen lips, her eyes hazy with passion when she opened them after climaxing all over his fingers. *Not the time, man. Get a grip. Her brother is standing right here!* He took a slow breath, wrangling his body in check. Man, he had it bad. All Garrett had to do was mention Jessa, and Eli's brain jumped tracks, forgetting anything else.

"I'm headed up to the lodge for some of the halibut she

caught. You and Ryan oughta come up. Think you could swing it?"

Garrett was being nothing but friendly. Eli had grown accustomed to the stream of social invitations in Diamond Creek. Locals were friendly and gregarious. Alaska contained a hodgepodge of residents—some born and raised here and many transplants. One commonality among residents was a mutual respect for the love of all things Alaskan. While Eli was a born and raised Alaskan, Juneau was large enough that he'd managed to mostly keep to himself. With the family he had, that worked just fine for him. When he moved to Diamond Creek, he'd initially been taken aback at how many locals invited him to various town events. Once his business was up and running, he'd fielded invitations to various town committees and the like. He'd yet to learn how to ease into the social world. He considered himself friendly, but he didn't have the easiness and gregariousness of people like Garrett and Jessa.

Exactly why Jessa just might be the best thing that ever happened to you. A previously quiet voice in his head interjected. He didn't know what the hell was going on with him, but when it came to Jessa, he thought the damnedest things. Between her and Ryan, his life was heading down a track he'd never contemplated—one that involved relationships he'd thought he was long past wanting. Before he realized what was happening, Garrett grinned and clapped him on the shoulder.

"Awesome! Delia's cooking and she's the best!"

Eli realized he was nodding his head. He'd just agreed to go have dinner at the lodge where he was guaranteed to see Jessa. The second that idea flashed through his mind, he couldn't even contemplate backing out. Yet, there was the rather awkward situation that he'd be surrounded by her family and friends, all of whom might pick up on the fact he could barely keep his eyes off of her. He managed a polite smile, which stretched when he saw the pride gleaming in Garrett's eyes. Garrett clearly adored Delia.

Oh right. Garrett just said Delia's cooking was the best. *Focus, man. Focus.* "I know when I've had dinner up at the lodge, the food was amazing."

Garrett's grin widened. "I don't know what magic Delia plans to do with the halibut, but we can always have extras from the dinner buffet. Ryan'll get a chance to see the lodge too."

Ryan turned away from the window, tuning into their conversation. "What's the lodge?"

Garrett launched into a brief description, while Eli's mind immediately swung back to Jessa and her smoky silver eyes.

CHAPTER 11

"Watch out!"

Jessa glanced behind her just as a badminton birdie bounced off her shoulder. Marley held her badminton racquet aloft and shrugged. "Sorry!" she called out, her auburn ponytail swinging as she jogged over to Jessa's side and picked up the birdie.

"No problem," Jessa replied with a chuckle.

Marley paused beside Jessa, tossing the birdie up and down in her palm. "Don't suppose you want to play some more? Or perhaps kicking the boys' butts once was enough?" Marley asked with a grin.

Jessa had joined in with Marley, her friend Ginger, and Marley's sister Lacey in a game earlier. They'd handily defeated Gage and the teammates he'd rounded up. Jessa returned Marley's grin. "Exactly. I like to quit when I'm ahead."

Marley shrugged. "I think we're about done now anyway. I need to go inside and check on Holly. My mom's with her, but she's due for a nap, so she's probably getting fussy."

At that, Marley jogged the short distance to the badminton net and stopped by Gage's side. Jessa watched while her oldest brother leaned down, his brown hair catching the faint rays from the sun. She smiled softly to witness the love in his eyes whenever he looked at Marley. Eli immediately flashed to mind. She couldn't help but wonder if he could look at her like that.

With a mental shake, Jessa turned and continued walking across the back lawn behind the lodge and up the steps onto the sprawling deck. Harry, Delia's ever-present manager and family friend, was arranging platters of food on a table. He glanced up. "How about a drink?" he asked, nudging his chin in the direction of the small bar he'd set up on the deck.

Jessa meandered over to the bar. "Do we have any of the gooseberry wine?"

Harry came to her side. "Sure do." Reaching past her, he snagged a bottle. He smoothly uncorked it and filled a glass. "Here you go," he said, handing it to her with flourish. Harry did everything with a touch of flourish.

Jessa was coming to enjoy working with Harry. She found keeping busy helped her stay grounded. Her mind flicked to Eli again. Her one and only outing outside of her family's orbit had been fishing with him. Oh and then the part where he blew her mind and sent her body into a tailspin of pleasure so intense, she flushed even now thinking about it. She was a bit embarrassed at how carried away she'd gotten, and yet she also couldn't stop wondering when she'd see Eli again.

She took a gulp of the gooseberry wine in an effort to distract herself. "I still can't believe how good this wine is," she commented to Harry. "Who knew gooseberry wine would be so delicious?"

Harry grinned and set the bottle of wine back on the bar.

At that moment, the door into the back hallway opened and Garrett stepped through.

"Hey sis!" Garrett threw an arm over her shoulders and hugged her close for a moment. "So good to have you here." His eyes landed on the bar. "Awesome! Can I grab a beer?" he asked, glancing to Harry.

"Thanks for asking, but you know the answer," Harry answered with a smile.

Garrett grabbed a beer and opened it, taking a long swallow. He glanced around when he set the beer on the edge of the bar. "Sorry I missed the badminton. I tried to get here sooner, but I got tied up at the office."

Gage clapped Garrett on the shoulder as he walked by them with Marley. "Yeah, I needed you. The girls kicked our ass. Be back in a few."

Harry followed Gage and Marley into the hallway leading to the lodge kitchen, and Garrett glanced to Jessa. "So, I met with your new friend Eli this afternoon."

The mere mention of Eli sent a wash of heat through her. *Seriously, Jessa. You can't be this idiotic over him.* The problem was…she was downright idiotic. She'd spent most of the night and today thinking about him in any spare moment. All through high school, she remembered watching her friends take turns going gaga over different guys. She seemed to have missed that phase of life. She dated here and there, but she'd never been infatuated with anyone. She'd chalked it up to never meeting the right guy. Until Eli. The part she hadn't contemplated was what it might mean to meet the right guy.

Garrett arched a brow, at which point Jessa realized she'd lost track of the fact she was in a conversation. Eli had hijacked her brain. "Oh, right. He mentioned he needed an attorney, so I gave him your number. What did he need?"

"Well, not sure how much he told you, but he's filing for

guardianship of his little brother. He brought Ryan with him. Seems like a good kid."

Jessa's curiosity shot through the roof. Eli had casually mentioned yesterday during the fishing trip that he was hoping Ryan would be able to stay in Diamond Creek, but he'd been vague about any problems at home for Ryan. She wanted to grill Garrett, but that would make her interest in Eli more than obvious. Much as she loved Garrett, he loved to tease. It was hard enough to manage her responses to Eli without being teased about them.

"Oh. He mentioned hoping Ryan would stay here, but that's all I knew. Is everything okay?"

"Everything's fine for now, but it sounds like home might not be the greatest place for Ryan to be. He wants to stay with Eli, and Eli's determined to make sure he can." Garrett paused, his gaze somber. "Eli's a good guy. He's stepping up for his brother without hesitation."

Jessa took in Garrett's words, her heart tightening. On top of everything else, Eli was going above and beyond for Ryan. At that moment, the door to the back hallway opened. Eli stepped through with Ryan and Cliff following him. He held a small cooler in his hand. Garrett immediately turned to Eli. "Hey! Glad you guys could make it." Garrett glanced to Jessa. "I invited them up this evening. Figured the more the merrier." His easy grin encompassed all of them when he gestured a hand toward the table laden with food and the bar. "Grab a bite and a drink. Only soda for you though," he said with a wink in Ryan's direction.

Eli caught Jessa eyes. "Hey there. How's it going?"

Flutters spun in her belly and heat slid through her veins. Her breath went shallow. She took a gulp of wine and managed a smile. "Pretty good. How about you? Did you guys go fishing again today?"

Eli held up the small cooler in his hand. "We didn't run a charter, but we stopped by the harbor after we finished up at your office," he paused with a nod in Garrett's direction. "I showed Ryan the best spot to fish from the beach there, and he pulled in two silvers. Thought you guys might want to grill them up with the halibut."

"Most definitely! Let me take those inside to Delia."

Eli handed over the cooler. Garrett started to walk off, but turned back. "You guys can meander around if you'd like. If you can rustle up enough people, there's badminton. There's also horseshoes set up on the far side of the lawn there," he said, gesturing vaguely toward the corner of the lodge.

Ryan glanced to Eli, a question in his eyes.

"You heard him. Do what you want, just let me know if you're doing anything other than hanging around here."

Ryan and Cliff headed off the deck. While Gage and Marley hosted casual gatherings for family and friends almost nightly, there were also always lodge customers around. At the moment, a group of kids of mixed ages were clustered near the badminton net. Jessa watched Ryan walk alongside Cliff. "Cliff seems like a good guy," she commented.

Eli looked out beyond the deck, his eyes following Ryan and Cliff as they walked. "He is. I'm glad he's around right now. Well, I'm always glad he's around because he's a damn hard worker, but he's good for Ryan. He's mature, but he's nice enough to not mind Ryan tagging along. He's also got twin brothers who are close to Ryan's age. They'll be up tonight, so I figured it was good to bring Ryan. He could use the chance to hang with somebody other than me."

"Garrett mentioned you're filing for guardianship. I hope it works out. I don't know all the details, but Ryan's lucky to have you."

Eli's shoulders rose and fell with a deep breath. He leaned an elbow against the bar beside them and hooked a hand in his jeans pockets. "Maybe. I, uh, don't talk about it much, but my childhood wasn't exactly great. My dad's, well, he's a jerk with an alcohol problem and a tendency to make life miserable for whoever happens to be around. I tried to make sure he stayed away from my mom and Ryan, but he showed back up a while ago. I don't want to hurt my mom, but I'll be damned if I let Ryan go through what I did."

Eli stared out to the mountains rising up behind the lodge. A raven called nearby, taking flight from the spruce trees near the bottom of the slope. Jessa's heart gave a hard thump. Even though she hadn't known Eli long, mere days, she knew without doubt he was a good man. It hurt her to realize what he'd experienced, although the details were sketchy to her. If there was one thing she'd always been able to count on, it was her family. Even when they drove her nuts, they were there. A flash of anger ran through her. Eli didn't deserve the childhood he described, no more than Ryan. Ryan was a sweet kid, a hard worker and eager to please. Jessa now realized what she saw in his eyes when Ryan looked to Eli—so much hope. He looked up to the brother who'd managed to rise above what his childhood had offered, and Ryan wanted that same chance.

Without thinking, she stepped closer to Eli and slipped her hand around his elbow, giving it a quick squeeze. "I'm sorry. You're doing the right thing for Ryan." When she glanced up, Eli's eyes were there waiting. He looked slightly uncertain. He gave his head a little shake, a subtle flush cresting across his cheekbones. "I'm only doing what anyone would do in my position."

Jessa shook her head. "Some people would, but not everyone. Give yourself a little credit."

Eli chuckled softly. "Okay. Point taken."

He was quiet, his eyes locked to hers. The air hummed to life around them. Her body literally ached to feel him close against her again. His eyes darkened, and her breath caught in her throat. Eli tore his eyes away and cleared his throat.

She suddenly remembered where they were and slowly slid her hand out from the crook of his elbow, forcing herself to take a step back.

* * *

THE SUN HAD FINALLY FALLEN behind the mountains, leaving streaks of lavender and pink in the sky. Eli glanced around the deck at the lodge, wrestling with the strange sense of comfort he felt. Jessa's family was nothing other than warm and welcoming. They shared a lighthearted humor and easiness Eli wasn't accustomed to, at least not in any family setting he'd experienced. They'd had a slow dinner that unfolded amidst conversation. At the moment, Eli was seated with Gage, Garrett and Cam Nash after they persuaded him they needed a fourth for a game of rummy. They clearly played often and had a rather heated, but playful, competition. Cam's reputation as an elite backcountry skier had preceded him before he landed at Last Frontier Lodge. Eli was glad to learn Cam was nothing more than a laidback guy who happened to love the wilderness and skiing. At the moment, Cam caught Eli's eyes and shrugged. "This is what it's like with these guys," he said with a chuckle. "We're just props for their competition."

Eli grinned. "I noticed."

Gage said something to Cam, which drew his attention away. Eli glanced over to Jessa who sat at an adjacent table with Marley, Marley's sister Lacey, and Ginger who was both an old friend of Marley's and Cam's new wife. Delia had returned to the lodge kitchen, insisting she needed to help out before closing. The lodge deck had lights strung above, creating a festive atmosphere.

Jessa turned her head, her eyes colliding with his across the distance. It was as if a flame licked through the air between them and curled around him. The lust holding him in its grip twisted a little tighter. *What the hell are you thinking? Uh, that Jessa's the sexiest damn woman you've ever met and you like her, you really like her.* His mind had been lobbing points back and forth throughout the evening. He couldn't deny his draw to her, yet he wasn't accustomed to its depth. Jessa turned away to reply to something Marley said, the lights glinting off the gold streaks on her hair. He couldn't help but follow the slender line of her neck, his eyes trekking down to savor the generous curve of her breasts. He tore his eyes away and forced himself to focus on the card game. He was relieved the others were in the midst of debating the merits of silver salmon versus red salmon and didn't appear to have noticed Eli had been ogling Jessa.

Ryan had departed a little while ago with Cliff and his twin brothers. Eli wasn't the least bit accustomed to being asked permission for anything. When Ryan had come to ask if he could go spend the night with Cliff's brothers, Cliff had given him a funny look when Eli just stared at Ryan. Cliff had leaned close to explain they would be at his parents' house and assured him he would bring Ryan to the scheduled charter trip in the morning. Eli wanted Ryan to make friends, but found himself feeling oddly protective. Given that Cliff's parents were completely trustworthy, Eli had no reason to say no, but he'd had to remind himself of that.

Ryan's unexpected departure had sent Eli's mind and body into a reckless place. When Garrett had invited them up for dinner tonight, Eli had reasoned it would be no big deal to keep from entangling himself further with Jessa because Ryan would be with him, and he'd need to get him home at a reasonable hour. Instead, Eli was now free to do as he pleased and all he could think about was Jessa. As unsettled as he was by his intense attraction to her that went beyond physical and into a curiosity and interest he'd never entertained with any woman, he couldn't seem to talk himself out of it.

"Hey Eli, you're up." Garrett's voice knocked him back to the present.

Fortunately, he'd been zoning out while staring at the table. He glanced up and back to his cards, quickly playing a set of three sevens.

"Damn, you missed the memo where you're supposed to let one of us win," Gage commented with a chuckle.

Eli looked over at him. "Who says I'm gonna win?"

"Me and him with four cards apiece," Garrett added with a roll of his eyes as he angled his head toward Cam.

Eli had been so distracted by Jessa he hadn't noticed he only had two cards left, which happened to be two spades, a four and a five. Unless one of the others had a full meld or set, when it came back around to him, he'd be out. He grinned. "Well, you two are so damn competitive, I figured it'd be better if I won to keep you from duking it out."

Cam chuckled and added a card to a sequence of hearts. Garrett laid down two more cards to the same sequence before Eli went out, adding his cards to a sequence of spades.

Gage gathered the cards together before shuffling them and returning them to their box. He pushed his chair back. "That's it for me guys. Gotta get Holly to bed, and I'm due up early tomorrow to drive to Kenai for some shopping." He caught Eli's eyes when Eli stood. "Thanks for coming tonight. You're welcome anytime. I'll be by later this week to talk about another gear order."

"The thanks are all mine. Dinner was amazing. As for the gear, you know where to find me. If you're hoping to catch me, call ahead so you don't miss me when I'm out on a charter."

Gage clapped Garrett on the shoulder before heading over to Marley's side and taking their sleepy young daughter out of her arms as they walked into the lodge. Cam stood and gave a small wave before stepping to the table by Ginger. Eli felt an odd pang when he saw Ginger stand and slip into a quick embrace with Cam. The comfort and intimacy between them was evident. Eli's eyes landed on Jessa and he wondered what it would be like to have that with her.

Garrett stood up as well. He glanced to Eli. "I'll call in the morning before I head over to file that petition, okay?"

Almost relieved at the interruption of his thoughts, Eli looked up and nodded. "Sounds like a plan. Thanks again for helping out."

"It's what I do. Otherwise, good to see you tonight. I'm going to track down Delia, so I'll catch you later."

At that, Garrett walked quickly into the lodge, leaving Eli on the back deck with Jessa, Lacey, and a few customers over in the far corner. Eli strode to the table where Jessa sat with Lacey. Lacey bore a strong resemblance to Marley, sharing her auburn hair and green eyes. She had a bold, athletic presence. Eli knew her fairly well as she often stopped by his store to stock up on gear before heading out on the guided trips she ran. She'd backed off doing as many as she used to, but she'd started her own small business and coordinated high-end wilderness treks for eco-tourists seeking remote vacations. She glanced up when Eli reached their table.

"Hey Eli! It's so great to see you. It's been weeks since I needed to go by Game to Fish. How's business been?"

"Crazy, but it's always crazy this time of year. I'll run myself ragged until fall and then I might be able to breathe."

Lacey grinned. "That's life in Alaska. I was telling Jessa she should give Alaska more than a few weeks. Don't you think? She might fall in love with it."

Eli's heart gave a swift kick, startling him. Just the thought of Jessa being around on a more than passing basis did strange things to his insides. He mentally shook himself and aimed for casual and nonchalant in his reply. "Maybe. Lots of people stay in Alaska after they come for a visit."

Jessa glanced up at him, her silver gray eyes flashing in the lights. "Just like I'm telling everyone who asks, I'm open to the possibilities. Right now, I'm enjoying it. Seeing as I don't have a home to go back to, I can take my time."

Eli had been curious to know what had brought Jessa here other than a visit with her brothers. Just as he was about to ask, Lacey chimed in. "I still can't believe your whole apartment building burned down. It's crazy! I'm so glad you're okay."

Eli recalled Jessa's bandaged hand and how she'd held her arm protectively the first time he saw her. He couldn't help but ask about it. "Did you burn your hand in the fire? Is that why you had bandaging on it before?"

Jessa nodded, lines of tension bracketing her mouth. "Yeah. It wasn't too bad. I got singed when I was climbing out the window. I'm counting myself lucky, all things considered."

A wash of protectiveness rolled through Eli. He didn't even like thinking about the fact Jessa had been in the building when it caught on fire, and he certainly didn't like realizing she'd gotten injured. Even though she sat here in front of him clearly fine and clearly safe, his chest tightened at the possibilities that hadn't come to be.

Lacey stood up. "You're damn lucky! I don't even like thinking about what could've happened." She collected the wineglasses on the table. "I'll drop these in the kitchen. I've gotta get going for an early morning start tomorrow. See you guys!" she called with a wave of an empty wineglass.

CHAPTER 12

*J*essa looked over at Eli, trying to tamp down the runaway gallop of her pulse. Having him near with her family around only seemed to exacerbate her hyper awareness of him. Restless, she stood and walked over to the deck railing. The mountains behind the lodge and in the distance created staggered shadows against the darkening sky. A crescent moon was rising above the mountains over to one side, heralding the arrival of night. She felt Eli come to her side. He rested an elbow on the railing. Her heart was pounding so hard and fast, she feared he could hear it. Daring a glance to the side, the strong lines of his profile sent a flash of heat through her. He turned, just as she was trying to tear her eyes away from him, and caught her in his green gaze.

Her breath hitched and her low belly clenched. This evening had been a long, slow tease as far as her body was concerned. A gust of wind blew across the deck, sending tendrils of her hair in a lazy spin. Eli moved incrementally, angling his body toward hers and lifting a hand to catch a loose lock of hair. He brushed it out of her eyes, slowly tucking it behind her ear. A heated shiver raced through her at the casual touch. His hand slowly slid down the side of her neck, his thumb brushing across the beat of her pulse.

The air around them felt weighted—with anticipation and the heavy pulse of desire. Another gust of wind came just as he dipped his head and brought his lips to hers. She shivered at the contrast of the chilly air and the heat of his mouth. His hand threaded into her hair, cupping the nape of her neck. Her skin prickled everywhere he touched. He stepped closer, the hard-muscled planes of his body coming against hers, and she gasped. Their kiss went wild—raw, hot, and wet. He swept his tongue into her mouth, stroking against hers. Arching into him, she was frantic to assuage the need thundering through her. He broke free, his lips traveling in a heated path down her neck, licking, nipping and kissing his way down into the valley between her breasts. Meanwhile, she couldn't seem to get close enough. Desperate to feel more of him, she stroked a hand up his back under his shirt, gasping at the heat of his skin and the flex of his muscles under her touch.

He stroked a hand up her abdomen to cup her breast. A soft moan escaped, and he suddenly froze, lifting his head. His ragged breathing filtered through her awareness, and she dragged her eyes open. His gaze was dark and intent. "I just remembered where we were," he said, his voice gravelly.

"Oh!"

Even with her mind telling her she should take a step back, she couldn't. Her body wanted to be exactly where she was—tight against Eli where she could feel the heat emanating from him and the evidence of his desire, hot and hard against her belly. She tried to gather her thoughts, but the only thing she could think was she needed more. Now.

Eli's features were shadowed in the dim light. He cleared his throat. "I don't think we should keep this up out here. Any more and I won't be able to stop," he said bluntly, the roughened timbre of his voice sending shivers over her skin.

Drenched with need, she only knew one thing in this moment. She needed Eli—all of him—now. The depth of her longing for him drowned out the uncertainties that would usually chorus above any other voice inside. She didn't want to miss out on the chance to feel her way through this, all of it.

"I don't want to stop," she whispered.

He was quiet for several beats. The wind blew through the trees, and an owl called softly in the distance. A thread of uncertainty wove into Jessa's thoughts as the silence extended. Perhaps she'd been a touch too bold.

"Good to know because I don't either," Eli finally said.

All she wanted was to dive right back to where they'd been, but she forced herself to remember where they were. While they happened to be the only people out on the deck at this moment, the restaurant was still full and she wasn't up for having Gage or Marley happen to glance outside and see her making out with Eli. She forced herself to step back, instantly missing the feel of Eli's hard body against hers. She reached for his hand and walked swiftly across the deck. The walk up the back stairs and down the hallway to her suite felt endless. By the time they reached the door, she was awash in heat with liquid need coiling tightly inside. She fumbled with the key card and shoved the door open.

Eli kicked it shut behind them with his boot, reaching for her as she turned to face him. Their lips met in a fierce kiss. It was as if now they'd blown past any hesitation, they'd let go the reins holding anything back. Thought fled, and Jessa dove into sensation. Their kiss exposed the pure, hot need pounding between them—lips, teeth and tongues tangling and clashing. They were in the narrow entryway into her suite, and her shoulder bounced against the wall as she yanked at his clothing. He swore and took a step back.

Her eyes slammed into his and what she saw there took her breath away—raw, intent desire focused solely on her.

The next few moments passed in a heated blur as they fumbled and tugged at each other's clothing in between consuming kisses. Jessa caught her foot on Eli's jacket, which had been tossed to the floor, and stumbled. Eli steadied her with his hands. She couldn't hold back her giggle. When she glanced up to see his mouth hook in a half-smile, a jolt of need shot through her. She leaned against the wall and reached her hand blindly to one side, flicking on the light switch. The tiny entry hall led into a small suite with a king-sized bed on one side and an efficiency kitchen on the other. A bathroom was off to the side of the bed.

Her breath came in heaves. Eli had tossed her shirt aside moments ago, and she stood before him in her leggings and a black silk bra. Her nipples were taut against the silk. His eyes traveled down, and she felt his gaze as if he'd touched her. She could feel the moisture between her thighs. The moment offered her the chance to see him. His brown hair was mussed from her hands running roughly through it. His chambray shirt hung open, revealing his muscled chest, lightly dusted with hair. She reached and stroked her hand up his chest, savoring the feel of his muscles. His heart pounded, strong and steady under her palm. His eyes rose again and caught hers. His hand was curled on her shoulder where he'd steadied her. He traced along her collarbone with his thumb, trailed his hand down between her breasts and paused there. Held in place by his eyes, her breath became shallow as he slowly slid his thumb under the clasp of her bra.

With a flick, her bra fell open, and her breasts—heavy and aching with need—tumbled loose. She heard his sharp intake of breath and then he slowly drew his fingers along the undersides of her breasts, tracing the curves. By the time he lightly circled a nipple with his finger, she was on fire, suffused with heat and near desperation. Her channel clenched and she shifted her legs restlessly. He rolled a nipple between his thumb and forefinger. A low moan broke from her. He finally, *finally*, dipped his head and swirled his tongue around a nipple, drawing it into his mouth. She arched into him, pleasure streaking through her as he alternated between her nipples, toying with one with his fingers and the other with his mouth. By the time he drew away, she was so hot and bothered, she was on the verge of a climax. She placed a palm on his chest and shoved him back. She snatched his hand and tugged him behind her, aiming straight for the bed.

Just as she reached it, his hands gripped her hips, bringing them to a stop.

"Eli, I want..."

"Just let me..."

His words broke off as he hooked his hands over her waistband and shoved her legging over her hips, his movements rough.

"Holy hell," he muttered as his hands traced her hips, lingering over the curves. She didn't spend a ton of time thinking about her body, a side benefit to generally not focusing too much on men, but she experienced a flash of insecurity. She wasn't one of those thin, lithe women. Once she'd hit adolescence, her curves came out in full force. Just as her mind started to kick in and interfere, his touch traveled over her hips and down along her legs as he dragged her leggings off. She kicked them free and turned, left in nothing but her cotton panties, scattered with daisies, and her bra hanging off one shoulder. She shook the bra loose and tossed it aside before reaching for him.

He caught her hands. "Not yet," he said, his voice almost a growl.

Moving with deliberation, he stroked a hand down over

her abdomen, her belly fluttering under his touch. He kept moving, his palm cupping her mound. Her breath came out in a ragged gasp when he dragged his fingers across the damp cotton between her thighs, his eyes on her the whole time. The need coiling inside her was burning so hot and fierce, all she knew was she needed to find relief. He moved swiftly, lifting her and bringing them both down on the bed as he stretched beside her. He proceeded to drive her beyond mad between his hands and his mouth—mapping her body. Long, hot minutes later, he pushed her knees apart and dragged his fingers back and forth in a maddening tease over her panties.

"Please…" She distantly heard her plea and almost didn't recognize herself. She was too far gone to care and cried out when he hooked a finger over the edge of her underwear and yanked them down her legs in one motion. He immediately delved into her folds. He slid one finger into her channel, another following. Her channel throbbed around him. Her hips arched, rising to meet the slow tease of his touch. When he brought his mouth to her and swirled his tongue over the nub of her desire, she shattered, a fierce climax rushing through her.

Awash in sensation, she felt him slowly move away and stand. She dragged her eyes open and looked at him in the soft light from two lamps in the corners of the room. He shrugged his shirt off, his skin gleaming. Dear God, the man had one hell of a body—all muscle and brawn. He reached into his pocket and yanked out his wallet, a condom following. He moved quickly and efficiently, shoving his jeans off his hips and kicking them free. His arousal was evident in his fitted briefs. Her body, even after the most intense orgasm she'd ever experienced, immediately tightened, another hot rush of need scoring through her. In seconds, he'd kicked his briefs off and rolled the condom on.

The mattress gave under his weight as he knelt between

her thighs. His palms slid up her legs, the calloused surface lighting tiny fires under her skin. It felt as if the air around them was alive, nearly vibrating with the force of pure desire between them. He slowly stretched out over her, lacing his hands in hers. When he was fully atop her, she could feel his cock, hard and hot, against her folds. He dipped his head, bringing his lips to hers in another devouring kiss. She lost herself again in wave after wave of sensation as he rocked his hips against her, his cock sliding in her folds, slowly driving her back into that wild, frantic place inside where she chased after more and more.

He tore his lips free and lifted his head. "Jessa," he whispered gruffly.

Opening her eyes, the touch of his hot gaze tightened the spool of need within her. His hands gripped hers when he moved swiftly and surged into her, seating himself deeply. He held still for a long moment as her body adjusted to the delicious stretch of him filling her.

* * *

ELI FORCED himself to hold still in Jessa's clutching heat. She was tight around him and felt so damn good—hot and slick. He was at the end of his restraint, but he felt her body tighten around him, so he hung on and waited. Her silver-smoky eyes held his. A sense of intimacy he'd never experienced curled around his heart, rattling him. Yet, he couldn't turn away and his body was ten steps ahead. When he felt her channel relax around him, he started to move, trying to keep it slow. She arched into him, curling her legs around his hips and rising to meet him. She dragged her hands down his back, her nails scoring his skin. He lost the thin thread of control he'd been hanging onto and began pounding into her.

When she cried out and her channel began the clench

around him, he surged into her once more, his release thundering through him. Collapsing against her, he shifted his weight to the side. Her body eased around him, and awareness gradually filtered into his mind. He was stunned and near immobilized by what had just happened. He enjoyed sex just as much as any man, but he'd generally viewed it as a means to an end. He didn't set out to use anyone, but he kept relationships casual because he'd never been inclined to anything more than that. This, whatever the hell this was with Jessa, had simply overtaken him. He didn't want to untangle himself from her and only wanted to curl up beside her and soak in the warmth of the feeling he experienced with her.

CHAPTER 13

$\mathcal{J}$essa came awake slowly, feeling more rested than she had in months. Eli was spooned behind her, his hand resting on the curve of her hip. It felt *sooo* good to wake up in his arms. Opening her eyes, the clock indicated it was five in the morning. The wispy light of dawn was breaking over the mountains, heralding the sun's arrival with faint streaks of gold and orange reaching into the sky.

She felt Eli shift behind her and then stretch, his body going taut for a second before relaxing against her again.

"Mmm. Time?" he asked in a mumble against her neck.

The feel of his lips on her skin sent a soft shiver through her. "Five."

He didn't move, but she felt him take a deep breath. "I have to get up. Fishing charter today." His voice gained a touch of strength.

His hand stroked down her hip and back up to brush her hair away from her face. She rolled over in his arms, smiling when she saw his disheveled hair. She reached up and ran a hand through it, straightening the brown locks. His mouth hooked in a smile and he dipped his head, catching her lips in a quick kiss. When he pulled back, heat was rolling through her and all she wanted was to tumble right back to where they'd been last night.

He gave his head a little shake. "I don't wanna go, but I have to. We have a full boat today. Cliff and Ryan are probably already on their way."

She kicked the covers back and rolled out of his arms quickly. "I'll get up with you," she announced, flinging the covers off of him. When her eyes angled down, she saw the clear evidence of his desire. Damn, the man had a body to die for. He was all muscle, but he didn't have the polished look of a man who spent hours at the gym. His gym was his life—working and living on the ocean and in the wilds of Alaska. When he caught her eyes, his held a gleam. He shrugged, unabashed, and quickly stood, heading straight for the bathroom.

"Mind if I jump in the shower?"

Dry-mouthed, nearly speechless at the depth of her response to him, she shook her head. "Go for it," she finally managed to reply.

Moments later, she'd wrapped herself in a robe and gathered their scattered clothing off the floor. She carefully set his on the counter in the bathroom. She started a pot of coffee and had a to-go cup ready for Eli when he stepped out of the bathroom. She held it out as he walked over to her, buttoning his shirt.

"Thanks," he said as he accepted the small paper cup from her. He took a sip and closed his eyes. "This'll get me to town." He paused and looked over at her, his eyes searching. "I, uh… Well, I don't know what the hell I meant to say. I don't suppose we could plan to see each other again? Soon?"

He seemed to be stumbling as much with this as much as she was, which eased her own uncertainty. She might not have expected this with Eli, but she couldn't turn away from it either. It felt too good to be with him. She took a gulp of coffee, nothing amazing but serviceable enough to help her speak, and nodded. "I'd like that."

She was rewarded with one of his half-grins, so sexy it took her breath away. He took a step and dipped his head, dropping a kiss on the curve of her neck. Goosebumps rose along her skin and sent a ripple through her. He lifted his head and caught her lips in a swift kiss—his tongue stroking in to tangle with hers briefly before he pulled back. His eyes met hers. "I'll call you."

At that, he turned and strode to the door, grabbing his jacket off the hook where she'd hung it only minutes earlier. His hand was on the doorknob when he stopped and looked back. "Soon," he said firmly. With a wink, he was gone.

She stayed where she was by the counter and placed her fingers against her lips, as if she could contain the feel of his against hers.

* * *

SEVERAL HOURS LATER, Jessa followed Marley across a parking lot along Diamond Creek's shoreline. Marley adjusted the straps on the carrier she wore for Holly. Holly was going on six months old now and full of curiosity. Her chubby little legs dangled from the carrier, she had one hand latched onto a lock of Marley's hair with the other in her mouth. She looked around from her perch on Marley's shoulders, her green eyes alert as she took in the world around them. What a world it was. Jessa took a deep breath, savoring the salty ocean air coming in soft gusts off of Kachemak Bay. Diamond Creek's tourist draw came from its breathtaking view, which included the ocean, the mountains, glittering glaciers, and abundant wildlife. Marley had insisted she come along with her to pick up some signs from a local gallery.

The gallery was located in a small run of shops set on a boardwalk along the ocean. Gulls called and flew above. A lone eagle sat on the corner of the deck railing along the boardwalk, its gaze intent and fierce as the bird calmly tracked their approach. Jessa still wasn't accustomed to how common eagles were in Alaska. Every single day she'd been here, she'd seen several eagles. As she eyed the eagle on the deck railing, another flew overhead, calling its shrill call as it flew past them toward the ocean.

Jessa nudged Marley's shoulder. "What's that?" she asked, pointing to a cluster floating in the water.

Marley grinned and brushed her hair out of her eyes when the wind caught it. "That's a raft of otters. If they float close enough you can see their furry little faces. They hang together like that all the time."

"Oh, that's so cool!" Jessa watched the otters as they continued walking toward the gallery.

She glanced up at the sign—Midnight Sun Arts—as they walked through the door. The gallery was a bright, open space with displays on the walls and scattered throughout the room. There was a collection of blown glass in one corner, pottery in another and paintings throughout the space. Jessa could have spent hours here, just looking around. While they might be in a tiny town in Alaska, whoever ran this gallery clearly knew their art because the selection was excellent and eclectic. A ping of anxiety ran through her as she realized she'd been completely avoiding thinking about what to do with her life. The small, budding art business she'd established in Seattle had literally gone up in smoke. She knew she could try to start over, but at the moment, she was weary of worrying about money and trying to make ends meet. This feeling—of anxiety and worry—had taken root firmly since the fire. It was what led her to pack up Blue—her beloved little truck—and head to Diamond Creek when she didn't know what else to do.

Being here in this gallery, filled to the brim with art, sent a whoosh of wishful thinking through her, reminding her of those old hopes and dreams she'd tried to make happen. She shook her head and took a breath. She hadn't realized she'd stopped in the center of the gallery all by herself while Marley was at the counter talking to a woman with short dark hair in a stylish, tousled bob. Jessa gathered herself and walked to Marley's side.

Marley glanced over, pausing in whatever she'd been saying. "Jessa, this is Risa Thomas. She's the manager and part owner of the gallery. I was just telling her about your furniture," she said as she glanced from Jessa to Risa. "Her furniture is so much fun! I have a few pieces in the house. I'll…"

Jessa couldn't stop her head from shaking. She knew Marley was trying to be helpful, but the problem was she didn't have much to sell at the moment. The few pieces that had survived the fire because they happened to be stored away from her apartment were still in the back of her truck. She needed time and to find a space where she could paint before she considered trying to sell anything anywhere. Not to mention she wasn't so sure she should keep trying to follow her silly dreams. Perhaps she needed to focus on something more practical. "Marley, you don't…"

Marley waved a hand and paused to remove the half of her ponytail that Holly was chewing on. "Don't tell me I can't try to promote your work! You had plenty of buyers in Seattle, but there was a lot more competition there. I already mentioned your work to Risa when I called her about our signs, and she said she'd seen your stuff online and would love to have some pieces to sell."

Jessa flushed, while Risa nodded emphatically, her dark brown eyes warm. "I meant what I said to Marley—I would be happy to offer your work here. We like to stay ahead of the curve with our inventory and artsy furniture likes yours is getting more and more popular. While Seattle is definitely busy and a hopping arts scene, you wouldn't believe how much inventory passes through here. Probably double that of the average gallery in Seattle. It's just a different market—tourists want to buy, not just look. Anytime you want to talk more about it, just let me know and we'll come up with a plan." Risa paused, her smile deepening. "Nice to meet you, by the way."

That tiny sprout of hope inside that just wouldn't quit unfurled another leaf, a whisper of possibility rising along with it. Jessa smiled softly. "You too. Well, uh, thanks for the offer about my furniture. I'd love to talk more about it with you, but the problem is I lost most of my inventory when my apartment building burned down. I used the second bedroom there for storage, so everything went 'poof.' I'm just trying to figure out what to do next. First, I need to find somewhere to work. Maybe when I figure that out, I'll give you a call."

"You mean somewhere to paint?" Risa asked.

At Jessa's nod, she grinned. "We've got some offices spaces upstairs. Right now, one of them is sitting empty. You're free to use it if you'd like."

Marley grinned and clapped her hands. "See! I told you it'd be a good idea to come talk to her." Her expression sobered. "Although if you'd mentioned you needed a space to paint, Gage would be happy to set something up for you. Garrett would probably clear out a room at his office. I wish..." She paused and took a breath, her eyes softening. "I'm sorry. I don't mean to be so pushy. I know what it's like to have things feel like they're turned all upside down. I know you need time to sort this out without us barging into your life. Although I *was* hoping maybe you'd want to give Risa's gallery a shot."

Jessa had started to feel defensive, but Marley's understanding dissipated it. She took a breath and let it out, the knot of anxiety in her chest easing. "I know you're trying to help. No need to apologize." She took another breath, wondering if she was about to do something crazy and forging ahead anyway. "If you don't mind, maybe I could take a look at the office space upstairs. How much is the monthly rent?"

Risa shook her head with a soft laugh. "Nothing."

"You have to charge something," Jessa insisted. "It won't feel right."

"Look, I'm part owner of the gallery, but I don't own the building. I share ownership with my old bosses in Anchorage and they own this building. They rent out a small hotel suite above here for major bucks all summer, but the two offices aren't convenient for most year-round businesses. The gallery stays open all year, but locals like to have their offices downtown, not by the ocean. Ethan and Jack would be tickled if you used the space. If you're worried about the rent, maybe we can work out a deal after you have some inventory to sell."

Hope rooted itself a tad more firmly inside of Jessa. Maybe she didn't know how long she'd be here or what might happen next. Maybe she didn't have a place to call home anymore, unless she counted her truck Blue. But, maybe, just maybe, starting to do what she loved again would help her find a path. Even if she didn't stay in Diamond Creek, selling her furniture in this lovely gallery by the sea would be worth doing whether she remained here or not. She looked across the counter at Risa and smiled. "Maybe we can do that." She turned to Marley who was preoccupied with Holly who'd somehow managed to get one of her feet stuck in her backpack carrier.

"There!" Marley exclaimed when she gently tugged Holly's chubby little foot back through the harness where she was seated. Holly continued fiddling with a bright red toy tied to the carrier strap. Marley looked over at Risa and Jessa and shrugged sheepishly. "I can't seem to master this backpack thing. Anyway, did I hear right? You're going to check out the space upstairs?" she asked, looking to Jessa.

Jessa grinned. "Yes, you heard right. Aren't we here for something though? Signs?"

Risa threw her head back with a laugh. "Right. Those are actually upstairs. Why don't you two follow me?"

Moments later, Jessa stood inside a small room. It was perfectly square with soft, cream colored paint, dark hardwood flooring, and sunlight streaming through the windows on one wall. The office overlooked Kachemak Bay. Sunlight glittered on the surface today. A breeze ruffled the water. Jessa took a deep breath, that sense of hope unfurling another leaf inside. For what she needed, this was absolutely perfect. Tears welled in her eyes and she wiped them away. After weeks of feeling like her chance at keeping her life afloat with her artwork had burned up, she might find a way to get back on her feet. Intellectually, she'd known all along she could rebuild, but she'd felt so defeated and tired. Right now, in this lovely little room with a breathtaking view, she felt like she'd been handed a chance to get back on her feet in a way she'd never imagined. Her imaginings had included sky-high rent in a tiny apartment in Seattle and trying to make do on less while she scrambled to create some inventory to sell fast enough to pay the bills. By the grace of her family and a kind stranger in Diamond Creek, she had a cushion for now.

Risa poked her head around the doorframe. "What do you think?"

"It's perfect. Would you mind if I put drop cloths on the floor? That's the only thing I'd be worried about."

Risa grinned and gestured for Jessa to follow her. She stepped into the short hallway and followed Risa to the end where Marley was in another office. This one was a replica of the other office and its entire floor was covered in drop cloths. She looked to Risa whose grin morphed into a laugh.

"I have some extra drop clothes here if you need them," Risa offered once she stopped laughing. "I use this space for painting signs." She gestured to the ones arranged on a table.

Marley turned, holding a sign up. "They look great! Gage is going to be so excited."

"Glad they turned out how you wanted. Let me help you load them up," Risa replied, striding to the table and carefully stacking the signs.

That evening, Jessa stood by the windows in her room and looked out over the mountains. She was about to go downstairs for another shift in the restaurant. She'd come to count on the work and enjoyed bantering with Harry, Delia and the customers, along with seeing a rotating collection of Gage and Marley's social circle. Her mind spun to thoughts of Eli. Most of her morning had kept her so busy, she managed to function without her entire body tingling at the memory of last night. Yet, here in her room, alone in the quiet, heat flashed through her and liquid need built inside. The way she felt with him was beyond anything she'd ever felt with a man. She felt as if she was standing on the edge of a precipice, or she might have already tumbled over, but she didn't recognize the feeling. Everything with him was just plain...amazing. She wished she knew what to do about it.

CHAPTER 14

Eli checked the mooring lines and turned to look out over the bay one last time. It was late evening with the sun hovering low over the mountains, its orb shimmering and painting the sky with streaks of gold and orange. The day had been beyond busy. They had a boat full of six today. Eli was coming to wonder how he'd managed these charters without Ryan's help. He'd been indispensable today between helping generally with anything and everything and spending a good hour assisting a customer with a badly tangled line and broken reel. They kept extra equipment on the boat for situations like that, but the man had insisted he only wanted to fish with his own equipment. Ryan's patience was greater than Eli's, so he'd happily turned the job over to him. Cliff and Ryan had left a few minutes earlier to ferry the customers over to the Fish Factory to get their daily catch flash frozen and overnighted to wherever they wanted it to go. Eli would pick Ryan up after he grabbed a pizza for the boys.

He took a breath, savoring the briny scent of the ocean. At the sound of the water surface breaking, he glanced to the side to find a seal looking at him curiously. Seals frequented the harbor docks for sunning and seeking out fish scraps. The seal's dark round eyes stared at him for a long moment before the seal curled and dipped back under the water, undulating along the surface. Eli turned to walk up the dock, grinning when he realized the seal was following and watching him.

Jessa had been flitting in his thoughts all day. Any moment he wasn't entirely preoccupied with whatever he was doing, he thought of her—her flashing silver eyes, the feel of her soft curves under his touch, the way it felt to sink inside of her, and the incandescent buzz of joy he felt being close to her. Joy wasn't a familiar feeling to him. His childhood had offered little of it, and his choice to keep his emotional distance as an adult had somewhat boxed the opportunity for that kind of joy out of his life. Oh, he experienced joy when he was on the ocean or in the wilderness, but that was a different kind of joy. This thing he felt with Jessa—it made him feel out of control, which he didn't particularly like. Except it felt so good to be with her. It almost hurt to think of not experiencing more of her. So while he was most definitely stumbling along in uncharted territory for him, he wasn't about to stop.

When he reached his truck, he impulsively pulled his phone out and texted her. He was taking Ryan shopping tomorrow and for some inexplicable reason, he wanted her to go with them.

Hey, would you be up for a shopping trip for Ryan tomorrow?

He didn't wait for her reply because she'd mentioned she was working in the restaurant tonight. He slipped his phone back in his pocket and headed over to pick up the promised pizza for Ryan and Cliff.

Later that night, Eli leaned into the couch cushions and sighed. Ryan had just gone up to bed after devouring most of the pizza. Eli figured Ryan would be asleep the second his head hit the pillow. He'd looked as exhausted as Eli felt. Long days on the water did that. Eli heard a faint buzz. He knew it must be his phone, but he figured he'd ignore it. Then, he realized Jessa might be replying to his text earlier. What little energy he had left propelled him off the couch to search for his phone. He found it on the counter by the refrigerator. Sure enough, Jessa's name blinked on the screen. He swiped the screen to read her message.

Shopping for Ryan? Sounds interesting. I'd love to go! Where do we meet?

Eli quickly typed his reply.

How about I pick you up at the lodge around 10am?

Her answer was quick.

Perfect! I'll meet you out front. Gotta go...busy here tonight.

Eli found himself standing alone in the kitchen smiling at his phone. When he snapped into awareness, he experienced a moment of foolishness. He was feeling goofily pleased that Jessa had agreed to go shopping with him. For good measure, his mind repeated it. *Shopping.* The thing was he hadn't the slightest idea of everything he needed to make sure Ryan had. Thus far, Ryan was making do with the surplus of Eli's t-shirts. Because Ryan was much lankier than Eli, he was wearing the jeans he'd arrived in and a few pairs of pants Eli had in stock at the store. Given that he was fishing or outside almost daily, Ryan was running through clothes much too rapidly for it to be practical to continue this pattern. Eli had determined they'd drive to Kenai and stock up on whatever Ryan needed. From Eli's experience in childhood, he doubted Ryan had many choices before. Eli considered himself lucky since he'd moved to Diamond Creek. Between his retail store, fishing charters and guided hunting, he made damn good money. Up to now, he had no one but himself to spend it on. He was strangely excited to spend it on Ryan, although he hadn't the faintest idea where to start. He hoped Jessa could help.

Dude, it's great she can help, but that's not why you invited her. Face it, you'll take any chance you can get to see her. Eli shook his head to himself and shrugged. He knew perfectly well all he wanted was to see Jessa. The feeling was strange and disconcerting, but he was damned if he could make it go away.

* * *

Early the next morning, Eli stood in the kitchen and waited for the coffee pot to beep. He planned to do a few hours of paperwork this morning, mostly plowing his way through invoices and payments for the month. Ryan would sleep until Eli woke him. He'd come to learn Ryan could wake early, but only if prompted, unlike Eli who was up early no matter what. The coffee maker finally beeped, and he quickly poured a cup before sitting down at the kitchen table. A solid hour later, his phone buzzed. Without glancing at the screen, he answered, figuring it was Cliff who was opening the store today.

"Eli?"

His mother's voice came softly through the phone. He took a breath, fighting the tightness welling in his throat. He'd expected her to call any day now. He'd left her a message after his meeting with Garrett and explained his plans. He'd asked her to call as soon as she could, but he was guessing she'd hoped it would all go away. That's how his mother approached life—with passive hope. Her passivity hadn't led to anything good over the years. He figured her call this morning came after she was served the guardianship petition Garrett had filed.

"Hey Mom. What's up?"

He heard her shaky breath before she spoke and shoved

his sadness away. He had to put Ryan's needs before his mother's.

"Eli, I didn't think you'd really go through with this. A man stopped by yesterday at work to serve the court papers. Ryan needs to be here. With me. How could you...?"

Eli cut her off. "Mom, you know exactly what it means for Ryan to stay with you. Four more years of Dad's garbage. If you want a chance to have a relationship with Ryan, a real one, I'd suggest you let him stay with me, or he's going to do just what I did and leave as soon as he can. Hell, he already did!"

His mother's breath drew in sharply. He waited. He didn't like what he had to say, but it was what it was.

"Eli, I'm sorry. More sorry than you know about how your father was when you were growing up, but he's doing better now. He's not drinking as much, he's trying to find work. Don't punish Ryan for the way your father was when you were here."

All of these flimsy arguments were what Eli expected from his mother, so he was no longer surprised and no longer hopeful something would be different. He'd also had Garrett hire an investigator in Juneau just to cover his bases. He didn't want to make assumptions about his father if he was wrong.

"Mom, I had my lawyer here hire an investigator. In less than an hour, he confirmed Dad hasn't worked in over ten years, and his arrest record for petty bullshit has almost doubled since I moved away. He was arrested just last week for assault after another bar fight. All this guy did was a preliminary online search and this is what came up. I don't even want to know what I'd find if I asked him to dig deeper. You can wish Dad would change as long as you want, but I won't stand by and let him put Ryan through the hell he put me through. Ryan's here with me, he's safe and

I'll take care of him. You can either stand in the way, or accept it."

There was a long silence. Eli eventually heard a soft sob and closed his eyes to keep ahold of himself. He hated, absolutely hated, that he had to do what he was doing. He hated that he knew it would hurt his mother, but he wasn't going to sit by and force Ryan to return there.

"Okay, okay. I understand. I really do. I just wish it could be different," his mother said, so softly Eli could barely hear her. That old guilt tightened like a knot in his chest. He could picture her worn, pained expression—the one he'd seen time and again after his father lashed out at him or her. But he couldn't let that stop him from protecting Ryan.

"Mom, if you want help getting out of there, I'll help you. All you have to do is ask."

Years ago before he moved away, he'd thrown himself into trying to get his mother to leave his father behind. Although she'd somehow tolerated Eli forcing his father out of the home with the threat of reporting him, she'd managed it because she knew Eli was paying his way. He knew she couldn't stomach just up and leaving his father behind. She'd been a victim so long, she didn't know anything else, and she felt responsible for taking care of the very man who'd made her life a living hell. Eli meant it when he said he'd help if she asked, but he wouldn't try to force his help on her again. It had taken him years to accept the reality that he couldn't rescue her if she didn't want to be rescued.

"I know you'll help if I ask. Is Ryan awake?" she asked, abruptly shifting gears.

"Not yet. I can have him give you a call when he is."

"That would be nice. Just tell him I love him, okay?"

"Of course, Mom."

"Can I call to check in every week?"

Eli gritted his teeth. He knew she thought she had to ask

permission because she'd spent most of her adult life connected to a man who she *always* had to be careful around. She couldn't make any assumptions. It didn't change the fact that Eli hated how her habit of constantly asking for permission applied to everyone. He'd never question her desire to call and check on her son, but she wouldn't trust that, so he had to reassure her.

"You don't have to ask, Mom. Call every day if you like."

"Okay." There was another long pause. Eli could feel his mother gathering herself. "I'm not sure how your father feels about this guardianship thing, so I don't know what he'll do. I'll try to explain and maybe that will help."

"Doesn't matter to me how he feels. He doesn't have a chance in hell of winning, so he can waste his time if he wants."

"I know, I know. I'll go now. Tell Ryan to call me at work, okay?"

"You got it." Eli swallowed against the tightness in his throat and started to pull the phone away from his ear before he stopped. "Mom?"

"Yes?"

"It may not seem like it, but I wouldn't be doing this if I didn't care about you."

He waited, his throat tight and an old familiar worry knotting in his chest.

"I know, Eli. I know it might be hard to believe sometimes, but I love you and Ryan more than I can say."

Eli managed to say goodbye and listened to the line go quiet in his ear. He slowly set his phone down on the table, his breath coming out in a slow sigh. He didn't doubt his mother loved him and Ryan, but to this day he didn't think she understood how much damage his father had inflicted on him. In his years away, he'd come to terms with understanding that due to the emotional wringer his father had put her through over years and the constant threat of violence, she'd been shredded—emotionally and psychologically. Even if he didn't blame her, he couldn't stand by and allow Ryan to get hurt.

* * *

JESSA STOOD in front of the bathroom mirror, fiddling with her hair. The brown locks were lightened with streaks of blonde throughout. At times, she added bright streaks of color here and there for the fun of it. With Eli about to arrive to pick her up, she was inexplicably obsessed with looking just right. Her hair tended to be a tousled mess most of the time. It still was, but she was pointlessly trying to straighten the locks. With a sigh, she grabbed her hairbrush and ran it through quickly before fluffing her hair with her fingers. To make matters worse, she wanted to look good, and Ryan would be with them all day. So, she somehow wanted to look good and as if she wasn't trying...at all.

She'd gone with her usual leggings, navy blue today, and a cotton shirt that gathered at the waist and had cinch ties on the sides with a scoop neck. She slipped on a pair of silver hoop earrings and her silver charm bracelet before turning for the door. She came to an abrupt stop when there was a knock at her door. Puzzled, she stepped to the door and opened it to find Marley in the hallway.

Marley held Holly in her arms, her eyes widening when she saw Jessa. "You look like you might be going somewhere."

Jessa felt the flush bloom on her cheeks. She wasn't trying to hide anything about Eli, but what was happening between them felt so intimate. Marley's eyes held a gleam. "Hmm. Let me guess. You're going to do something with Eli, aren't you?"

Jessa couldn't help the grin that spread across her face. "Maybe."

Marley threw her head back in a laugh and quickly paused to free her hair from Holly's grip when she reached out and grabbed ahold of Marley's ponytail. "Just admit it. You have a thing for him, and he definitely has a thing for you!"

Jessa's cheeks got even hotter. She chewed her lip and rolled her eyes. "You hardly know him, how can you tell he has a thing for me?"

Marley put her free hand on her hip, somehow managing to look affronted even while adjusting Holly in her arms. "I know Eli more than hardly! Gage has been buying gear and whatnot from him for over a year now. Eli's a great guy. Honestly, I'd started to wonder if I knew someone to set him up with. He's nice, he runs a solid business, and he's pretty easy on the eyes. I'd have to be blind not to notice he has a thing for you. Every time I looked his way the other night, his eyes were glued to you. Gage even noticed, and he almost never comments on things like that!"

Jessa leaned her shoulder against the doorframe and sighed. "Oh God. Don't tell me Gage has some kind of opinion about…"

"About what?" Marley countered with a sly grin.

"I don't know what's happening. Eli, well he just happened. I mean, I only met him because I backed into him in a parking lot! Then he invited me to go fishing and somehow Garrett ended up inviting him for dinner here. Then he asked if I wanted to go shopping with him and Ryan, and now I am and I have no idea what's going on." Jessa spoke so quickly, she wasn't sure if she stopped because she ran out of words or breath.

Marley's expression softened, her gaze warm and kind. "I didn't mean to tease. Go have fun shopping and stop worrying so much. I'll be the first to admit, I'm not so great at taking my own advice and I worry like crazy. But...like I said, Eli's a great guy. No reason not to see where things go."

Jessa pushed away from the wall and hooked her purse over her shoulder. "I know you're just teasing. It's just my life feels upside down. I don't really do the whole dating thing, and I don't even know if that's what I'd call whatever's happening with Eli." A memory from the other night when he surged inside her flashed through her mind. Maybe she didn't know if they were dating, but she sure as hell knew *something* was going on between them. Something much bigger and more powerful than she'd ever felt.

"How about you just enjoy the day? I heard from Garrett that Eli's filing for guardianship of his little brother. I bet he could use a little help shopping for him," Marley offered with a soft smile. "Come on, I'll walk downstairs with you. I stopped by to see if you wanted to have breakfast together, but I'll manage without you."

Jessa grinned and followed Marley into the hallway. Being the youngest of five siblings, she'd spent much of her life chafing at the ever-present monitoring that automatically came with siblings likes hers—on the nosy side, opinionated, and loving. As the youngest in the Hamilton clan, Jessa had been determined to show everyone she could make it on her own. She'd tried to carve her own path even though doubts dogged her along the way. Once the fire sent her life spinning sideways, she'd started to wonder if her doubts had been right all along. At the moment, here in this tiny, breathtaking corner of the world, she soaked in the embrace of her family. Marley was a newer member of that circle, but Jessa adored her. There was a time when she'd have been beyond annoyed to have anyone notice something between her and Eli, but right now, it didn't really bother her. If anything, it was nice to feel like she wasn't alone. Being here at the lodge, she was starting to feel grounded again.

When they reached the lower floor, Marley paused beside the massive wooden entry doors and glanced to Jessa. "Is that Eli's truck?" she asked, gesturing to the black truck Jessa had backed into the day she arrived.

"That's the one." Anticipation fluttered in her belly. *All you're doing is shopping with him. And his brother. Don't forget that. Yeah, but I get a whole day with him.* Her mind bantered with itself. Her last thought brought a smile inside her heart. Because that's what she wanted—another day with Eli. She didn't really care about the details, although she was happy to help shop for Ryan.

Marley draped her arm over Jessa's shoulders and squeezed. "Have fun! See you when you get back."

Jessa squeezed Marley's hand on her shoulder. "Bye! Text me if you think of something you need me to pick up."

Marley's arm slid off Jessa's shoulders, her eyes widening. "I didn't even think of that. I'm running back upstairs to check with Gage before he starts working outside on the trails. I can think of a few things right off, but I'll text a list later."

Before Jessa could reply, Marley dashed off. She heard a chuckle from the reception desk and looked up to find Harry grinning at her. He gave a small wave. "Haven't you noticed yet that, in Alaska, it's perfectly normal to ask someone else to do half your shopping for you? If you stick around, you'd better get used to it."

"Why is that?" she asked, bemused.

"Because everything local is expensive. The closer you get to the few cities here, the cheaper everything is. Diamond Creek has plenty of places to shop if you're after high-end touristy stuff, not so much if you just need groceries for a good price."

Jessa nodded slowly. "Makes sense. Hey, do you need me to work tonight? You didn't mention it last night."

Harry clicked something on the computer screen, his

eyes quickly scanning it. "Nope. We're good tonight, but if you're up for it, I could use you for the next two nights after that. We still don't know when Natalie's coming back. Rumor has it she has a new boyfriend up in Anchorage. If that's the case, we'll keep you plenty busy, so you'd better let me know if you want to keep working."

"I'll work as much as you need," Jessa replied without thinking.

Harry's brows hitched up with his grin. "Okay then. You'd better get going before your new boyfriend drives off without you." He winked and turned away.

Her cheeks hot again, Jessa tugged the heavy door open and jogged down the steps. Eli was walking up to the lodge entrance, his stride long and loose. She paused at the foot of the stairs, her breath catching in her throat. Damn. He was just all kinds of rugged and sexy between his muscled body, his dark brown hair and those green eyes landing on her like she was water and he was parched.

Eli leaned on the counter in the department store and watched while Jessa held up several shirts for Ryan. Ryan said yes to basically anything Jessa suggested. He'd been a good sport for most of the day, although he seemed almost befuddled by the process. A few minutes later, Jessa and Ryan approached Eli at the counter with Ryan's arms filled with a collection of t-shirts and long-sleeve cotton shirts.

"We're done!" Jessa announced firmly as she patted the stack of jeans and other clothing already waiting at the register.

Ryan shrugged sheepishly. "Are you sure about this? This seems like a lot of clothes."

Eli clapped him on the back. "You'll wear them. Don't worry about it. Plus, this means doing laundry less."

Ryan flushed and laughed nervously as he handed over the armful of shirts to the woman waiting to check them out. In the short time Ryan had been staying with Eli, Eli had done a load of laundry almost daily to keep up with it.

After Eli finished paying, they headed out to the parking

lot. "Last stop is the grocery store," Eli said as he started the truck. "Let me know if you have any requests."

"Pizza," Ryan commented from his seat in the back.

"Let me guess, you're living off frozen pizza?" Jessa asked, grinning over her shoulder.

Eli recalled he'd had a cart full of frozen pizza the day he'd meandered about the grocery store hoping to see her. "Yup, and we're completely out of it. Pretty sure Ryan could eat ten of those a day and still be hungry."

"Definitely," Ryan added with his shy grin.

After a longer than usual stop at the grocery store between Jessa piling her cart full of requests from Marley and Delia, and Ryan adding one thing after another, they were finally on the highway back to Diamond Creek. On the way back, Ryan asked to be dropped off at Ben and Jeff's house. They'd texted him during the day to invite him for a barbecue and video games.

"What the hell do you mean, barbecue and video games? How do those even go together?" Eli asked, legitimately puzzled with the combination.

Ryan sighed elaborately before explaining. "They went silver salmon fishing today, so I guess their parents are grilling the salmon and some other stuff. After we eat, they want to play some online games. Think of it like when you watch TV."

Eli nodded and glanced sideways at Jessa's muffled laugh. Her silver eyes flashed with mirth. He resisted the urge to reach over and stroke his hand along her curves. He'd discovered today that Ryan was an excellent chaperone. Not because he was actually chaperoning, but because Eli definitely didn't want to do anything inappropriate around him, so he'd spent most of the day shackling his urges to touch Jessa. Damn if she wasn't about the most touchable woman he'd ever laid eyes on. With her tousled hair, her gorgeous eyes and her luscious body, he'd spent almost all day itching to touch her.

He forgot he was in mid-banter with Ryan until Ryan cleared his throat audibly. He tore his eyes from Jessa and glanced in the rearview mirror to catch Ryan rolling his eyes. "Okay, like TV. I get it then. We have to drop Jessa off first, and then I'll take you over to their place. Okay?"

"Cool."

Eli pondered how to persuade Jessa to have dinner with him since he actually had the night to himself. It occurred to him perhaps he should simply ask instead of going in circles in his mind. Another glance in the rearview mirror told him Ryan had put on the new headphones Eli picked up for him today and was staring out the window while he nodded along to whatever was playing on the smartphone Eli had gotten him.

"Don't suppose you'd want to have dinner with me after I drop everything off at the house?"

Eli held his breath. The sense of anticipation he experienced around Jessa was unfamiliar to him. He wasn't used to wanting someone so damn much. She saved him from himself with a quick answer. "I'd love to! Why don't you drop Ryan off first? Then we can go deliver the groceries to Marley and Delia. That way, you save yourself from the back and forth."

Eli kept his eyes on the road and nodded, that sense of joy only Jessa could elicit blooming in his chest. "That works for me. Do we need to go by Delia and Garrett's place to drop off their stuff?"

"Nah. Delia said just to bring it to the lodge. She can take it home from there."

"Alright then. Any preferences on where to go for dinner?"

He felt Jessa's gaze and glanced her way. In that tiny

moment, all he wanted to do was stare into her dreamy gray eyes. He mentally shook himself and glanced ahead again.

"Well, no. Aside from the coffee places, I wouldn't really know where to go. What would you suggest?"

Eli pondered for a moment, wondering what Jessa would like the most. "We could try Diamond Creek Brewery, Sally's or the Boathouse. Those are all local favorites. The Boathouse is a touch more high end. Sally's is an all-American bar type restaurant. The Brewery is somewhere in between the two. Take your pick."

"Diamond Creek Brewery," Jessa replied firmly.

Eli grinned. "Good choice."

* * *

JESSA LOOKED around the restaurant while Eli stepped away to the restroom. When Eli had pulled up in front of the building, Jessa had thought for a moment he must've been confused when she saw they were parked in front of a plane hangar. Then, she saw the brightly painted sign above the doors into the building. While the brewery was located in what was once a plane hangar, the owners had done wonders with the inside. The far side of the building held the brewery part of the business with the stainless steel brewing equipment partially visible behind a brick wall dividing the space. Decorative copper storage vessels marked the entrance into the actual brewery. The tall ceiling was filled with model planes hanging above. The hangar had been renovated with extra windows cut into the walls, providing a view of a marshy field where moose often gathered against the backdrop of the bay and mountains. Booths lined the walls with tables scattered in the center. The kitchen sat on the opposite side from the brewery with a bar separating it from the rest of the room. The space was decorated with fabric wall hangings, photographs and colorful rugs, which softened what could have been a noisy space.

She took another sip of her wine and marveled at how busy the place was. Eli had called ahead to reserve a table, which she'd thought unnecessary until they arrived to find the entry way crowded and almost all of the tables full. As she looked around, she saw Eli making his way back to their booth in the corner. A prickle of awareness ran up her spine. Today had been one long tease. All he had to do was exist and her body hummed. Now that she had a better sense of how Ryan ended up here with him, it made her like Eli even more. He didn't offer much about his childhood other than to say he'd be damned if he'd let Ryan stay there now that his father had returned. Without hesitation, he'd shouldered the responsibility of becoming Ryan's guardian, even if it meant going through a legal fight to make it happen. Beyond the fact the man was sexy as all get out, he just had to go and be a caring and kind brother. Family meant a lot to her, and it almost pained her physically to realize that Eli had never really had a family he could rely on. Fortunately for Ryan, Eli was stepping up to be the kind of family he could have used himself when he was Ryan's age.

Eli slipped into the booth across from her, his mouth hooking in a half-grin. His green eyes were bright against his sun-burnished skin. "So, are you about ready to go, or do you want to stay for a bit?"

Jessa glanced to the line of customers waiting near the entryway. "We should go. The salmon burger was amazing and the wine is delicious, but the longer we sit, the longer other people have to wait."

"How about I pick up a bottle of the wine on the way out?"

"We can do that?"

"Sure can. They sell everything they make in the brewery here."

Eli caught the eye of one of the waiters passing by and made his request. Moments later, they were threading through the tables and the small crowd by the doors. Jessa felt the heat of Eli's palm on her low back through the thin cotton of her shirt. Heat radiated outward from his touch. The chilly summer air washed over them when they stepped outside. It was late evening with the sun making its glorious bow behind the mountains and sending streaks of lavender and pink into the sky. She took a deep breath, savoring the woodsy scent mingling with the hint of the ocean.

Eli had parked over toward the marshy field. As they walked in that direction, her eye caught on a cluster of moose in the field. "Oh look! Marley kept telling me I'd see moose soon, and there they are!"

Eli's soft laugh sent a hot shiver through her. "Hard not to see moose around here. Let's go onto the viewing platform after I leave this in the truck," he said, holding aloft the bottle of wine. He paused and left it inside the truck cab before guiding her with his hand toward a wooden walkway hidden by the tall grasses.

In seconds they stood on the small platform looking out over the field. There was a full-grown moose and two tiny calves. "Oh, the babies are so small!"

"Yeah. They're much smaller than people expect. It's mid-summer though, so those two are probably a good month or more old now. They look to be a set of twins too."

"Oh, wow," she breathed, feeling a sense of wonder steal over her.

Alaska was renowned for its expansive wilderness and beauty, but Jessa hadn't truly understood what that meant until she'd come to visit. Every time she was here, she felt like she stepped a little further into the wild wonderland

Alaska offered. The sense of being so far removed from the bustle of civilization added depth to its beauty.

"I never get tired of seeing the moose calves. They're so damn cute. Well, I never get tired of any of the wildlife. Makes me remember what matters. We're just a speck in the universe."

Jessa glanced to Eli. "That's why you do what you do, huh?"

Eli shrugged, his eyes on the moose and scanning the horizon behind them before he looked to her. "I love the outdoors. When I was growing up, it was the only place I found peace. Now, I still get the peace, but it's also plain fun to take tourists out and see some minds get blown."

As they stood there by the field with nothing but the soft sound of the wind rustling the tall grass and the call of a raven nearby, she felt suspended in time. Eli's eyes darkened. His hand was still resting on her low back. With the slightest pressure, he turned her toward him as he angled himself to face her. A step and he was flush against her, his hand sliding over her bottom to cup it.

"Jessa…" His voice was low and gruff, sending a prickle over her skin.

The angles of his face were in shadow, brightening his eyes. Heat suffused her when he incrementally pulled her against him, and she felt the hard evidence of his arousal. Suddenly, they were kissing—a wild, out of control kiss, so hot, so wet and so deep. He explored her mouth boldly with his tongue and lips, and she couldn't get enough. She plastered herself against him and dragged her hands up over his chest—that glorious, sculpted hard chest of his. She gasped when he tore his lips free and dragged them down her neck, licking and nipping. She was drenched, her thighs clenching with the need spiraling wildly through her.

Eli swore and pulled back. Their breath heaved in the chilled air. He looked down at her. "I'm not going to be able to stop if we go any further and seeing as we're on a viewing platform..." He gestured around them and in the direction of the brewery just by them. They were in full view of anyone who happened to look in their direction.

Jessa flushed, a giggle bubbling out of her. "Oh my. I forgot where we were. Maybe we should..." She paused, uncertain what to say. What she wanted to say was they should go anywhere private. Immediately. The desire pumping through her was so powerful, she wouldn't have been surprised if she'd tackled him right here without a thought for where they were.

"Go back to my place," Eli finished her sentence.

She nodded with alacrity. He moved swiftly, turning and curling one of his warm, strong hands around hers as they walked to his truck. The moment they were in the truck, it felt as if the entire space was alive with electricity, snapping with the force of their desire.

Eli kicked the door shut behind him just as Jessa whirled around and shoved him against the door. She shimmied her lush body against him, slid a hand around his neck and yanked him down to meet her lips for a kiss. The lust pounding through him had been on pause during the short drive back to his house from the brewery. The second her tongue tangled with his, it thundered through him. The next few moments passed in a fumbled blur as they tore at each other's clothes. One of his boots landed all the way over by the kitchen counter when he kicked it free, while Jessa's jacket hung sloppily off the edge of the couch.

His breath came in heaves and he fought to keep some semblance of control. They hadn't even moved away from the door yet. He leaned his head back and dragged his eyes open to find Jessa standing before him, making quick work of the buttons on his jeans and sliding her palm inside to stroke the length of his cock. Her shirt had been tossed aside, but her dark blue silk bra hugged the curves of her breasts, making him itch to touch her. He reached a hand out and stroked his thumb across the tight bead of her nipple through the silk only to groan when she shoved his jeans and briefs down around his hips to free his cock. The feel of her hand curling around him and sliding up and down buckled his knees. He braced a hand against the door behind him.

"Jessa," he choked her name out.

"Hmmm?"

Her reply was smothered as she leaned forward and dipped her head to drag her tongue along one side of his shaft and then the other.

Whatever he'd meant to say next was lost in the maelstrom of need claiming him. He looked down at the sexy curve of her back. Every inch of her was beyond tempting. He kept one hand braced against the door because he couldn't stand if he didn't, while he dragged the other down along her spine to grip one of her hips. Meanwhile, she drove him beyond madness between her bold exploration of him—licking, stroking, and sucking until she finally took him all the way into her mouth, swirling her tongue as she did. She drew back, her fist stroking in a wet grip. He was teetering on the edge of control, so he reached for her, tugging her up.

Her smoky gaze collided with his, her lips plump and swollen. He kicked his jeans off while she shimmied out of her leggings. Somehow they made it to the couch. His rough and ragged breath mingled with her breathy pants. He found himself seated on the couch with Jessa straddling him in nothing but a scrap of dark blue silk matching her silky bra. He could feel the damp heat of her sliding against his cock as she rolled her hips slightly. He latched onto the barest thread of control and gripped her hips to hold her still.

She dragged a hand down his chest, those smoky eyes on him every second. He refused to be rushed just yet and eased his grip on her hips to slide his hands up her waist and cup her breasts. A sense of satisfaction rolled through him when she bit her lip and moaned as he teased her nipples through the silk. He dipped his head and laved his tongue over the silk, dampening it and biting a nipple lightly while he rolled the other between his fingers. When she arched into his touch, he couldn't hold back anymore and flicked the clasp on her bra, groaning at the feel of her silky skin under his touch as her breasts tumbled loose. She flung her bra across the room and shifted her hips back to stroke her palm boldly over him.

"Hang on..." He glanced around, looking for his jeans where he'd made sure he'd tucked a condom into his wallet.

Jessa followed his gaze and leaned backwards to snag his jeans. He yanked his wallet out of the pocket and tore the condom out. She was ever helpful with trying to open the packet and roll the condom on, knocking her head with his in the process. Her eyes slammed up, and she giggled.

Her giggle nearly undid him. Though his body was practically on fire and so driven with need he could barely think, his heart gave a hard kick. Jessa had this way of reaching right to his heart without even trying. Her blithe warmth and bubbly nature knocked him sideways. The combination of that with her bold sensuality brought him to his knees—physically and emotionally.

He felt her shift against him again and the lust thundering through him took over. He reached between her thighs, stroking his fingers across the wet silk. Her eyes closed and she pressed down into his touch. He shoved the flimsy fabric aside and delved into her slick folds. She was restless, urging him on. He dragged his fingers out and positioned his cock at her entrance, driving in and seating himself to the hilt in one surge.

* * *

JESSA'S BREATH escaped in a soft moan when Eli filled her, stretching her deliciously. She held still, savoring the fullness. She was so close to the edge of a climax, she wanted to hold back because it felt so good, so, so good to be with him like this. She didn't quite recognize who she was with him. She wasn't reserved sexually, but she'd never been as wildly turned on by anyone before. Simply touching him and any reserve she had fell away. All she wanted was to be close and to twine herself into the heartbeat of passion that pulsed and shimmered around them.

"Jessa..."

She looked up at his gruff whisper, straight into his heated green gaze. He lifted a hand, stroking it into her hair, as he started to move, rolling his hips slowly. She moved with him, tumbling into sensation. His hand tightened in her hair as he stroked deeper into her. She rose up, savoring the stretch as she sank down onto him again and again and again. Arrows of pleasure shot through her when he reached between them and circled her clit with his thumb. Tremors began to wrack her body as she chased after the sweet release, dancing just beyond her reach. Another swirl of his thumb and her release broke over her in wave after wave, her channel convulsing around him.

His hand tightened in her hair again, his body going taut and his head thrown back as a guttural cry broke from him. His head fell forward into the dip of her shoulder just as she curled against him. Her body still shuddering from the echoes of her climax, she lifted a hand and slowly stroked through his hair. They remained still, their breath slowing in unison. As the heat gradually dissipated, a shiver chased over her skin when she felt a soft breeze.

He loosened his hand in her hair, letting his palm slide slowly down her back. "Left a window open earlier," he said, his voice husky.

She lifted her head to find his gaze on her, as if he'd been waiting. His mouth curled in a small smile, which she felt right in the center of her chest. Joy bloomed inside and she flushed. Another gust came through the window, sending goose bumps prickling over her skin.

Eli's warm palm stroked in a circle before he shifted his hips, easing her up. She resisted for a second, not wanting to move away from him. "Just wanna close that window," he said.

She giggled and scrambled off of his lap, watching while he strode across the living room. The kitchen lights, which must have been on when they came in, filtered into this area. His body was nothing but muscle. She savored the sight of his back flexing as he leaned over easily to close the window in the corner. He turned back, tossing his condom in the trash by the kitchen counter on his way back to her. He stopped by the couch, looking down. "Do I need to plan to take you back to the lodge?" he asked.

She shook her head. In her mind, there was no question. She didn't want to be anywhere but here with Eli, so it seemed entirely silly to insist he return her to the lodge. Not that she needed to report her whereabouts to Gage and Marley, but out of courtesy, she felt she should since she was a guest of theirs, family or not. She'd told Marley earlier she probably wouldn't be back until tomorrow and had tolerated Marley's sly smile in response.

Eli held a hand out. She placed hers in it, reveling in the feel of his calloused palm curling around hers. He tugged her up. "Where are we going?" she asked, almost giddy inside.

"Bedroom," came his succinct reply. He walked to the side opposite the kitchen in the cathedral ceilinged living room and pushed through a door in the corner. He flicked the light on, and she looked around as he kept walking. His bedroom was sparsely furnished with a king-sized built-in bed with sleek lines and topped with a dark quilt.

In another second, they were in a large bathroom with a shower, an oval shaped bathtub and double sinks. He flicked on another light and started the shower, pulling her inside with him. The steamy water was pure heaven. She fell asleep a while later, snuggled under the downy quilt and tucked into Eli's shoulder, his body emanating warmth and strength.

* * *

JESSA WOKE WITH A START, the choking smoke of her dream clearing once she opened her eyes. The now-familiar feeling of disorientation and fear raced through her in loops. Her heart was racing wildly and her breath was coming in rough pants.

"You okay?" Eli's question was soft and threaded with concern. His low voice reminded her of where she was.

She gulped in air and tried to slow her heart rate, mortified she'd had one of her nightmares here. They'd been gradually decreasing in frequency since she'd arrived in Diamond Creek. It figured she'd have her first nightmare in several nights when she happened to be with Eli. She felt his palm resting on the curve of her hip, the point of contact anchoring her to this moment. There was no choking, thick smoke filling the room and no fire. A sliver of air—cool and scented with spruce—slipped in through the small gap of the one window Eli had barely opened before they tumbled into bed. He'd explained that he slept better with fresh air.

Right now, that whisper of fresh air was so soothing, she almost wept. Each time she awoke from these muddled, frightening dreams, she reminded herself she'd gotten out safely during the fire and she didn't need to be afraid. Fear was a strange force. It had a way of burrowing inside, free from the rules of logic. Eli's palm traced the curve of her hip, traveling up her side and over her shoulder to sift through her hair. He was quiet and for that she was relieved. The level of comfort she felt with him startled her. He seemed to understand her, just as now when she didn't want questions. She merely wanted a few minutes to pass through to the other side of this feeling of fear and confusion.

With his fingers idly untangling her hair and the warmth and strength of his presence easing the tension bundled inside of her, she eventually rolled over in his arms. When she glanced his way, his eyes opened to meet hers in the shadowy room. She considered what to say and decided the truth was the simplest.

"Since the fire, I have nightmares sometimes. I got out okay, except for the burn on my arm," she said, lifting the arm in question. "I lost just about everything. I didn't mean to wake you, I..."

"Please don't apologize for having a nightmare. I've never woken up in the middle of a fire, but I can bet it was terrifying."

He kept stroking her hair, and she sighed. "It was. I'd rather not go through it again."

"I don't even like thinking about what you went through."

In the quiet night, her heartbeat gradually stopped its fear-fueled pounding and she relaxed again. She fell asleep again with Eli's hand stroking through her hair, safe and warm with the cool breeze whispering through the window.

CHAPTER 17

$\mathcal{E}$li carefully tightened the mount on a customer's shiny new roof rack. He glanced across at the customer, a young man named Adam. "How's it feel over there now?"

Adam gripped the base of the roof rack and gave it a good shake, or rather he failed to budge it even a tiny bit. "Rock solid. Awesome!" Adam jumped down from where he'd been standing on the inner edge of the passenger door to his truck.

Eli stepped down and tucked his screwdriver in his back pocket, turning to face Adam who'd walked around to meet him. Adam was grinning ear to ear. He brushed his blondish-brown hair out of his eyes and held a hand out to shake Eli's, his grip firm and enthusiastic.

"Thanks man! Just what we needed. Mind if we stay parked here for a few minutes while I get our bikes and kayaks off that crappy rack we have on the back?"

Eli chuckled, glancing to the taped together rack mounted to the rear of Adam's truck. "No, take all the time you need. If you need any help, just holler."

"Got it. We'll probably stop in again. Janet's trying to talk me into a new tent. When we have some more time, we'll come back. We plan to be here for at least a week." Adam was referring to his girlfriend whom Eli had met briefly when they stopped by the other day. Adam and Janet were two of thousands of like-minded tourists passing through Diamond Creek for various outdoor expeditions.

"We're open seven days a week. Stop by when you can." At that, Eli nodded and headed back into the store.

Game to Fish was bustling today, although that was the case most days. Eli tended to feel pulled in two directions in the summer. He loved being out on the water for charters, but the store got so busy, he liked to be here to make sure things ran smoothly. Cliff was his main employee, but he had a rotating collection of employees who covered shifts in the store, most of them friends of Cliff's. Today, their scheduled charter had canceled after one of the members became seasick the day prior on another trip. As such, Eli took advantage of the freed up time to catch up on things in the store. He'd conveniently forgotten there was no such thing as catching up on anything during the height of summer. From the moment he walked in, the store had been mobbed.

Game to Fish served a wide range of customers—from those who were casual wilderness sightseers looking for the best binoculars to be found up through hard-core backcountry hikers, fishermen and hunters constantly looking to replace whatever item had just died in its given quest. He enjoyed the range because it enabled him to share his love of the outdoors with everyone. The bright spot of his childhood had been the gift of the Alaskan wilderness right outside his doorstep. He would escape the toxic tension always simmering from his father and spend hour upon hour outside, exploring trails, walking along the beach, and absorbing the peace offered. His first job in high school was on the docks in Aurora Harbor, the largest boat harbor in the Juneau area. He helped haul fish off of commercial fishing boats and made extra cash filleting fish for tourists. He'd moved on to work for a charter company in Juneau where he'd learned everything he knew about boats and fishing.

At twenty-two years old when he'd clung to his control in the wake of another vicious talking to from his father, he'd made the only decision he thought he could—to get away. He was so afraid he'd become like his father, he couldn't stand to be there anymore. Diamond Creek was considered one of Alaska's coastal jewels and ripe for tourist dollars. Looking back, he realized he'd had no idea what he was really doing. He took a glimmer of a dream and made it happen out of sheer will. Every penny he'd saved up in his adolescent and early adult years had been sitting in a savings account. Somehow, he pulled off getting a loan to start his business, and here he was today. Game to Fish was thriving. He might be worn out most of the summer, but he loved it.

He threaded his way through the displays of gear and clothing and headed for his office. With Ryan and Cliff here to help, he had four employees working out front and could try to steal a few minutes to update orders. He'd started paying Ryan last week, although Ryan had tried to persuade him it wasn't necessary. Eli ignored him and put him on the payroll. Ryan worked as hard as anyone, and Eli wasn't content to let him work for free. Considering that his own work ethic was what had gotten him out of the hellhole of his father's orbit, he figured it was a good thing to support.

He managed to reach his office without getting stopped and quickly closed the door. His phone message light was blinking, but he ignored it to make sure he put in the orders for stock of what he called the staples—the basic gear they blew through all summer long, such as water bottles, day trip backpacks, windbreakers and the like. Every spring, he settled on a set inventory for those items and made sure to stay on top of it.

After that, he checked his email and finally checked his messages. His chest tightened when he heard his mother's voice. She rarely called his cell, although she had it. Sometimes he wondered if she called here because she knew he'd be less likely to answer.

It's Mom, Eli. I talked to your father about Ryan. I'm sure you won't be surprised to hear he's angry. I don't think he plans to fight it though. I just thought you'd want to know. Tell Ryan I love him.

Eli listened to the line click dead and sat there for a several beats before tapping the speaker off on his phone. He leaned back and ran a hand through his hair. He was relieved to hear his father didn't plan to make this guardianship situation ugly. For Ryan's sake, Eli wanted him to know he could stay here and stop worrying about it. Ryan didn't talk about it much, but Eli saw the worry lingering in the back of his eyes. Eli couldn't shake the muddle of feelings this whole situation brought up for him. Oddly, the way he felt for Jessa kept bouncing his mind onto tracks of worry he thought he'd long ago jumped off. Jessa had so effortlessly knocked down his defenses, he didn't know what to do. He'd made a very clear, purposeful decision years ago that he wouldn't try to do the whole commitment thing. Hell, he hardly even dated. He didn't *ever* want to find himself in anything resembling his parents' marriage. He feared because of his father there might be some part of him waiting to be triggered. He figured if he didn't seek out relationships, he wouldn't have to worry. This decision hadn't been a problem for him. Until Jessa.

Jessa was lightness, joy, warmth and mind-blowingly sexy. The way he felt with her was almost too good to be true and damned if he knew what to do about it. His conundrum now was he was afraid of letting things go too much further because he couldn't bear it if he somehow hurt her. His fear about becoming like his father stemmed from a conversation he'd overheard his mother having when he was around ten years old. She'd been talking to her sister, who'd since passed away, and making excuses for his father. She'd repeated over and over through tears that Norm hadn't been abusive when they met. Looking back, Eli wasn't sure it was true, but it stuck with him. He couldn't imagine ever being like his father, but he couldn't shake the worry he could become like him.

A vision of Jessa flashed through his mind, the way she looked arching above him when he drove into her. His body reacted instantly at the thought of her. His heart clenched and that unfamiliar feeling of intimacy she elicited pinged in his center. His mind spun to waking beside her when he heard her cry out in her sleep. He could tell himself over and over she was fine, and she clearly was, but it almost physically pained him to think about the fire. He had only the sketchy details, but it terrified him to realize she could have been hurt far worse than she was. There was a loud knock on his office door, nudging his mind back to where he was.

"Yeah?" he called out.

Ryan poked his head around the door. "Hey, um, Gage Hamilton is here. He said he was hoping to talk with you about some orders."

"Oh right. Just have him come back here. It's too busy out there. You guys handling everything okay?"

Ryan shrugged. "Think so. I mean, there's four of us and we're busy, but customers are moving through. I'll go get Gage, okay?"

"Yup. Just point him this way."

A minute later, Gage strode into his office, his eyes quickly scanning the room. Eli knew Gage was a former Navy SEAL, and he looked the part. He was in prime physical condition and carried himself with a somber alertness. The only time Eli saw another side of him was when he was with Marley and around his family. Then, Gage softened. Eli had enjoyed spending time with the Hamilton family the other night. They were so unlike his own family, it was almost surreal.

Gage looked to him and nodded quickly. "Hey, thanks for taking a few minutes. He held up a folder. "I took a look at these catalogs. I tried looking online, but it drives me crazy trying to click through all the screens, so I circled what we'd like to order in these."

Eli grinned and gestured to the chair on the opposite side of his desk. "Have a seat. Let me take a look."

He quickly scanned what Gage handed over, seeing Gage was clearly looking to stock up on skis and ski gear for the lodge before winter rolled in. He pulled up his ordering screen and immediately transferred over what Gage had noted. As he handed the folders back to Gage, he thought of something. "You know, we could think about having a small area at the lodge where you kept some winter gear for sale. Not the heavy stuff you're getting here, but jackets, hats, and gloves. That type of thing. It would save you from sending customers to town and help me hone in on what you guys need up there. Just a thought."

Gage gave him a considering look. Eli suddenly realized Gage's gray eyes were quite similar to Jessa's. He mentally shook himself to keep his attention from wandering to Jessa.

"You know, that's a damn good idea. Let me think on it and see if we can figure out how to make it work." Gage glanced out the window to his side before his gaze locked onto Eli again. Eli sensed a shift in topic. "Jessa likes you," Gage said firmly. "A lot."

Eli sat there, definitely uncertain about how to reply to this announcement from Gage. Considering that he'd avoided relationships of any kind for his entire adult life, it was safe to say he'd never had to worry about a conversation with an older brother of a woman he was suspecting he was in way too deep with. When it became obvious Gage wasn't going to say anything else just yet, Eli nodded slowly. "Uh, you think so?"

Gage leaned back in his chair, resting his elbows on the arms and steepling his fingers under his chin. "Yes. I think so. Look, I try not to be that brother, the one who thinks he has to clear any guy his sisters might date. With Jessa though, she's, well, she's never really been into anyone the way she seems to be you. She's one of the nicest people I know, definitely the nicest person in our whole family. You seem like a good guy, but I have no idea what you're after. Just figured it'd be better if you knew I won't stand by and watch anyone hurt her. If you're hoping for a fun fling, you'd better know right now it's obvious she likes you a lot more than that. If you think you're moving on, don't toy with her."

After a few quiet moments, Eli realized he must look like a fish. He kept opening his mouth to say something and then closing it when he couldn't figure out what the hell to say. *You are in over your head, way over your head here. Get a clue and back off. Gage is probably doing you a favor.* That was one side of his suddenly argumentative mind. *Yeah, but I can't just walk away from her. I...* He had to cut off the other side of his mind because what he was about to say shocked the hell out of him. He'd almost said the word 'love' in his mind, albeit silently. But still. How could he even think the word? He didn't do love. Yet, he couldn't conceive of walking away from Jessa and cutting himself off from all that was good about her and how he felt when he was with her. What he said next startled him.

"Look, I don't know what to say or how to handle this. You say Jessa likes me. Well, I like her. A lot. I'm not going sit here and tell you I know what's going to happen because I sure as hell don't. The one thing I can promise you is I'm not out to hurt her. I know she's special. I wish…" He paused and ran a hand through his hair. He wished all kinds of things, mostly that he had faith he could be the kind of man Jessa deserved. If only he knew that, he wouldn't be worried about any of this.

Gage's hands fell and he angled his head to one side, narrowing his eyes. "You wish what?"

Eli wanted to ask Gage's advice, but it seemed odd given the circumstances. Eli shrugged. "I guess I wish this kind of thing was easy to figure out ahead of time," he said.

Gage threw his head back with a laugh. "Right. If only. Look, whatever happens, I'll try to stay out of the way. I know Jessa can take care of herself, and now I know you might be in worse shape than her. Be good to her, and we're good."

CHAPTER 18

*J*essa carefully maneuvered the folding table she held up the back stairs at the gallery. Risa had given her a key to the back hallway to start setting up her studio. Once she reached the top of the stairs, she walked quickly to the end of the hall where her space was and leaned the table against the wall. She spun in a slow circle, trying to decide the best spot for it. She'd already covered the floor in two layers of heavy fabric drop cloths. She laughed to herself when she realized she had more space in this small room than she'd ever had in the second room in her apartment. The ceiling angled up to a point with light spilling in from the windows facing the bay. She settled on putting the table in front of the windows. That way, she could enjoy the view while she worked.

Several hours later, she took a last look around for the day. Aside from the table, she'd set up shelving along one wall to store her paints, brushes and supplies. On the other wall, she'd carefully organized her meager collection of unpainted furniture. The fire had burned up most of that, but she'd had enough to fill the back of her little truck from what had been stored away from her home. A smile bloomed when her eyes landed on the small project she'd completed this afternoon. She'd promised herself she'd try to finish one item, so she'd painted a pair of chairs and a small table for a garden. They were brightly colored and painted with swirling flowers, intended to be outside on a porch, or in a flower garden. She'd gone for a design based on fireweed and lupine after her visit last summer when those flowers were in bloom. At the moment, the set was sitting in the center of the room with the paint drying.

As she turned away, there was a soft knock on the door. "Come in!" she called out.

Risa poked her head around the door, her brown eyes bright and a warm smile spreading across her face. "Hey! Thought I'd pop in to see if you got everything situated. I meant to be more available to help, but the gallery kept me too busy." She paused, her eyes landing on the decorative set. "Oh! It's lovely!" She glanced back to Jessa. "I could sell that this afternoon if it was ready," she said with a grin.

Jessa flushed, joy bubbling up inside. "You think?"

Risa put her hands on her hips. "You know your work is good! Of course I could sell it," she said emphatically.

Jessa shrugged. "I try. I know it really hasn't been that long since I've had a chance to paint, but it felt like forever. It made me doubt whether I could get back to it."

Risa nodded. "Makes sense. Looks like you're right back at it." A bell chimed from downstairs. Risa turned back into the hall. "I need to get back down there. You've got a key, so just come and go as you please. Bye!"

At that, Risa jogged down the stairs leading to the gallery. Jessa picked up her purse and closed the door behind her as she made her way out. When she got outside, she took a deep breath, savoring the salty air, and looked around. Gulls circled above, and an eagle flew low across the water behind the gallery. Emotion welled inside of her.

After her apartment building burned down, she'd felt so dejected and weary. Living on the edge of her budget had pushed her to a point of hopelessness when she realized she'd have to find a way to pull her art business together again on almost nothing. Risa's offer to let her use the space here as her studio was such a gift, she felt overwhelmed. Possibility seemed possible again.

She jogged to her truck, tucked her purse inside and turned back for a walk on the beach. Marley kept telling her she should explore the beaches here, so she figured now was a perfect time. The wind gusted off the water, cool and refreshing. The tide was on its way back in, but tide pools were still visible along the damp sand in eddies near rocks and dips on the ground. She watched as a wave rolled up and caught a pink starfish in its tow, pulling it out into the ocean with it. The beach here was scattered with rocks, ranging in color from gray to green to orange to red. As she walked along, she saw a raft of otters, likely the same group she'd seen the other day. They floated together in the water, rising and falling with the soft roll of the waves.

Eli danced in the edges of her thoughts most of the day. The other night with him had been...so, so, so good. He was just plain good—nice, caring, funny, and sexy as hell. Just thinking about him and the other night sent a hot flush racing through her. A chilly gust of wind soothed the rush of heat. She stopped on the beach and looked out over the bay. A glacier glittered on the far side, its translucent blue color alluring and magical. She finally turned back and retraced her path, watching as her footsteps from her walk out dissolved in the waves rolling over them as the tideline crept further up along the beach.

When she climbed into her truck, she realized she needed to get back to the lodge fast. She was scheduled to work tonight and had gotten so absorbed in her painting that she'd lost track of time. She pushed Blue to go as fast as she could on the way up the winding road to Last Frontier Lodge. When the brightly painted sign for the lodge came into view, she smiled. She raced inside and up to her suite to shower and change. While she'd come to learn she could dress far more casually than she'd expect to in a restaurant in Seattle, she couldn't show up with paint spattered on her arms and face.

In record time, she pushed through the swinging door into the kitchen and glanced around for Harry. While Delia managed the restaurant overall, Harry was in charge of managing everything that happened out front. At the moment, Delia was stirring something on the stove and giving directions to one of the line cooks nearby. She caught Jessa's eye and mouthed a hello.

"Jessa, Jessa! You're here!" Harry greeted her with a grin, his brown eyes gleaming with an ever-present hint of mischief.

"Of course I'm here! Did you think I wouldn't be?"

Harry glanced at the clock on the wall above the door into the restaurant. "You're usually early, so I didn't know if you forgot."

She rolled her eyes and strode past him to pour a cup of coffee. "I didn't forget. Hand over the specials list and I'll go out front."

She took a swallow of coffee and paused at his side. Harry chuckled and slipped a list out of his pocket. She snagged the list and made her way to the reception desk out front. Within minutes, she was busy bantering with customers, serving samples of wine and whirling between the reception desk and the restaurant. By the time she turned the sign to closed, her legs were starting to tire. The restaurant had finally started to empty with only a few customers lingering. She loved this time of evening when she could walk around and quietly clear off and tidy tables. She waved goodnight to the final batch of customers who made their way out into the chilly night and paused to look out over the mountains behind the lodge. Dusk in Alaska was a long, slow bow. The smudgy gray light cast shadows everywhere. The moon was rising to one side of the mountains through the lingering burst of color from the sun, which had set behind the mountains some time ago. She marveled at the late Alaskan evenings. It was close to eleven and only now was darkness taking hold.

"Thought I might find you here."

Eli's voice was low and reached right into her center. Her heart gave a swift kick and heat flooded her belly. She turned to find him leaning against the archway leading into the restaurant. He was just delicious. He wore a denim jacket that fell open to reveal a t-shirt that hugged his sculpted chest and abs. Even from across the room, her fingers itched to touch him. He was all heat, strength, and pure man.

"Hey," she called as she turned and walked toward him. "I didn't know you were stopping by."

"Hope you don't mind. Ryan went off to Jeff and Ben's for the night again, so it's just me and… Well, I guess I just drove up here hoping I might find you."

She reached him and stopped right in front of him. "You found me," she said softly, a giddiness rising inside.

He smiled and lifted a hand to stroke through her hair, his hand coming to rest in the curve of her neck. Her pulse shot forward and her breath hitched.

"I have to do a few things to finish…"

"No need to stay. Not much left to do." Harry's voice came from behind her.

She turned, and Eli's hand followed her turn, sliding over her shoulder and down her back, coming to rest on the curve of her bottom. She could barely focus, but forced herself to pay attention to Harry. He stood by the door into the kitchen.

"You sure?"

Harry grinned and glanced around the restaurant. "I'm sure. There's nothing left to do out here. I know you like to help in the kitchen, but it's not necessary. Go," he said firmly with a wave as he turned and exited the restaurant into the kitchen.

Eli's hand caressed her bottom, and liquid heat swirled in her center. She turned back to face him. His dark green gaze locked onto hers. For several beats, they simply stood there, the air heavy with the weight of their desire. In slow motion with her heart thundering in her ears, she watched as he dipped his head and brought his lips to hers. His kiss started soft and almost instantly morphed into fierce. He fit his mouth over hers, slid his hand into her hair and swept his tongue into her mouth. In seconds, she was on fire, heat suffusing her and need racing through her. A muffled clatter came from the kitchen, and Eli tore his lips away. She stood in his arms as he stroked a hand roughly through her hair. Their mingled gasps were loud in the empty restaurant.

In a stumbling rush, Jessa dragged Eli up the back stairs and down the hall to her suite. Once the door slammed shut behind them, they tore at each other's clothes, leaving a trail from the door to the bed. When the back of her knees bumped against the mattress, she paused and looked over at Eli. He kicked out of his jeans, lifting them as he did to yank a condom out of the pocket. With his eyes on her, he made quick work of rolling the condom on and took a step to close the distance between them. He lifted a hand and traced from her shoulder, around the curve of her breast, into the dip of her waist and over the contour of her hip. Her breath came in shallow pants as she lifted her eyes to meet his. With their eyes locked together, he dropped a knee on the bed while hers buckled under the tremors running through her.

Heat blazed through her as he stretched out beside her, his hands and lips mapping her body. She was impatient and needy for him, dragging her hands down the corded muscles of his spine, her nails scoring his skin. He rolled atop her, his cock resting against her folds. His hands curled into hers and stretched them up above her head. She curled her legs around his hips, arching into him.

"Eli..."

He mumbled something against her neck, the motion of his lips sending hot shivers through her. She flexed, frantic to feel him inside of her. He rocked his hips against her, the feel of his hard cock sliding over her clit nearly sending her over the edge.

"Eli...now!"

At her raspy demand, he lifted his head from where he'd been teasing her to madness with his lips. With his dark green gaze locked onto her, he gave her what she asked. In a swift surge, he seated himself fully within her. Without pause, he began to move, cycling into and out of her channel. She strove to meet each stroke, flying higher and higher until she spun loose. Hot pleasure spiraled outward through her. Through her own cries, she felt Eli stiffen and shudder against her, growling her name against her neck when his head fell forward.

What felt like hours later, Jessa stood in the shower in her suite, the steaming water sluicing over her as her body still vibrated from the explosive climax she'd just experienced. Eli had once again brought her to peaks of pleasure she'd never even thought possible. His palm stroked down her back, his touch slippery under the water. She titled her head back, resting it against his shoulder. The connection between them stitched tighter.

She fell asleep in his arms again. There were no nightmares tonight.

CHAPTER 19

"Please rise," the court clerk announced in a calm, authoritative tone.

Eli stood in unison with Garrett. Ryan rose quickly a second behind them. Eli's only experience in court had been a few times when he was young and his mother brought him along for hearings related to his father. He didn't remember what he wore, but he did remember his father never bothered to clean up. Eli had insisted Ryan wear navy slacks and a button-down shirt today. When he'd realized he hadn't thought ahead when he took Ryan shopping, Jessa had immediately volunteered to pick something up for Ryan on a shopping trip with Marley.

Eli himself wore matching navy slacks—double thanks to Jessa—and a button-down shirt. Garrett matched them with the addition of a suit jacket and tie. He was clearly at home in court, relaxed and confident. Eli hadn't expected to feel nervous, but he did. Somehow, the formal setting brought home how much meaning this official hearing had. If all went as Garrett confidently claimed it would, they would be walking out shortly with Eli legally identified as

Ryan's guardian. Although Eli hadn't even hesitated to do this, now that they were standing in front of a judge, the weight of what was happening was starting to sink in. He was about to assume legal responsibility for his younger brother. He couldn't help but ponder the meaning of it. Beyond making things right for Ryan, he was getting a chance to do what he wished someone could've done for him. He could feel Ryan's anxiety humming beside him.

They waited as the judge, a petite woman with dark hair flecked with white, entered the courtroom. After the clerk announced they could be seated, they collectively sat. The next few moments were remarkably dry. Garrett verbally reviewed the petition, which seemed a pointless formality, as it was quite clear the judge had reviewed everything thoroughly. She asked a few questions of Garrett and then turned her gaze to Eli and Ryan.

She addressed Eli first. "Mr. Brooks, as I understand it, you are fully prepared to serve as your brother's guardian, correct?"

He started to stand, but the judge waved him back. "Yes, Your Honor," he finally managed.

Eli's heart pounded hard and fast as he waited. The judge looked down at the paperwork in front of her and then back up. "I'm familiar with Mr. Hamilton's work, so I trust he's thoroughly explained your responsibilities. Do you have any questions for me?"

"No, Your Honor."

She nodded and looked to Ryan. "I've read your letter attached to the petition, but is there anything else you'd like to say before I make my ruling?"

Ryan shook his head, his hair falling over his eyes. He brushed it back nervously and swallowed.

The judge nodded and glanced between them before looking back to Ryan. "I've had a chance to read a letter sent by your father."

A flash of anger rose in Eli. Garrett had called him last week to tell him his father had filed a written dispute of the guardianship petition. Eli had stopped by Garrett's office to review a full two-pages of garbage written by his father. It was handwritten, which led Eli to believe his father hadn't enlisted his mother to help. If he had, the letter would have been typed. The letter mainly consisted of denials and accused Eli of influencing his impressionable younger brother for financial gain.

The judge looked back to Eli before she spoke. "After reviewing the materials Mr. Hamilton submitted with the petition, I'm not inclined to consider your father a reliable historian about the events. My sole concern after review of all the materials is how you intend to support Ryan's relationship with his mother. Have you considered that?"

Eli took a breath to steady himself and nodded. Garrett had prepared him for this question, but it didn't change the slight emotional pang. He wasn't doing any of this to put a wedge in Ryan's relationship with their mother. If anything, he hoped giving Ryan the chance to be free from the influence of their father might actually prevent Ryan from resenting their mother the way Eli had when he was younger. Yet, it didn't make it any easier when he thought of how his mother felt.

"Yes, Your Honor," he finally replied. He paused for a breath, almost laughing at how many times he'd said 'Your Honor.' Garrett had politely instructed him on courtroom manners and even suggested he practice a few times for good measure. "I've spoken with our mother and plan to ensure Ryan visits her at least twice a year. I'm willing to support more, but I'm not willing to allow Ryan to stay there as long as our father is staying in the home."

Garrett interjected. "Your Honor, if I may?"

She nodded and Garrett continued. "As I've noted in the petition, Mr. Brooks is willing to be legally bound to cover the expenses associated with visitation, including travel expenses for their mother to be flown here to visit Ryan monthly if she agrees."

The judge nodded firmly. "I noted that. I'd like to have the record note the commitment to twice yearly visits at a minimum with the limitation of not staying at the family home." She paused and looked to Ryan. "I'm assuming this is acceptable to you?"

Ryan nodded quickly. "I, um, Your Honor, I want to see my mom. I know if my father's not around, Eli will let me visit more, so I'm okay with it."

Another slow nod from the judge. Moments later, she verbally declared Eli to be Ryan's legal guardian, read the orders for the record and signed the petition. Eli walked out of the courtroom at Ryan's side, emotion tightening his chest and relief rushing through him. For a second, tears pushed at the back of his eyes, but he took in several gulps of air and pulled himself together. When they stepped into the waiting area and then through the doors outside, Garrett clapped him on the shoulder. "Done!"

Eli met Garrett's eyes and took a deep breath, the tight feeling in his chest easing with the fresh air flowing into his lungs. "Thank you. That went just as smoothly as you predicted."

Garrett's gaze grew sober. "I don't mislead clients. If you hadn't had a good case, I wouldn't have said so."

Ryan stood beside them, his hands stuffed in his pockets. He looked between Eli and Garrett and swallowed. "Um, thanks," he finally said. His eyes were bright with tears, and he turned and stared out over the parking lot.

Garrett caught Eli's gaze and nodded. "He's got one hell of a brother," Garrett said softly.

They stood quietly for a moment until a moose happened to saunter into the parking lot on the far side. A second later, a calf followed its mother into the open.

"Suppose we should either get in our cars or wait inside," Garrett said with a low laugh.

Eli glanced to the moose and her calf and the distance to his truck and Garrett's car. The moose kept walking, her calf following, all legs and tentative steps. "Looks like they're just passing through. Give 'em a sec and they'll get to the alder over there," he said, gesturing to a cluster of alder on the far side of the parking lot.

His prediction proved true a moment later when the moose stopped and began to nibble on the alder, helpfully tugging a branch down for her calf to reach. They made their way to their vehicles. After waving goodbye to Garrett, Eli started his truck and glanced to Ryan. "How ya doin'?"

Ryan looked over at him, relief evident in his face and his shoulders slumping. "Good, but I'm tired. Can we go home, so I can change before we go to the store?"

Eli grinned. "You didn't think I could stand to wear these clothes any longer, did you?"

Ryan laughed and shook his head. "No, I guess not."

* * *

Jessa carefully swirled her paintbrush to finish off a purple starfish in the center of a small table. She stepped back and surveyed the table in question. Unbeknownst to her, Risa had started spreading the word about her work and last week a family had commissioned her to paint a pair of tables and chairs for a greenhouse room in their home. They specifically wanted a tide pool themed set, which was what she was currently working on. The legs of the table had wavy fronds of seaweed, and she was gradually adding in various sea creatures found in tide pools on Alaskan beaches.

There was a knock at the door. "Come in!" she called out.

She didn't look behind her, expecting it to be Risa who popped in every day she was here. She jumped when she felt a warm hand stroke down her back. Before she glanced over her shoulder, she instantly knew it was Eli because she felt his presence the second he stepped into the room. She angled her head back just as his lips met the curve of her neck. "Hey," he said, the movement of his lips against her skin sending prickles along her skin.

"Hey. I didn't know you were stopping by." She rotated to face him.

He lifted one shoulder in a shrug. "I was on my way back from the harbor and thought I'd stop in. Risa said to just come on up." He stepped back and glanced around. "This is a great little spot." He took a few steps to the table she was painting. "Wow! This is...amazing."

His eyes scanned the room, pausing over the growing collection of finished projects against the back wall. He turned back to her. "So, this is what you do. I bet people love these."

Jessa flushed. "It's what I do. Maybe not what you'd get for yourself, but I managed to make decent money before. I'm hoping to get things back on track."

Eli's eyes bounced from her to the table in the middle of the room and back to her. "Just because I have no sense of decorating style doesn't mean I can't tell a good thing when I see it," he said. He eyed her for a long moment. "Risa mentioned she's started to sell your pieces and lined up a few commissions. That's just what you're hoping for, right?"

She shrugged, feeling self-conscious. "Well, yeah. But these days I'm not so sure how much I should focus on this or something else." She paused and looked over at the cheerful, wild pieces she'd finished and glanced back to him. "I kind of stumbled into this because I love to paint, but I wanted what I painted to be something other than flat on a wall. Since the fire though, when I had to face the fact I had almost no savings to speak of, I've been wondering if I need to do something else. Right now, it's working at the lodge and this, but..."

Eli shook his head sharply. "But what? You looked happier than I've ever seen you until you started to talk about it. Risa knows what sells and she seems pretty damn confident she'll sell plenty of your work. Don't beat yourself up for not having savings. Anyone who tries to do their own thing runs that risk. If my store had burned down those first few years, I'd have been in the same situation. Focus on how much it means to you and listen to Risa. I'd hate to see that glow fade from your eyes just because you let your doubts get in the way."

Jessa stared at him, stunned at his firm belief in her. A smile spread from her heart to her cheeks and she threw her arms around him. "Thank you. I needed that," she mumbled into his shoulder. She slipped down and glanced up at him. He looked slightly startled and gave his head a little shake.

"Just telling the truth," he said with a shrug.

She stretched up and kissed his stubble-rough cheek.

His phone beeped in his pocket, snapping the moment. "I need to get that," he said as he stepped back. "It's probably Ryan and he's waiting for me to pick him up at the Fish Factory." He slipped his phone out, glancing down at the screen. "Yup, it's Ryan." He glanced back to her. "Thought maybe I'd see if you wanted to grab dinner tonight. Ryan's packing up for a camping trip with Cliff and his brothers this afternoon."

She was nodding before she even thought about it. He grinned and stepped close again, dipping his head and catching her lips in a quick kiss. Though brief, every kiss from Eli sent her body into a state of heated anticipation. With one deep stroke of his tongue against hers, he drew back, catching her bottom lip in his teeth for a second before he straightened. His green gaze reflected the heat swirling inside of her.

"Should I pick you up later?" he asked.

"How about I meet you at your place? I need to get to the lodge and wash this paint off first though," she gestured to the streaks of paint on her arms.

He lifted a finger and traced a line on her neck. "I like the paint."

Dear God. One simple touch of his finger on her neck, and she was melting inside. With her pulse leaping, she flushed and shrugged. "This is me every day when I'm working."

He nodded slowly, his hand falling away. "So, it's…" he glanced to his watch "…three now. Anytime after an hour, and I'll be ready to go. Just come by."

His phone beeped again. "I'm outta here. See you in a bit."

At that, he turned and left. Jessa stood there, her heart beating wildly. She unconsciously reached up to trace her fingertip along the very place Eli had just touched her. Her mind spun over the last few weeks. Somehow, they'd slid into some sort of relationship, but she didn't know what it meant. They saw each other every few days in between her busy schedule at the lodge restaurant, working in her studio, and his insanely busy summer schedule with his store and fishing charters almost every day. She felt like she'd tumbled into this, whatever this was, between them. If she allowed herself to stop and think, which she tried to avoid most of the time, she worried she was falling too far and too fast. What little she'd been able to glean about him from Marley, Delia and others was that he'd never been known to date anyone seriously. She didn't know how to interpret that. She was as puzzled with her own feelings. Given that she'd never felt about anyone the way she felt about him, she felt like she was flying blind. The hard part was...she was afraid he was coming to mean far too much to her. Meanwhile, she had to consider that she'd come to Diamond Creek to lick her wounds and find a way forward for her life. She didn't know if that meant staying here, or finding a way to pull her life together back in Seattle.

You know what you want. Stop pretending like you don't. Her heart spoke up, clamoring sternly for her to listen. *But I don't know if it makes sense, and I don't know what he wants. You'd better pay attention before it's too late. Maybe you don't know what he wants, but you won't know unless you try to find out.*

Jessa sighed and gave her head a little shake. These internal conversations were happening with frequency, and she was betwixt and between about the way forward. Not just with Eli, but with her life. Somehow, Eli and the way she felt about him, which she didn't dare label yet, had gotten all tangled up in what she should do with her life. She got to work cleaning her paintbrushes and putting her supplies away. Conveniently, the tasks needed to get done, but they also distracted her mind from obsessing about Eli.

CHAPTER 20

The low hum of voices surrounding them, the soft buzz of wine flowing through her, and Eli simply existing nearby left Jessa swinging between a comfortable sense of relaxation and a feverish sense of anticipation. Eli had insisted she needed to try the Boathouse Café'. It had been everything promised—delicious local seafood and a touch more high-end than many restaurants in Diamond Creek. The restaurant sat on a bluff overlooking Kachemak Bay. At the moment, the sun was in the midst of its slow descent behind the mountains. Its fading rays cast long beams of light across the water. She turned back to Eli when she heard someone say his name. She watched while he grinned and waved at the man who'd greeted him. Eli turned to her when the man reached their table.

"Travis, this is Jessa Hamilton, sister of Gage and Garrett Hamilton. She's visiting for a bit," Eli said before gesturing to the man. "And this is Travis Wilkes. He's a local fisherman and yet another Alaskan who has a few more jobs I can't keep track of."

Travis grinned, his blue eyes glinting. Like so many men

Jessa had seen around Diamond Creek, Travis had a rugged, sexy, outdoorsy quality to him. His light-brown hair was windblown, his skin burnished bronze from probably hours and hours on the ocean and outside, and his body fit and muscled. "Nice to meet another member of the Hamilton clan. I've gotten to know both Gage and Garrett. Gage is everyone's local favorite hometown boy come home now that he's reopened Last Frontier Lodge, and Garrett saved my ass when I ran into some problems with my neighbors over a property line dispute. You planning to stick around like your brothers?"

Jessa's eyes automatically flicked to Eli. His had sharpened with interest. She couldn't help but wonder if he hoped she'd stay. She forced her attention back to Travis. "I'm not sure. I came up for a surprise visit after my apartment building in Seattle burned down. I don't really have a plan, so I'm winging it right now."

Travis nodded firmly. "You'll stay."

"I will?" she asked, startled at his quick assessment.

He grinned again. "Yup. If you weren't falling in love with Diamond Creek, you'd already have other plans," he replied with a chuckle. "Anyway, nice to meet you. I've gotta get going. Just wanted to say hi." He glanced to Eli. "I'll stop by your store later this week. I need some new gear for a trip out to Bristol Bay."

"If you're hoping to catch me there, call ahead because I might be out on a charter," Eli said.

"Will do. See ya." With a wave, Travis walked past their table and toward the entrance.

Eli caught her eyes. "Let me run to the restroom and then we can go." At her nod, he stood and walked toward the restrooms on the far side of the restaurant.

Jessa took a look around while she waited for him to return. The Boathouse Café would fit in well in any city. It had a warm feeling, comforting and modern at once. The dining area overlooked the bay with the back wall lined with windows. To one side, the kitchen grill was open and adjacent to part of the bar, which was polished mahogany with copper cookware hanging above. A wide selection of wines was visible in decorative racks. Polished wooden tables and booths with crisp white linens made up the seating, and a variety of rich colored curtains added a vibrant touch.

The restaurant was filled to capacity with an ever-present cluster of customers waiting to be seated. She took another sip of wine and glanced up to see Eli returning. He walked with an unconscious swagger—masculine, strong and confident. He slipped into the chair across from her, his eyes immediately locking onto hers. She swore he could tell how much she wanted him as his eyes darkened and a current of electricity buzzed between them. He cleared his throat, the rough sound sending a jolt through her. "You ready to go?"

"Uh huh," she managed.

They stood, and he rested a hand on her low back as they wove through the tables on their way to the register. His touch was like a hot brand. She was starting to think she was half-crazy when she was around him for any length of time. Her body had a mind of its own, constantly humming and on edge when he was near. Moments later, they were walking outside. The contrast of the cool air only served to notch up the heat inside. Eli glanced down, his features shadowed in the dusky light. "Walk to the harbor with me."

His words were a statement, but they held a hint of a question. Considering that she might have walked through fire with him right about now, her answer was a given. She nodded before a thought passed through her mind. His palm slid off of her back and reached to curl around her hand, his grip warm and strong. Otter Cove Harbor was adjacent to the Boathouse Café, so they walked across the parking lot onto a small path winding through the tall grasses near the beach and down toward the harbor.

When they stepped onto the docks, the rhythmic roll of the waves under the floating docks matched the dreaminess Jessa felt. Her entire being was focused solely on being closer to Eli. The air hummed around them. They reached Eli's charter boat, and he tugged one of the mooring lines, bringing the boat flush with the dock. Without a word, he helped her climb into the boat, following behind her. Jessa waited while he moved quickly around the boat, checking the lines. When he reached her again, he stopped right in front of her. "I thought you might like to see the moonrise from the harbor," he said, his gravelly voice sending shivers over her skin.

"Oh." The single word came out on a breath. With Eli standing inches away, she felt as if a flame lit the air around them. She gulped in a breath, attempting to marshal her thoughts and behave rationally. Yet, all she wanted was him. Now.

So, she took a step, until nothing but a whisper of air separated them. "When will the moon rise?" she asked, her voice rasping.

"In a little bit." His voice was low and taut.

"Then maybe we have time for this," she said as she slipped a hand boldly up his chest to curl around his neck. With only the slightest tug, his mouth came to meet hers. Their kiss was long, hot, slow and deep. Every stroke of his tongue against hers sent pleasure curling through her. She dove into the sensation, throwing herself into the kiss while she slipped her hands under his shirt. *Oh yes*. She needed to feel his hot skin and hard muscles under her palms. With a low growl, his lips traveled down her neck in a heated path, licking and nipping. He tugged her against him, his palm cupping her bottom. She moaned at the feel of his hard shaft against her. His knee slipped between her thighs sending a sharp spike of pleasure through her.

With one hand holding her firmly against him, he brought the other between them, tugging her scoop-neck shirt down roughly and flicking the clasp between her breasts. Her breath came out in a sharp cry when he leaned down and sucked a nipple into his mouth—his touch rough, hot and wet. He alternated between her breasts, swirling his tongue around, nipping lightly and generally making her wild with need. Her hips rolled of their own accord against his knee, hot, sweet spikes of pleasure with every subtle motion. She was so wet, she could hardly bear it.

A gust of wind came off the water, just cold enough to nudge her awareness. For a second, she realized where they were—on Eli's boat in the harbor, likely in view of anyone who happened to be nearby if they cared to look. She was so turned on, so driven with need, she just didn't care. She tugged at his jeans, swiftly unbuttoning his fly and sliding her hand in to stroke the length of his cock. He groaned against her skin and lifted his head.

"Turn around," he said.

She responded automatically to his gruff command and turned. His palms slid down her sides to caress the curve of her hips. She wore leggings paired with a flowing cotton shirt. Her nipples tightened in the cool air, exposed as they were with the neck of her shirt stretched below them. Eli hooked his thumbs over the waistband of her leggings and dragged them over her hips. He drew a finger along the line of her thong panties, sliding across the silk and down between her thighs. She was wet, so wet.

He stroked back and forth over the silk. Her channel throbbed. She was so close to the edge, she almost came right then and there, but he pulled his hand away. She gripped the boat railing in front of her when her knees started to give out. She heard the rustle of clothing and the tear of foil before Eli stroked his finger over the silk between her thighs again, this time pushing it out of the way and delving into her slick folds. He slid one finger into her channel and then another. She arched into his touch, driving her hips back into his hand, soft pants falling from her lips. She cried out when he drew his fingers away, but then she felt the head of his cock at her entrance. He dragged it back and forth, pushing her to the delicious edge of madness. The pressure built and built within, her channel starting to convulse as she thundered closer and closer to tumbling over.

In one swift surge, he seated himself deeply inside of her. She cried out and arched her back, trying to bring him deeper and deeper into her. He held still, sliding his palm down her spine, anchoring her hips in place as he started a cycle of slow strokes.

* * *

ELI LOOKED down at the sight of Jessa's luscious bottom. Her breath came in pants and gasps, low cries breaking through. He could barely hold on through the lust thundering through him. Again and again, he surged into her creamy, hot clench. Her channel throbbed around him. He reached a hand around and slipped it under the silk to circle over her clit. Her body stiffened, her channel tightening around his cock in pulses. She cried out, her head falling forward, and he finally let go. His own release crashed over him, so rough and raw, it rocked him to his core.

As he shuddered into her, he gripped her hip tightly. When his release ebbed, he gulped in air and slowly eased his grip on her. Her hands were curled over the boat railing, her channel still reverberating around him. He slowly straightened and drew back. Only then did it sink in for him of where they were. It wasn't that he didn't factually know they were on his charter boat in the harbor. It was that he'd been so overtaken by his need to be close to Jessa —a need that went far beyond purely physical—he'd forgotten they were in public view of anyone nearby.

He quickly removed his condom and turned to toss it in a small trash bin they kept on the boat for clean up. He'd never considered the kind of clean up he was doing now. He yanked his clothes into place and buttoned his jeans, while Jessa slowly straightened and tugged her leggings back up. When she turned around, her breasts were still exposed, and he itched to touch her again. She quickly pulled her bra and shirt into place. A flush crested her cheekbones when she looked up at him. The light was almost gone now, but her silvery-gray eyes shone through. She ran her fingers through her hair.

He forced himself to breathe over the hammering of his heart. The way he felt with her—this deep connection, a physical need that drove him like no other, and a warm, buzzing joy—was like nothing he'd ever experienced. He shook himself mentally and looked out over the water. The moon was rising over the bay, hanging low and round above the mountains.

"Look. There's the moonrise I wanted you to see," he said, pointing over her shoulder.

Jessa spun around, her hand coming to her chest. "Oh! It's so beautiful."

He stepped to her side, leaning against the railing. She stood still for a long moment. He glanced over, and she had a look of wonder on her face. She turned to look up at him, her eyes shining. "It's amazing. Thank you for bringing me out here." Her words were simple and reached right in and grabbed ahold of his heart.

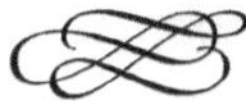

"Hey Ryan, we're leaving soon!" Eli called out as he grabbed a few granola bars out of a kitchen cabinet and stuffed them in his backpack.

He paused to listen and chuckled to himself when he heard Ryan's feet hit the floor upstairs and move in the direction of the bathroom. The sound of water running commenced. Eli sat down at the kitchen table and opened his laptop. A few minutes later, Ryan came downstairs, dressed and ready to go for another day of work on the charter boat.

As Eli drove toward the harbor, Ryan spoke. "I'm not sure it's okay to ask this, but do you think we could somehow get Mom to send my stuff here? I don't have much in my room, but it'd be nice to get what I have."

Eli was momentarily startled, but he immediately realized he should have expected this. Of course, Ryan wouldn't even want to consider asking until the guardianship was finalized. He glanced to the side when he came to a stop sign. Ryan was staring intently out the window at a small field by the road. Only the slight flush on Ryan's cheeks cued Eli that he had probably been nervous to ask and was worried about Eli's possible answer.

"We can ask, but I'm not so sure how likely it is. Even if I send money to cover it, with Dad there, it's a gamble. If you want, we could take a few days off and fly down there. What do you think about that?" Eli wasn't so sure how he felt about it, but he figured the only way Ryan would get any of his stuff was if they went there to get it.

Ryan whipped his head to look at Eli, his eyes wide. "Really? You'd do that?"

Eli nodded. "Of course. That way, you can see Mom, maybe see a few of your friends and get your stuff. It's no big deal."

"You're not worried about seeing Dad?"

"I'm not thrilled to see him, but whatever. He'll be an ass, but it's nothing I can't deal with. How about I make some reservations tonight? We'll go as soon as we can. I'll need to work around the charter schedule, but I think we have a few charter free days next week."

Eli drove through the intersection, turning onto the road leading to the harbor. "Let's grab some coffee for me and get you something to eat," he said as Red Truck Coffee came into view.

Ryan was quiet until they were in line at the coffee truck. A brisk breeze gusted off the bay, and he shivered in his t-shirt. Typical teenager that he was, Ryan rarely bothered to dress with the weather in mind. Eli had quickly discovered it was best to keep an extra windbreaker in his truck and on the boat for Ryan.

His eyes scanning the mountains across the bay, Ryan spoke. "Thanks for offering to take me to get my stuff. I kinda figured I might just have to forget it."

"No problem. We'll get your stuff, and it'll be good for me to see Mom."

Ryan nodded, his eyes still focused on the mountains.

Within a few minutes, they were walking back to the truck. Eli had a strong cup of coffee in hand, while Ryan was already nibbling on a blueberry muffin.

Later that evening after a busy day on the water, Eli reviewed their charter calendar and clicked through options for flights to Juneau next week. They had only two days without any charters scheduled, so that's when they'd go to Juneau. Ryan sat down in the chair across from Eli and slid a plate across the table. Eli glanced down to see a perfectly grilled fillet of silver salmon. Ryan seemed to like trying to cook things, so Eli had encouraged him to try grilling some of their catch tonight. After some guidance, Ryan had insisted he could handle it on his own. Eli took a bite and looked over at Ryan. "Damn good."

Ryan grinned ear to ear and took a bite for himself. "It came out pretty good," he said, a touch of wonder in his voice.

Unless things had changed, Ryan likely hadn't had many chances for fresh seafood growing up, which was a sad state given the plentiful seafood on the docks on Juneau. When Eli was young, his mother's long hours didn't leave much time for her to cook. Once upon a time, there had been a grill on the tiny back deck. In a fit of rage, his father had kicked it over, breaking the hinges and bending the cooking surface. It had never been repaired. Eli's work on the docks gave him opportunities to enjoy barbecues with his work buddies, but unlike so many Alaskans, he hadn't been spoiled with the bounty of seafood Alaska had to offer. As such, he thoroughly appreciated the side benefit of running charters, which meant fresh seafood of whatever happened to be in season. Between Ryan's arrival and Jessa's explosion into his life, he realized he had forgotten to replace the chest freezer.

After they finished eating, Eli stood and gathered their plates. "I can help," Ryan said, starting to get up.

"Nah. You cooked, so I clean up. Give me a sec, and let's confirm out flights next week."

He put their dishes in the dishwasher and snagged a beer before returning to the table. "I'm looking at booking us on a flight next Tuesday morning and returning Wednesday evening. I'm assuming that works for you. I wish we had a little more time for your sake, but the calendar for charters is just too damn full. Honestly, if we don't go next week, there's not another two days free until halfway through September. You ready for me to confirm?"

Ryan, who'd been fiddling with his phone, glanced up. A flash of worry flickered in his eyes. "You sure it'll be okay?"

"You mean going, or me taking you?"

"Just going."

"Look, Dad's gonna be exactly what he's always been— an ass. But we're not staying there. I'll take you to the house to get your stuff and we can maybe take Mom out, but as far as Dad making this miserable, I don't plan to give him much of a chance. I get that you're worried, but let's just get through it."

Ryan looked at him for a long moment, the worry lingering in his eyes. He finally nodded. "Okay. Do you think maybe I could stop by my friend's house? The one whose parents let me go with them to Whittier."

"Sure. I'm guessing you can text him or something."

Ryan was already looking down at his phone, likely doing just that. Eli took a swallow of his beer and snagged his laptop to move to the couch. He used evenings to manage the business end of his business—matching up daily totals, replying to the endless stream of online inquiries about scheduling charters and guided trips in the fall, and generally getting to what he usually only managed in fits and starts during days at the store.

Ryan followed him over and plunked down in the other

corner of the couch. Eli clicked the remote and turned the television on before tossing the remote to Ryan. "You pick."

They'd developed this habit in the evenings when Ryan was home and when Eli wasn't out with Jessa, those events usually occurring in sync. Ryan was a casual sports fan and usually selected something to do with sports or sci-fi. Tonight, he settled on some sci-fi movie while Eli stayed focused on work.

Much later after Ryan went to bed and Eli finally put his work away, Jessa came to mind. The truth was, she came to mind so much, it was distracting. They'd fallen into a pattern, a pattern Eli had *never* fallen into with any woman ever. In the last few weeks, they saw each other every few days at a minimum. The nights between, Eli thought of her just before he fell asleep, as soon as he woke and any minute he wasn't completely occupied with something else. Because he missed her—her warmth, her quirky sense of humor, her generosity, her lack of cynicism, and of course her alluring, knee-buckling beauty and sensuality. When Travis had run into them the other night at the Boathouse Café, Eli had held his breath when Travis asked her what her plans were. Her indecisive answer wasn't a surprise. What was a surprise was the fact he was worried about her plans. In his usual state, he'd be able to be relaxed about it and just figure they were having an amazing time that would eventually end. The idea of ending what he had with Jessa knotted his chest and not in a good way. To complicate matters, he most definitely didn't like how he felt and wanted to knock his feelings into submission, so he felt like he had some semblance of control once again. Keeping a clear boundary between himself and any possibility of a relationship had been his way of ensuring he never had to worry about becoming like his father. Problem was, with Jessa, he wanted more, so much more, and it sent that old worry spinning through him.

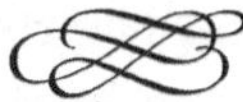

Jessa closed her studio door behind her and headed downstairs to the gallery. Risa had asked her to drop in to see the display area she'd set up for Jessa's furniture. Jessa glanced around when she entered the gallery from the back hall. Risa was at the register talking with a customer even though it was past closing time for the gallery. She caught Jessa's eye and gestured toward the front corner of the gallery, immediately turning back to continue her conversation. Jessa wove through the displays, pausing to admire a collection of soapstone carvings, before reaching the front corner.

She stopped and simply stood there. Risa had created a charming display. She'd assembled a miniature rock garden, likely with rocks straight off the beach behind the gallery, and artfully arranged several of Jessa's pieces around it. She'd included a small tea table set, brightly painted with fireweed flowers. Jessa clasped her hands together and sighed. Relief and joy rolled through her. She knew this was only one step, and certainly not enough of a step to get her back to financial independence, but it was putting her on the path.

The bell to the entrance jingled as the customer exited the gallery. Footsteps sounded on the hardwood flooring as Risa walked to the door to lock it and then came to Jessa's side. "What do you think?" she asked.

"It's lovely. I see why your gallery does so well. You have a knack for bringing out the best in everything you display." She paused and turned to face Risa. "Thank you. I know you didn't have to give me a chance like this. It means more than you know."

Risa smiled warmly, her brown eyes twinkling. "Maybe it doesn't seem that way to you, but this is a mutually beneficial arrangement. I don't know if you noticed..." She paused and pointed to a small tag on the chair leg. "But, I already sold this set. Fortunately, they didn't want to pick it up for three days, so I figure you can let me know what you'd like to display next."

Tears welled in Jessa's eyes, and she felt silly. It was such a small thing, the sale of one set, but it was huge for her. After the fire, she hadn't been certain she could pull everything together again. Risa tugged her in for a quick hug. "See! I told you I could sell your pieces. Don't you dare try to pretend it's because I'm a good salesperson either. I'll take the compliment on my displays, but I have to have something good to work with. So...we need a plan for inventory. After I sold this, I had three other requests to buy it today. Please tell me you have some other sets ready. They don't have to be the same, but anything with an Alaskan theme will probably sell more quickly."

Jessa turned away, looking back over her shoulder. "Come see what I have so far, and we'll decide what might be best."

A while later, Jessa drove up the winding road to Last Frontier Lodge, which was strangely starting to feel like home. She was buzzing with energy after her impromptu planning meeting with Risa. They'd established a plan for inventory Risa had permission to put on the floor when needed, and Jessa had a short list of projects to start. Risa knew what would sell and wasn't hesitant to let Jessa know. As far as Jessa was concerned, it was an ideal partnership. While she loved to be creative and go off on tangents with her designs, she was also practical.

When she pulled into the parking lot at the lodge, light was spilling out of the front entrance. Harry often propped the double doors open in early evening. The parking lot was close to full, so Jessa took a spot in the back corner before making her way inside. She paused by the reception desk. "Hey Harry, I'll be down in about a half hour. I need to get the paint out of my hair," she said, lifting a lock with dried paint streaked on it.

Harry grinned. "See you in a few then."

After she showered, she was getting dressed when her phone beeped, indicating a text had arrived. She tugged a stretchy blue min-skirt over a pair of black leggings and strode over to the table where she'd left her phone. Picking it up, she saw Eli's name blinking on the screen. With a swipe, his full message showed.

Hey Jessa, wanted you to know I'm taking Ryan to Juneau in a few days. Between now and then, we just booked a two-day charter trip with an overnight in Halibut Cove. Guess this means I won't be seeing you for a few days unless you can see me tonight.

She froze, her heart clamoring for her to call down to Harry and ask if she could have the night off. She didn't want to go that many days without seeing Eli, and just what the hell did that mean for her? Eli was coming to mean so much, it was starting to bother her that they never spoke about anything between them. She glanced at the time on her phone and called downstairs quickly. Harry picked up.

"Didn't I just see you?" he asked in greeting.

"How'd you know it was me?"

"Um, you know we have caller ID here, right? Gage must've listed you, along with the rest of the family, because whenever any of you call, your name shows up. Anyway, what's up?"

"What are the chances I could leave a little early tonight?" she asked, biting her lip, hoping he would say yes. She didn't feel right calling out completely, but she thought if she worked the first two hours, the busiest time of the night, that would be a good compromise.

"What are the chances you'll tell me why you're asking?" Harry countered.

Jessa could practically feel his sly grin through the phone. She flushed even though she was all by herself in her room with no one to see. "I'm asking because Eli has to go out on an overnight charter trip and then he's taking Ryan to Juneau for a few days, so if I want to see him before he goes, tonight's the night."

"That's an automatic yes," Harry said with a chuckle.

"Really?" Jessa couldn't hide the glee in her voice.

"Of course! I'm all about romance, and Eli has seriously got a thing for you."

"Yay! Okay, how about I cover until eight?"

"Sounds good." He paused and she heard him say something to someone in the background. His voice came back on the phone. "Gotta go. See you in a few."

The line clicked dead in her ear, and Jessa immediately sent Eli a text. *Tonight. 8pm. Meet me at the lodge.*

Eli's reply was swift, her phone beeping again as she adjusted the small bow at the center of her blouse. Fiddling with the bow with one hand, she spun the phone on the table. *See you then.*

He wasn't much for conversation via text and kept to the basics, but right now, the basics were just fine. She'd have one more night with him before he was gone for more days than she wanted to consider.

* * *

ELI LAY in the dark with a shaft of moonlight falling across the bed. Jessa was curled against him, the feel of her curves and soft skin so damn good he didn't know what to do about it. He was becoming more and more muddled inside about her. He couldn't seem to stay away, yet he was unsettled by that fact and by how good he felt with her. This wasn't supposed to happen for him. Steering clear of relationships had been a simple matter up until now. Even worse, Jessa was so *good* in so many ways that he was terrified of letting this go further because he couldn't tolerate considering how he might hurt Jessa if he ever became anything like this father.

He figured a few days away from her would be a good thing. Maybe he just needed time to get his footing back under him. He turned to look at her, her skin limned by the silvery light of the moon. His heart clenched and that unfamiliar feeling she elicited—longing mingled with hope—rose inside.

A few days later, Eli slung his backpack over his shoulder and walked alongside Ryan toward the car rental place at the airport in Juneau. Ryan was keyed up and had been ever since they'd boarded the plane to Juneau in Anchorage. Eli himself was wired given this was the first time he'd returned to Juneau since he moved away a decade ago. Situated in Southeast Alaska, Juneau was simply breathtaking. While it shared similarities to Southcentral Alaska, this sliver of Alaska was its own world with rainforests surrounding it and mountains flanking it on all sides. None of this part of Alaska was accessible by road, so one could only travel here by boat or plane. Juneau was the largest city in the area, really the only place that could be called a city. If it hadn't been established as the state's capital, it likely would have stayed much smaller due to its geographic isolation. Yet, with legislators flying in each year and its location along the fabled Inside Passage, Juneau was a bustling port city, host to commercial and sport fishing and cruise ships.

Once they were driving away from the airport, Eli took stock. Not much had changed, the mountains rose steeply to one side of the town with the ocean on the other. Driving through downtown with its colorful storefronts and streets busy with tourists, Eli felt detached. He'd spent more time, mathematically speaking, here than anywhere else—a full twenty-two years. Yet, the ten he'd spent in Diamond Creek held so many more positive memories that the place felt like home. While Juneau felt familiar, it didn't feel like home. Probably because he'd never been comfortable here, always on edge, always waiting for the next blow up.

That evening, Eli waited in the living room of his mother's apartment. He supposed he should consider it his parents' apartment, although he never had, even though for most of his childhood his father lived there. At the moment, Ryan was packing up his belongings. Eli had made sure Ryan had two extra duffel bags and assured him they could box up and mail anything he couldn't fit in the bags. Eli glanced around the living room. Not much had changed since he moved away. The apartment was in a small building with every apartment comprised of the same layout with a living room, kitchen, bathroom and two bedrooms. The living room and kitchen were essentially one room with the doors for the other rooms directly off the living room. A couch and a recliner sat against one wall. An old television sat on a small wooden table on the opposite wall. A cluster of daisies sat on the round kitchen table, the only bright spot in the apartment.

His mother, Beverly, came through the front door. She'd gone outside to check the mail in the parking lot. She held a few envelopes in hand and carefully set them on the kitchen table. Her brown hair was held back in a braid that hung hallway down her back. Her green eyes were tired and sad. Eli knew she didn't want this—Ryan packing up to leave—but he'd steeled himself to tolerate her sadness.

She clasped her hands behind her back and looked over at Eli where he sat on the armrest of the couch. "So how is Ryan adjusting?" she asked softly.

"You might want to ask him, but he's doing great as far as I'm concerned. He works at my store and helps out on charter trips. He's a hard worker." He paused and glanced to the bedroom door where he could see Ryan removing clothes from a dresser. "He's a good kid, Mom. You get the credit for that. I'm sorry it's worked out this way, but I'm not leaving him here as long as Dad's around."

Beverly nodded, her gaze somber. She gave a small shrug. "I won't pretend I like it, but I suppose I understand." She paused and looked away, her eyes traveling out the kitchen windows to the parking lot. Eli guessed she was checking to see if his father's car was there. His father had lost his license many times due to drinking while driving tickets, but he'd never let that stop him. Eli had no idea if he had his license back right now. Beverly turned back, a hint of anger in her eyes. "Maybe I understand, but you turned out okay and your father was here all the way up until you moved away. I mean, I'm so proud of you. You have your own business, and you're doing great. I don't understand why…"

Eli interrupted her because he simply couldn't take the excuses. "Mom, I'm damn lucky to be in the position I am, but just because I'm running a business doesn't mean everything's okay. It's not likely I'll ever be in a relationship because I don't ever want anything like what you and Dad have. I'd give anything to have a family I could turn to. I refuse to force Ryan to deal with the same thing. You know how bad it got when I was old enough to talk back. Why the hell did you let Dad move back in?"

His mother's eyes widened and her breath came in sharply. She was quiet for several beats. "He got evicted from the place you found for him and didn't have anywhere to go. Maybe I can see he's not a good influence, but I couldn't stand by and leave him without a place to stay."

As if she had a sixth sense, her eyes traveled to the kitchen window again where Eli saw his father stepping out of his battered hatchback car. Eli's gut clenched. He'd hoped to avoid this encounter, but he wasn't so lucky. He stood and strode to Ryan's bedroom door. The room was almost empty. Ryan was currently checking the dresser drawers.

"Hey," Eli said softly.

Ryan swung to face him. "What?"

"Just a heads up, Dad's here."

Ryan didn't say a word. He left an empty dresser drawer open and turned to gather up the duffel bags. Eli stepped into the room. "You got everything? We can take however long you'll need. I'll deal with Dad."

Ryan shrugged. "Got everything. I was just checking to make sure."

Eli hooked his hand around one of the bag handles and threw it over his shoulder. He followed Ryan into the living room just as their father entered through the front door.

Norm Brooks had aged in the decade since Eli had last seen him. His once dark hair was mostly gray, his eyes weary and tinged with only a hint of the rage that used to simmer there, and his skin was weathered. When Eli was young, he'd grown terrified of his father and then he'd shot up in adolescence and finally felt big enough to defend himself and his mother. That was when he became a more frequent target of his father. Looking across the room at his father now, he'd expected to feel that old anger, but he didn't. He felt nothing but pity.

Ryan was right on his heels, and Eli felt the tension radiating from him. Another surprise was Eli had expected to be the target of his father's anger, yet he wasn't. He watched his father's flat brown gaze land on Ryan, seething with anger. Awareness sliced through Eli. Norm's targets were only those over whom he thought he might have power. Eli wasn't in that position anymore. Eli stepped past Ryan and nodded to his father. "Hey Norm."

Norm's gaze swung to Eli, bouncing off of him and to the wall beyond his shoulder. "Hey." An entire word comprised his greeting. Eli didn't suppose he could hold that against his father seeing as he couldn't manage much more than the two words he'd uttered. He forced himself to wait, sensing Ryan was about to bolt past him out the door.

Norm turned back to Ryan. "Well, you got what you wanted. Hope you're happy about it."

Ryan lifted his chin. "It's good to be with Eli, but I'm not happy about any of this. I wish I could stay with Mom, but ever since you moved back, it's been hell."

Norm was quiet, that low-level fury simmering under the surface of his gaze. Eli's guess was their father would either take off tonight and go for a bender at the bars, or take his anger out on their mother. He hoped for the former. There wasn't much point in staying long and trying to make polite conversation. Eli turned to their mother. "We'll go. We're here until tomorrow afternoon, so if you want to have lunch or something tomorrow, let me know."

Beverly nodded. Eli knew, down to his bones, she wouldn't dare say she'd like that, although he knew she would love any chance to spend time with Ryan and perhaps even him. She'd pay a price if she said anything now, so she simply nodded. Ryan walked over to her and gave her a quick hug. Eli followed suit and they left, leaving silence and angry tension behind when the door clicked shut.

CHAPTER 23

Jessa checked her phone for the umpteenth time, hoping to see a text from Eli. Nothing. Since he'd left for his charter trip and onto Juneau after that, he'd fallen silent. She'd gotten accustomed to at least a text or two per day from him, so his complete lack of communication was bothering her. He wasn't due back from Juneau until tomorrow, so she told herself she'd wait until then. It didn't help that she was all stirred up inside. She grabbed her purse and left her suite. Marley had convinced her she should join her and Delia for a girls' night out with their friend Ginger.

Shoving Eli to the back of her mind, no small feat, she jogged down the stairs to find Marley waiting at the main doors. Marley walked to meet her, hooking her hand through Jessa's elbow. "Let's go!"

A short drive later, Jessa followed Marley into Sally's. Jessa scanned the restaurant as they entered. Sally's was in an old renovated barn. As far as renovations went, the owners had kept it minimal. There was no question the restaurant was once a barn with the haylofts on either end still intact and balconies connecting them running along either side of the upstairs. The space had a polished rustic feel to it. A bar was situated in the center of the area and served as a divider of sorts with a closed in kitchen behind it. One side of the restaurant had tables and booths, while the other side had a small stage and scattered seating for watching music. Marley tugged her to the restaurant side and over to a booth where Delia was waiting with Ginger.

They slid in on opposite sides. Delia and Ginger smiled in unison with Ginger lifting a beer in greeting. "Hey ladies! We were just marveling that we beat both of you here."

Marley shrugged. "Seeing as you're almost always late, enjoy it while it lasts," she said with a sly grin.

Ginger threw her head back with a laugh and took a swallow of her beer. Her gaze swung to Jessa. "So, how's it going? You've been here over a month now. That must mean you're staying," she said bluntly.

Jessa knew Ginger to be Marley's best friend and outspoken and blunt no matter the circumstances. Eli instantly flitted in her mind. It wasn't that she'd make a decision to stay in Diamond Creek because of him, but she'd be lying to herself if she didn't admit the idea of leaving him behind almost physically pained her. She batted those thoughts away and focused on Ginger. "I just might," she said with a shrug.

Marley squealed. "I knew it! I told Gage the other day I thought you might stay. Risa told me how good your sales have been at the gallery, and she told me she's already coordinating with her partners in Anchorage to show your stuff up there and in Juneau. There's as much reason for you to stay here as there would be to go back to Seattle when it comes to work."

There was a flurry of comments from Delia and Ginger before Marley interjected again. "Of course, there's Eli too," she said with a grin.

"Do tell!" Ginger declared.

Jessa felt the flush creep up her cheeks. "There's not a whole lot to tell. We've, uh… Well, I guess we've been seeing each other. I'm not really sure where it's going. If I decide to stay in Diamond Creek, it'll be because of family and my artwork. Eli might be a bonus in all that, but…" Her words trailed off because she didn't really know what else to say. She wished she had a clearer sense of what she and Eli were to each other. *Um, hello? You know exactly what he is to you. The most amazing man you've ever met who makes you feel like a dream and who's an all around good guy. He's everything you want and you know how much he means to you. Stop being a chicken about it.* She mentally shook herself and swatted her thoughts away.

Ginger nodded firmly. "So, he's awesome and you're afraid to say so. Totally get it. I only have one piece of advice for you."

Jessa's mouth fell open at Ginger's mind-reading capabilities. "How…?" She paused and shook her head, not quite ready to admit Ginger zeroed in on the truth. "Okay, what's your advice?"

"Don't waste time not telling him how you feel. I did that with Cam and almost messed up big time because of it. You've got a lot more to lose if you don't tell him how you feel. If you tell him and it doesn't work out, at least you won't wonder if it's because you never said a damn thing."

Jessa felt the eyes of all three women on her as she took in Ginger's words. She glanced around and felt her cheeks get even hotter. "Is it that obvious?" she asked generally.

Delia smiled that warm smile of hers and slipped her arm over Jessa's shoulders. "Maybe, but don't worry about it."

Marley and Ginger weren't so subtle or gentle as they nodded in unison.

Jessa giggled. "Fine. I like Eli. A lot. Maybe more than a lot. I'll work on your advice," she said, pointing at Ginger.

As Ginger laughed, their waitress arrived. Conversation moved on through the evening. Later, when Jessa walked through the chilly night air in the lodge parking lot at Marley's side, she smiled to herself. Tonight had been fun. She had a small circle of friends in Seattle, but she was usually so busy with her artwork and arranging shows, she rarely had time to spend with friends and it was much harder to coordinate everyone's schedules. She'd already gotten accustomed to the impromptu gatherings at the lodge with Gage and Marley's friends and would miss the tight-knit feeling of Diamond Creek dearly if she left.

After parting with Marley in the hallway, Jessa entered her suite and walked to the windows. The stars stretched in a glittering glory across the dark sky. She left the shades open, so she could look at the sky as she fell asleep. Eli visited her thoughts, as he did just about any moment she wasn't actively focusing on something else. As she drifted into sleep, she made a decision. She would stop worrying about what Eli might be thinking and just tell him how she felt.

* * *

A LOUD THUMP had Eli turning to glance in the water beside him on the dock, only to take a face full of water when a harbor seal slipped off the dock nearby with a splash as it dove into the water. The thump must have been the seal as it wiggled across the dock. The seal in question had been napping in the sun on the narrow portion of the dock slip for the boat next to his when he arrived. Another much smaller splash rippled through the water when the seal rose back up, its' round, curious eyes landing on Eli. He shook his head with a chuckle and dragged his arm across his face to wipe the water off. The seal dove back under water, undulating just below the surface as it swam away.

Eli had been on the docks for several hours doing a late summer cleaning for the boat. They had another month of more of charters booked, but as summer wore on, the boat tended to need a few more thorough cleanings to keep equipment organized and make sure they were stocked with supplies. He'd left Ryan and Cliff behind at the store. He tugged his phone out of his pocket as he climbed onto the boat to grab a towel. He'd been ignoring it while he cleaned, mostly so he could actually get something done. Jessa's name flashed on the screen.

Hey! Stopped by to see you at the store, but Ryan and Cliff told me I'd find you at the harbor. Heading that way now.

He checked the time on her message and realized she'd probably be here any second. With his hair still dripping ocean water, he looked around for a spare towel, another thing they needed to stock up on.

"Hey Eli!" Jessa called, just as he found the sole clean towel left by the steering wheel.

He quickly rubbed the towel over his face and hair and stepped out into the rear of the boat. Jessa stood on the dock beside the boat, looking so damn sexy and cute, his throat tightened. She wore an unbuttoned flannel shirt over a fitted tank top, which hugged her generous curves. This was atop of stretchy mini-skirt and a pair of purple leggings. He'd come to learn leggings and mini-skirts were practically a uniform for her. A pair of bright red rubber boots completed her ensemble. He'd never been one to notice clothing much, but somehow Jessa made him notice mostly because her clothing matched her personality— quirky, colorful, lighthearted and practical all at once. A gust of wind off the water blew her hair wild, a blonde-streaked lock catching in a dangly silver earring. She carefully caught it and started to untangle it while she looked over at him.

He'd been home from Juneau for a few days. While he'd been unable to resist seeing her once for dinner and couldn't for the life of him stop texting her occasionally—because he enjoyed the light banter and missed it if it wasn't happening—he'd managed to come up with excuses for being too busy to do much more right now. In all honesty, he was so damn busy this time of year, the excuses were legitimate, yet he could've found time if he wanted. With Ryan here, he had a little more flexibility with the extra help. Eli was trying and failing to get a handle on the way he felt about Jessa. He wanted *so* much with her, and he was flat terrified he might not be able to do this whole 'relationship' thing. Seeing his parents and remembering how damn awful their marriage was only reinforced his decade old promise never to test the possibilities of romance.

He realized he'd yet to speak as her eyes began to look slightly puzzled. With a mental shake, he stepped to the side of the boat and climbed over the railing onto the dock beside her. "Hey there. Just saw your text a few minutes ago." He held up the towel in hand. "Got splashed by a seal," he offered with a rueful chuckle.

Her silvery eyes met his, and his heart gave a hard kick. She finally untangled her hair from the earring and clasped her hands together in front of her. "I know you're really busy, so I hope it's okay I came by."

"I'm always busy this time of year, but you can stop by whenever you like."

Why the hell did you say that? Because I like her, I like her a lot. Maybe it's more than like. Good grief. He felt like he had three personalities arguing in his brain—his old, protective, bitter side that had learned the hard way what it could mean to love someone; an in-between side that was sort of open to admitting how much Jessa meant to him, but on the fence; and then his heart, which was out of practice with conversation and used to staying silent. His heart was the part of him that felt so raw and exposed with Jessa, yet the very part that recognized just what she might mean to him.

Oblivious to his internal state, Jessa smiled widely. "Whenever I like, huh? You might regret saying that."

He managed a nod with a smile automatically forming because it was physically impossible not to smile when Jessa did—her effervescent joy was infectious. The next few minutes passed by as Jessa talked with him normally, like one would in their circumstances, discussed her latest progress on some gallery projects, how busy she'd been at the lodge restaurant and so on. Somewhere along the way, she became quiet, her gaze hesitant. He heard her take a deep breath and let it out quickly.

"Okay, I just need to say something," she murmured under her breath as if she was talking to herself.

"Huh?" he asked.

She looked up, biting her lip as she did. A bolt of need shot through him. Her teeth dented her plump bottom lip, so charmingly he just wanted to kiss her.

"I promised myself I'd say something, so I will," she announced, her voice stronger, although she looked nervous.

"Okay?"

"Here's the thing. We've been, I don't know, seeing each other for a bit now, but we never talk about what we are or what it means. I don't know what you want, or what you're hoping for, but..." she paused and took in a gulp of air before continuing "...I've never felt the way I do with you. I'm not sure what to call it, but I don't want to keep floating along in this sort of vague thing. I wasn't looking for anyone when I came up here, but you're everything I could have asked for if I was. You're nice, you're smart and family is really important to you." Her cheeks were flushed, and Eli wanted to step to her and wrap her in his arms, but he was frozen. She bit her lip again and grinned. "Plus, you're handsome as hell and kissing you is the best thing. Ever," she said firmly, her cheeks flushing a deeper shade of red.

She stopped speaking, her silvery-gray eyes on him as if she was waiting. For the life of him, he couldn't seem to speak. Emotion was galloping through him, a mixture of joy, fear and intense longing. The fear, so familiar and so used to keeping his heart behind walls, held its ground. Silence hung over them, while Eli stood there. An errant drop of seawater rolled down from his hair into his ear. He swiped the towel over the side of his face and shook his head.

Jessa closed her eyes and took a slow breath before opening them again. "Well. I promised myself I'd let you know how I felt because I didn't want to let something slip away, but I guess maybe I misread how you felt." Her gaze, usually so open and warm, shuttered, and she started to turn away.

"Jessa, don't..." he started to speak and froze when she turned back.

"Yes?" she asked, her eyes hopeful.

"I, uh..." *Seriously, man. You know how to talk, just do it. Say something!* "You startled me. I'm, uh, I'm not sure what to say right this second."

She was quiet, still waiting, so he floundered ahead. "I really appreciate you letting me know how you're feeling, and I, uh..."

He didn't know what the hell to say. Fear lashed at him— fear that she'd walk away because he couldn't seem to get through this moment sensibly, fear of letting her know how much she meant to him, fear of what he could become and on and on. "Look, I'm not so great at this kind of thing. I'm not sure what to say."

Jessa's eyes scanned his face, as if she was searching for

something. "Eli, I don't expect you to feel exactly how I do, but I'd think you could at least tell me what you want. That's kind of a general thing. Some people only want casual. That's fine, but I don't want you thinking that's what I want. If that's what you want, maybe we need to part as friends because you mean way too much for me to try to do that."

His heart battered against his ribs, so hard it was almost physically painful. Adrenaline surged inside, his emotions a tangled mess. Finally he shook himself and looked over at her. "I'm not sure what to say," he repeated, feeling flummoxed.

Jessa nodded slowly. "Okay. Maybe you can let me know if that changes. I'm not trying to pressure you, but I can't do this vague thing. Not with the way I feel about you."

At that, she turned away with a small wave. He almost called her name again, but he bit his tongue. *No point in just repeating yourself. Either get up the nerve to tell her how you feel or let her go.*

He watched as she walked down the dock, her hair catching the wind and blowing in a swirl. Her red boots were bright against the background as she climbed the steps to the parking lot and disappeared from sight. His heart and his head hurt.

CHAPTER 24

Jessa swung her backpack over her shoulder and grabbed her purse on the way out of her suite. In the days since she'd screwed up the courage to tell Eli how she felt, she'd been riding a pendulum of mixed emotions—angry, sad, frustrated and feeling plain stupid. The first day, she'd contemplated forgetting her burgeoning dreams of staying in Diamond Creek because she thought it might sting a bit too much to run into Eli. In her more rational moments, she'd managed to quiet her childish, embarrassed voice and recognize she had plenty of reasons to stay here, and none of them anything to do with Eli. If things had worked out with him, it would have been a major bonus, but it didn't appear that would be the case. Yet, she had family and a growing circle of friends, more leads for selling her furniture on a steady basis than she'd ever had in Seattle. At Midnight Sun Arts alone, she'd brought in more sales in the last few weeks than she ever had without a major arts show before. The market in Seattle was saturated and heavily competitive. With the flow of tourists in Alaska, she had a way to stand out and actually make a living that took so much more time and pure luck in Seattle.

After mulling it over herself, talking with Risa who was quickly becoming a friend, and finally talking with Marley, Gage, Delia, Garrett and her parents, she'd decided she would stay. She laughed to herself as she considered the list of family and friends who had something to say about where she lived. To finalize her plans, she needed to zip back to Seattle to transfer her bank accounts, settle a few bills with local businesses where she ordered arts supplies and officially say goodbye to friends. Because of the fire, she had nothing left to move, which created a mingled sense of freedom and loss. Garrett had insisted she let him apply his free air miles to her round-trip flight. She'd initially resisted, but then Delia shared Garrett only wanted to help and he had more air miles than he knew what to do with, so she'd let him make her reservations for her. She'd fly out tonight and return in three days.

She jogged down the stairs to the entrance of the lodge to find Gage waiting for her. His resting somber expression lightened when he saw her. Her oh-so-serious oldest brother had a soft side, but it only showed itself once in a while, although Marley's presence in his life brought it out with greater frequency.

"Ready?" he asked when she reached his side.

At her nod, he turned and walked outside. She followed him out to his truck. The ride to the small airport was quiet. Jessa was taking what Marley referred to as a "puddle jumper" to Anchorage where she would change planes for the flight to Seattle. When Gage pulled up at the airport, he parked his car and looked over at her. She leaned over to give him a quick hug and started to climb out when he said her name.

"Yeah?" she asked, angling back to face him in the seat.

"What's up with you and Eli?"

Annoyance flashed through her, mostly because it was hard enough to come to terms with her feelings that she'd prefer not to be reminded. "You're asking me this now?"

Gage shrugged. "Sure. Just wondering. Marley mentioned maybe things were, I don't know, confusing."

Jessa felt a prickly heat flush her skin. "As far as I can tell, Eli isn't interested in anything serious, so I guess that's it," she finally replied, her heart twisting painfully.

Gage nodded slowly. Meanwhile, Jessa was wondering just what the hell prompted his question. He lifted his eyes, his gaze considering. "For what it's worth, I think you might mean a lot more to Eli's than he knows how to deal with. Give it time."

She stared at Gage, annoyance with his interference and hope at his words warring inside of her. "How would you know how much I might mean to Eli?"

Gage's eyes softened and he smiled ruefully. "I have a hunch, and I might be another guy who kinda had a hard time getting a clue when it came to the woman I loved."

A giggle bubbled up because she knew perfectly well that sharing his feelings wasn't in Gage's comfort zone. Even now when it was plain as day to anyone with eyes that Gage was head over heels in love with Marley, he was still somewhat reserved. Jessa caught Gage's eyes. "I can imagine. I don't have much choice but to wait and see, so I will. In the meantime, I've got a plane to catch." She leaned over and kissed Gage on the cheek before leaping out of his truck and jogging into the airport.

* * *

ELI WALKED into his office and kicked the door shut behind him, sitting down at his desk with a thud. He'd just returned from a stop at the gallery, hoping to see Jessa only to learn from Risa that she'd left for Seattle. He'd had to fight the urge

215

to grill Risa for more information, but he could tell from the look on her face that she wasn't inclined to offer much. There was a quick knock on the door and then Ryan's face came around the corner. "Hey Eli, Gage Hamilton called and said he was hoping you could let him know when his order might be in. I told him you'd be here this afternoon, so he's here."

Eli ran a hand through his hair and nodded. "Okay, send him back."

Ryan stepped into his Eli's office. "You okay?"

Great, just great, your little brother is worried about you. You already feel like a damn fool and now this. Eli forced himself to take a breath and glanced to Ryan. "I'm fine."

"You don't look fine."

Holy hell. Am I gonna have to go through some kind of feelings talk?

"I am..." He stopped abruptly when he heard his tone, annoyed and irritated. "Look, I've got some stuff going on, but I'll be fine. Don't worry about me. Okay?"

Ryan either didn't take the hint, or didn't care. He looked over at Eli, those green eyes so familiar. "You know it's okay to get annoyed. I can deal with it. You're nothing like Dad."

"I wasn't trying to..." Eli stopped again, realizing he had been trying to choke off anything even close to anger with Ryan. Frankly, he'd done that for most of his life, so afraid to feel anything resembling anger. He leaned back in his chair and rolled his head from side to side, attempting to ease the tension bundled there. "Okay, maybe I was trying not to be annoyed, but whatever. It's no big deal."

"Is this about Jessa?"

"Really?" Eli asked, on the verge of exasperation. "You're gonna go there?"

Ryan nodded emphatically. "Uh huh. You haven't talked to her for like a week, and you're not all happy like you were whenever you saw her. It's not like you have to tell me the details, but I'm no dummy. Not that you're asking my opinion, but she's awesome and it's obvious you like her, so how come you're not talking to her?"

Eli gave up inside and started laughing, shaking his head as he did. "Damn, you don't give up, do you?"

Ryan shrugged. "Not really."

Eli's laugh faded and he looked at Ryan for several beats. "So you think she's awesome?"

Ryan angled his head to the side and shook it slowly. "Not that I should be giving you relationship advice, but yeah, she's awesome and you're way less cranky when she's around, so get a clue."

Eli burst out laughing, while Ryan turned away to head back to the front of the store. "Don't be dumb, man," he offered as a parting comment over his shoulder.

Less than a minute passed before Gage's shadow cast through the doorway. Eli had steeled himself to deal with facing Jessa's brother. He had no idea if she'd mentioned anything to Gage, nor did he have any idea if Gage would bring it up with him.

Gage nodded in greeting. "Hope it's okay I stopped by."

"Of course. How's it going?"

Eli gestured to the chair across from his desk. As Gage took a seat, he replied, "Busy as usual. You?"

"Same. Ryan mentioned you asked about your order. We just got a shipment of inventory in today, but I haven't had a chance to get through the boxes. I'll have time this afternoon if you don't mind waiting."

"Of course not." Gage said, glancing to the window and back to Eli. His eyes were sharp and assessing, making Eli feel as if he was under a microscope. "I didn't really come by to ask about the order."

Eli stomach churned, realizing Gage probably knew about his bumbling, fumbling response to Jessa. He forced himself to breathe slowly and cocked his head to the side. "Yeah?"

"Jessa seems to think you're not interested in anything serious with her. I think she might be wrong," Gage said flatly.

Eli felt as if he'd been knocked off his feet and hit the ground with a thud. He stared at Gage for a long moment, his heart banging against his ribs. He closed his eyes and tried to gather himself. When he opened them again, Gage's gray eyes, so like Jessa's were patiently waiting.

Eli nodded slowly. Much as he didn't want to talk about how he felt, Gage might be the only avenue he had to find out where Jessa was. "Look, I blew it. Jessa tried to talk to me, and I just plain froze. I didn't mean to hurt her, but I can see why I might've." He paused and steeled himself for Gage to tell him off.

Gage was quiet for so long, Eli's anxiety only ramped up further. Gage finally spoke. "Look, I know what I see when you look at her. Maybe you don't know it, but it sure looks like she means a hell of a lot to you. Mind telling me if you plan to do anything about that? Or are you going to just let her go?"

All kinds of thoughts barreled through Eli's mind, but the only thing he hung onto was that he couldn't stand the thought of letting Jessa go. So, damn his pride, he looked over at Gage and asked for help. "Okay, here's the thing. I have no idea what I'm doing here. My parents had a shitty marriage and my father made life a living hell for all of us. I didn't think I'd ever have to worry about, uh, a relationship. Then, I met Jessa. I thought maybe it'd be best if I put some distance between us because I don't ever want to end up doing anything like my father, but now I miss her like crazy. I went to look for her at the gallery and..."

Gage waved a hand sharply. "Back up for a sec. Why would you think you'd do something like your father? I don't even know the details, but have you ever done what you're worried about?"

Eli shook his head quickly. "No, never. Not that you need the details, but let's just say he had a temper and it came out with his fists sometimes."

Gage nodded. "I'll be more specific. Have you ever laid a hand on anyone when you were pissed off? Including your dad?"

"No. Never."

"So stop thinking you're something you're not. If that's the only reason you're blowing it with Jessa, stop being stupid." Gage's bluntness hit him right in the chest.

Eli was quiet, his heart thudding, as he took in Gage's words. Somehow, Gage's point-blank directness made him realize his own actions, or lack thereof, showed the opposite of what he'd been worried about all these years. He met Gage's eyes and nodded. "Okay then. Tell me how to find Jessa."

CHAPTER 25

A few days later, Eli stood outside a nondescript steel building. At best, he'd guess it was a warehouse. Gage had given him directions and assured him this was where Jessa was staying with their sister and brother-in-law. Apparently, the brother-in-law in question owned a private security business here in Seattle. After Gage's brutally blunt heart-to-heart with Eli, Gage had told him how to find Jessa. Eli thought about texting or calling, but he felt like he needed to do this in person.

He walked to the only door he could see on the building and entered. The inside wasn't any more informative than the outside of the building. A modern reception area awaited him with a sleek, simple industrial feel to the space. A petite woman with dark brown hair and eyes to match stood to greet him. "Can I help you?" she asked politely.

Eli felt like she could see right through him with her sharp gaze. She was all business in a tidy black suit. He nodded. "I hope so. I'm looking for Jessa Hamilton. Gage told me she was staying here, but I'm not sure…"

His words trailed off as the woman stepped to the side

of her desk. She glanced back to him quickly. "Your name?" After he stated it, she tapped a button on her phone. A male voice answered. "Hey Jo, what's up?"

"I have an Eli Brooks here to see Jessa."

"Be right out."

Eli's heartbeat, which felt like it was running on high idle between the adrenaline and the emotions cresting through him, kicked into a higher gear. He'd prepared himself to talk to Jessa and pour his heart out, but he wasn't so sure how much he could handle on his way there.

Only a few seconds passed and a door to the side of the waiting area opened. A tall man with dark hair, bright blue eyes and an intimidating presence approached him. Eli would bet money the man was ex-military. The man reached him and held a hand out. "Eli Brooks, I presume?"

At Eli's nod, the man shook his hand firmly. "Aidan McNamara. Better known to the Hamilton family as Becca's husband."

Eli nodded again and managed to utter brief, polite sentences, all the while wondering when this man would tell him where Jessa was. When he couldn't wait anymore he blurted his question out. "I was hoping to see Jessa. Is she here?"

Aidan's eyes, far too knowing and assessing, scanned Eli before he nodded slowly. "She is," he finally said firmly. "Follow me."

They went down a long hallway and up a flight of stairs before reaching a door. They went through two passcode doors before entering a spacious apartment. It was hard to believe an apartment was in this building. It was sleek and modern, like the downstairs, although soft touches of color brightened the space. Hardwood flooring and high ceilings made the area feel open and airy. The room they entered was an expansive living room and kitchen. A woman stood from the couch where she'd been reviewing some paperwork, which she set neatly on the coffee table. She was tall and dark and bore a striking resemblance to Garrett. Eli figured she must be his twin sister Becca.

She strode briskly around the couch and approached him, holding her hand out for a firm shake. "Becca Hamilton."

After he unnecessarily offered his name, she stepped back and crossed her arms. "Jessa is here, but you'd better have something good to say because if not, I'll be escorting you out."

Dear God. He had to find a way to get through this. Becca was, well, she was frightening. Before he had a chance to reply, he heard footsteps and turned to see Jessa walking into the room from the other side. His heart gave a hard thump and set to pounding so hard, he feared they could all hear it. He tried to take a breath, but his chest and throat were tight. What he wanted to do was walk to her and wrap his arms around her and soak in all that she was—warmth, lightness, joy, kindness and the sexiest damn woman he'd ever known. But he had an audience, a rather intimidating audience.

Jessa reached them, her eyes coasting over him and then landing on Becca. She surprised him by putting her hands on her hips and glaring at Becca. "I don't need you to be my guard, you know. I can handle this myself," she said firmly, a tinge of defiance in her tone.

Becca's eyes bounced from Jessa to Eli and back again. "Fine." She looked to Aidan. "Come on."

Aidan stepped to her side, his gaze bemused. "Where are we going?"

"Out to lunch," Becca replied with a grin. Hooking her hand in the crook of his elbow, she steered him to the door. "We'll be back in about an hour." With a wave, they exited the room, the door clicking shut behind them.

Eli's heart was about to pound its way out his chest, but

he forced himself to breathe and turned to face Jessa. Damn. She was beautiful. Her blonde streaked brown hair had an added streak of purple on one side and was pulled back in a loose ponytail with tendrils escaping and framing her face. She wore her usual leggings and a stretchy mini-skirt, both black today, paired with a fitted gray t-shirt that hugged every inch of her lush breasts. Making her ensemble just so *her,* she had on a pair of socks with cows all over them. The joy only she could elicit rose within him and he itched to touch her. But first, he had to make this right.

Her silver-gray gaze, slightly guarded, met his. "Hey there. I, uh, didn't expect to see you here."

He nodded slowly and managed to speak. "How are you?"

"I'm okay. You?"

He took a deep breath, marshaling every ounce of his courage. He felt so silly to be nearly paralyzed by this woman, but he was. She'd come to mean everything and he had to find a way to convince her to come back to Diamond Creek. He'd already planned to agree to some kind of long-distance relationship if that's all he could have.

Another deep breath and he met her eyes, steeling himself to do the thing that scared him the most. "I haven't been too good actually. I've, uh..." His words ran out. *You'd better do this, man. Don't chicken out now.* Another breath. He was getting really good at this whole breathe through it thing. "I've missed you. A lot. I'm, uh, I'm really sorry I blew it when you came to talk to me at the harbor. If you can believe it, Ryan told me to stop being such an idiot. I don't know how to explain, but because of how things were with my parents, I just decided it'd be better if I didn't try to do the whole relationship thing. It was never anything to worry about until I met you. I, uh...damn, this is hard." He paused and looked over at Jessa. Her gaze was pinned to him, her eyes bright with tears, and everything about her expression encouraging him to continue. So he did. "Look, I'm not sure what love is because I've never had any experience with it, but I'm pretty sure I love you…"

Jessa flew at him, flinging her arms around him. He lifted her and held her close, turning his head into her hair and just breathing her in. Tears clogged his throat and he swallowed against the tightness. The emotion almost overwhelmed him. Being able to hold her again after the week from hell was such a pure relief, he could hardly bear it. After several long moments, she leaned back and looked at him. She cupped her hands over his cheeks and smiled. "Wow! I didn't expect that," she said softly.

His heart swelled. "I didn't expect you," he finally managed.

She leaned forward and brought her lips to his. He felt as if he'd been underwater and finally came up for air. She was his air. The feel of her lips against his, her tongue stroking boldly into his mouth and her soft sigh when she drew away nearly undid him. She wiggled and slowly slipped from his arms and took a step back.

He'd pretty much wrung himself dry the last few days and didn't even know what else to say at this point, so he just soaked in the sight of her. She bit her lip and glanced over. "I suppose you might want to know that if I knew what love was, it would be what I feel when I'm with you," she said with a smile that morphed into a soft laugh.

He tugged her close and wrapped his arms around her again.

* * *

LATER THAT NIGHT after takeout Thai dinner with Becca and Aidan, Jessa glanced over when Eli rested his head against the headboard and rolled it to look at her, his eyes somber. His muscled chest gleamed in the low light cast from a lamp in the corner. His brown hair was mussed from her running her hands through it after he'd taken her to an explosive climax and made her forget where she ended and he began. She was languid and relaxed, completely at ease.

"So, I had one more thing to ask you," he said, his voice low and gravelly in the quiet room.

Her skin prickled at the mere sound of his voice. She turned to face him, crossing her legs and tucking the sheets over her lap. Her skin was bare and a bolt of need shot through her when he reached over and dragged a fingertip along the curve of her breast.

At her sharp intake, his eyes whipped up. "Couldn't help it."

"What did you want to ask me?"

"If you would come back to Diamond Creek…to stay with me."

Her heart leapt when she realized he'd come all this way to talk to her and somehow she'd neglected to mention she always meant to return to Diamond Creek. The way he put his heart on the line meant all that much more because of what he hadn't known. Tears pressed at the back of her eyes.

"Eli, I was already planning to come back. I just came down here to take care of a few logistics."

His green eyes widened and then he smiled, a slow, breathtaking smile. "Wow. I feel like an idiot. I was all ready to tell you we'd find a way to make it work even if you wanted to stay here. So, you were going to stay in Diamond Creek even if things didn't work out for us?"

She nodded, the wave of emotion easing inside. "I thought about coming back here, but I have more reasons to stay there. Don't get me wrong, I *really* want things to work out for us, but staying in Diamond Creek is the right thing for me. I have more family there than here. Things are going great with the gallery, and it just made sense. After today, you couldn't tear me away from there."

She leaned over and slid a hand into his hair as she brought her lips to his. When she pulled back, she saw her own feelings reflected in equal measure in his eyes.

Jessa walked down the dock at the harbor. A whistling sound caught her ears and she turned to see an eagle flying alongside the dock, mere feet away from her. Her breath caught and she stopped to watch as the eagle angled to the side, its wings catching a gust of the breeze, lifting it higher in the air as it turned. She turned to make her way down the dock. Eli was visible ahead as he leaned over the boat railing and handed a small cooler to Ryan. She breathed in the salty air and sighed, a warm joy blooming in her heart.

It was one day past the anniversary of the fire that spun her life on its compass and pointed her in the direction of Diamond Creek and ultimately Eli. Ryan had started to walk up the dock, two customers following behind him. He grinned when he saw her. "Hey Jessa, Eli's on the boat."

"Hey you too! Are you home for dinner tonight or something else?"

"Home. Eli said he's picking up pizza from Glacier Pizza on the way home. Jeff and Ben might stop by. Will that be okay?"

Jessa stopped and put her hands on her hips. "Did Eli say it was okay?"

Ryan nodded, his hair falling in front of his eyes. "Well, yeah, but if it wasn't cool with you, you could say so."

"Of course it's okay! Just don't leave dirty socks all over the place and I'm good."

Ryan burst out laughing and waved as she continued walking. When she reached the boat, Eli was waiting, having climbed out and slung his backpack over his shoulder.

He dipped his head and dropped his forehead to hers. "Hey."

"Hey. How was your day?" she asked, smiling widely because she couldn't be near Eli and not smile.

He brought his lips to hers before answering. In a flash, what started as a soft kiss morphed into hot and sense stealing when he swept his tongue into her mouth and nipped at her lips. By the time he pulled away, she was panting and arching into him.

He chuckled softly. "Sorry 'bout that. You kind of make me forget where I am."

"Ditto," she replied with a laugh. "I hear we're having pizza from Ryan's favorite place and maybe some company."

Eli stepped away and adjusted his backpack on one shoulder as he curled his palm around her hand. They started walking slowly along the dock back toward the harbor parking lot. "Yeah. Couldn't say no when he asked. He busted his butt today. We ran two charters—one this morning and one this afternoon. He never complains and just works. Makes it hard to say no when all he asks for is pizza and if his friends can come over. Hope you don't mind."

"I never mind. I don't know why you worry about it."

"Because it's your house too now, and if you did mind, it would matter to me."

They'd married a few months ago. Though Jessa had informally stayed with Eli for many months up to that point, she'd officially moved in after their honeymoon. The house was warmer now with her eye for decorating and some of her own furniture pieces to brighten up the space. She stopped on the dock and tugged him to face her. "When I married you, I knew Ryan was part of the deal. I love him too. He might not be my son technically, but he is in every way that matters. He needs to be able to have pizza and friends, so unless there's some other reason to say no, then it won't ever be because of me caring for some silly reason. Plus, all they ever do is stay upstairs. It's like the lair of teen boys with video games, TV, and stuff everywhere. Maybe we could agree that I get to make him do laundry a little bit more?" she asked with a grin.

"Deal," Eli said as he dipped his head for another kiss.

* * *

LATER THAT NIGHT with Ryan and his friends ensconced upstairs with two pizzas and engaged in a lively battle on some video game, Eli glanced over at Jessa. They were out on the back deck. The air was starting to lose its warmth from the sun and a soft breeze blew a loose lock of hair over her eyes. She brushed it away and turned to face him, leaning against the railing. She spun the almost empty wineglass in her hand and smiled at him. In the smudgy gray light of dusk with the sun setting in a glorious burst of red and gold behind her, all Eli could think was she was the absolute best thing that ever happened to him.

He stood from where he sat by the small wrought-iron table and stepped in front of her. She took the last sip of her wine and set the glass on the railing. He reached for her hands, holding them both in his.

"Tonight was perfect," he said.

Sometimes he felt silly because he felt so much with Jessa that words usually didn't capture it. Plus, he hadn't had much practice with words and feelings, not when they were paired together. Jessa didn't seem to mind, so he kept winging it.

"Takeout pizza is always perfect, especially when it's from Glacier Pizza. Although, I have to say living here has taught me the virtues of fish and moose and even caribou. I always promised myself I couldn't sanction mass-production of meat, but this whole hunting, fishing thing you do, well, that's something else altogether," she said with a teasing grin. "I still can't believe when I saw you last year with that grocery cart full of frozen foods. So not you!"

He chuckled, recalling his chest freezer had been broken and he'd wanted an excuse to find her in the grocery store. "Hey, I got to talk to you," he said with a shrug. "That's all I cared about."

She stepped closer and slipped her hand up behind his neck, her silver eyes shining through the dim light. "I'm so glad I backed into you," she whispered against his lips.

"Me too," he said on a sigh as her lips met his.

* * *

Thank you for reading Stay With Me - I hope you loved Jessa & Eli's story!

For more steamy, small town romance, Lacey & Quinn's story is next in When We Fall. Quinn is all kinds of sexy, and Lacey can't figure out how she missed that before. An epic friends to lovers romance! "… freaking fabulous!" Don't miss Quinn's story!

Keep reading for a sneak peek!

Be sure to sign up for my newsletter for the latest news, teasers & more! Click here to sign up: http://jhcroixauthor.com/subscribe/

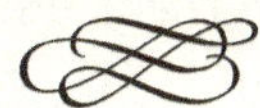

A rock came tumbling down the steep mountainside. Lacey Adams heard it before she saw it and quickly glanced up to see a small boulder hurtling toward her. She scrambled out of the way, only to lose her footing on the gravelly trail and crash to the ground onto her hip. "Ooomph!"

"How's it going up there?" Quinn Haynes called out.

"Great, just great!" Lacey called in reply. She waited until the boulder came to a thudding stop against a spruce tree at the bottom of the slope before pushing herself up on her hands. Once she was back on her feet, she took stock and figured she'd have a hell of a bruise on her hip when they got to camp tonight. Otherwise, it was all in a day's work for her. She and Quinn were leading a guided photography trip in Katmai National Forest. Katmai was renowned for its remote beauty and particularly for the brown bears that frequented the famed Katmai River Falls where remote video cameras recorded the massive bears feeding off salmon running through the river. They were many miles away from the river falls and trekking deep into the wilderness with a group of wildlife photographers committed to more pure forms of photography, namely capturing wildlife in more challenging circumstances than those of the convenient viewing platforms by the falls.

She'd volunteered to check this trail out before they took the group along this route to reach another mountain peak ahead. She'd confirmed what they suspected—the trail had been mostly washed out by the spring thaw when the melting snow turned into raging streams. The gravel here was loose, along with the rocks up above. If Lacey had her way, they'd take the slightly longer route through the trees. In her years of backcountry guiding, she'd learned it was usually wiser to go slow than to take potentially risky shortcuts. It was one thing to risk her own injury, another to risk that of her clients. She ran her own small business from Diamond Creek, Alaska and often paired with other guides she knew from her years of working in the wilds of Alaska. Quinn Haynes was an old friend and occasionally joined her on these trips. She hadn't seen him in over two years when they confirmed this trip. He'd taken a break from guiding to finish his medical degree. Now, he had a fancy title to go with living on the edge. He'd spent the last year overseas providing medical care in war torn regions.

Lacey carefully made her way back down the mountainside and met Quinn at the bottom where he was waiting. Their clients had taken a short hike to a nearby field to watch and wait for wildlife to pass by. Quinn grinned when he saw her. "I'm guessing we won't be using that shortcut. You okay?"

She had a slight limp from her hip's collision with the rocky ground. She figured it would work itself out once they got moving again. "I'm fine. The slope is rocky and loose. Let's take the longer way through the trees. Aside from not wanting anyone else to fall on their tail, I'd rather not worry about the expensive cameras they're hauling."

Quinn's amber hair glinted in the morning sun when he nodded. His eyes, almost a precise match with his hair, coasted over her. "You sure you're okay? You've got quite the limp."

Lacey sighed. "I'm fine. Give me a few minutes."

He turned to walk at her side when she reached him. They walked back toward the camp at a leisurely pace. Lacey's hip started to loosen as she'd predicted. By the time they arrived at camp, her limp had almost disappeared. Quinn strode to his tent and came out with a thermos.

"Coffee for you," he said as he handed it over with a grin.

Lacey plunked down in a camp chair and unscrewed the thermos lid. The coffee was plenty warm and dark. After a long swallow, she sighed and leaned back. "Thanks. I forgot you somehow manage to make the best coffee even when we're in the middle of nowhere."

Quinn chuckled and sat down across from her in another folding chair, his rangy form barely fitting in the chair. Lacey caught herself when her eyes began a slow investigation of Quinn. She didn't know what it was because she'd known Quinn for years, but ever since he'd met her at the start of this trip, she was uncomfortably aware of how handsome he was. He was in superb physical condition, rugged and fit, every inch of him honed muscle. His skin was bronzed from days living in the outdoors. He was a man who threw himself into whatever environment he happened to be in—whether it was the wilderness of Alaska, the beaches of a remote island, or the desert somewhere.

It wasn't that she hadn't noticed he was handsome before, but she'd never had any physical response to him. The last few days had been downright annoying for her. If she had a few spare minutes and he was nearby, he was like a magnet for her eyes and her body hummed with a buzz of awareness. She mentally shook herself and lifted her eyes above the trees. It was early fall, yet still quite warm for Alaska. The sun was up, brightening the snow-covered mountain peaks of the Katmai Range. Conveniently, the wilderness gave her plenty to stare at other than Quinn.

They sat in the quiet with nothing other than the sound of water sliding over rocks in the background. A stream was close to their camp, offering a place to bathe and easy water access for drinking and cooking. They had two more nights here before they hiked out.

Later that afternoon, Lacey was leading the way back from their hike when both of her knees buckled suddenly. Weakness like she'd never felt before crashed through her body. She stumbled sideways and gripped a birch tree to steady herself. After several deep breaths, she felt almost normal, so she pushed off the tree and began walking again. She glanced behind her to see Quinn had stopped with their group and was pointing at something in the distance. He was a veritable font of information about the geology of Alaska, so he was an extra plus as far as clients were concerned. She breathed a sigh of relief because it didn't appear any of them had noticed her stumble.

That night after the four photographers had retired to their tents, she glanced over at hers and sighed. Sometime during the hike away from camp, some type of animal, likely a marmot, had shredded a corner of the tent door, just enough that the fastener to the tent pole was torn and the tent leaned drunkenly to one side. That meant she would be sharing Quinn's tent tonight. Not such a great plan if her body's reaction to the idea told her anything. The moment she'd heard Quinn chuckle and comment she'd be sleeping with him tonight, heat had rolled through her body in a flash. She needed to get over this weird attraction to him as soon as possible. She didn't really do the whole relationship thing—too messy, too inconvenient. She'd also found that men tended to shy away from her anyway. She was too much of a tomboy.

She'd temporarily considered just sleeping outside under the stars, but that wasn't smart. Autumn nights were cold out in the wilderness and while a tent didn't offer too much protection, it was better than nothing. She looked across the dying fire to Quinn. His features were shadowed in the dim light, his amber hair gilded with gold in the flickering firelight. He glanced up and caught her eyes. For a flash, she thought she saw something in his gaze, but he shuttered it and his usual teasing smile hooked the corners of his mouth.

"I'm about to crash. You want me to help drag your sleeping bag in the tent?"

She stood swiftly. "Nah. I got it. Mind putting the fire out while I do that?"

She heard him stand as she strode toward her torn tent. She gathered her sleeping bag and carefully tidied up her backpack before carrying everything over to Quinn's tent. He was using a stick to sift through the coals and push them down into the pile of ash. Moments later, she was kneeling over trying to straighten out her sleeping bag when she heard the tent zipper. She scrambled to turn around. In her rush to turn, she fumbled and instead of him being up close and personal with her bottom, she found herself a mere inch or so from his face. For a beat, she wanted to close the space and see if his lips felt as good as they looked—full and sensual against his strong and masculine features.

Instead she scrambled back with her heart beating staccato in her chest and that inconvenient desire flooding her. Quinn merely grinned and crawled into the tent beside her. Without a word, he yanked his t-shirt off and slipped into his sleeping bag.

"G'night," he said, his voice gruff.

She could hear the smile in his voice because that's how

he always was. Everything held a hint of fun for him. Meanwhile, he'd left her dry-mouthed and nearly panting at the glimpse of his chest—all sculpted muscle and a true six-pack of abs. She'd seen him shirtless before, but she'd never thought much of it. What the hell was wrong with her? She shook her head and slipped into her own sleeping bag, grateful she'd be cocooned away from his body through the night.

She woke hours later, her hand—oh my god!—her hand was sliding over the hard planes of his chest. While somehow, her tank top had slid up and she was draped over him, one of her bare breasts pressing against his side and his hand cupping her bottom. She had absolutely no idea how they ended up tangled together like this, but both of their sleeping bags were unzipped and one of her legs was thrown over his. It felt *sooo* good to be close to him like this, her body was nearly aflame with need. This was not good, definitely not good.

* * *

QUINN CAME to slowly and realized he was rock hard with need and Lacey was draped all over him. He felt her lush bottom under his palm and almost groaned at how good it felt. Lacey Adams had been forbidden fruit for as long as he'd known her. She was always all business when she was around him, so he'd struck the same tone. But he couldn't help himself from appreciating how damn tempting she was with her auburn hair, her bright green eyes, and her body, which was nothing short of a work of art. She was completely fit. Her life demanded it with her years of leading hikes, dog sledding trips, cross-country skiing and then some in the wilderness. Somehow though, she retained her femininity with an hourglass figure, lush breasts and generous hips to soften her athletic build.

To wake with her like this sent his body and mind into all kinds of wild imaginings. Suddenly she stiffened against him. Ah hell, she was awake and now he had to find a way to be a gentleman about this. Because unless she made it crystal clear she wanted something more, he'd try to respect their friendship. Her hand stilled on his chest and she slowly lifted her head.

"Um, I'm not sure how this happened," she said, her words rough with sleep.

Seeing as he knew damn well she could feel his hard cock against the leg she'd thrown across him, he couldn't really deny his state. He chuckled. "Me neither."

Her eyes lifted and met his in the dark. He'd give anything for just enough light to be able to read her gaze. With his pulse thundering and lust lashing at him, he held his breath and willed his body under control.

She shifted her leg off of him. The feel of her silky skin sliding over his only served to tighten the need clawing at him. She slowly untangled herself from him, and he reluctantly let his hands ease off of her. She sat up and tugged her tank top down and looked over at him again. "Didn't mean to climb all over you like that," she said, her tone sheepish.

He aimed for nonchalant. "No need to apologize. We were asleep." He left unsaid the fact that he would have happily allowed her to climb all over him again, but he sensed he needed to bide his time if he was ever to have a chance with Lacey.

She was quiet for several beats before she spun around and slipped back inside her sleeping bag. "Right, we were sleeping," she said softly.

He listened to the sound of her breathing as she drifted back into sleep. He lay in the dark, wide-awake as his body settled down, the hot lust surging through him gradually ebbing away. An owl called in the trees nearby, another owl returning the call from a distance.

The following morning, Quinn woke before Lacey. He rolled his head to the side, a smile curling at the sight of her. Her auburn hair lay in a tousle around her face and shoulders. She was on her side facing him with her hands tucked under her chin. Her full lips were relaxed and tiny freckles were scattered across the bridge of her nose and her cheeks. He resisted the urge to lean over and kiss her. As if she sensed him looking at her, her eyes opened, green with flecks of gold and bright in the gray light of dawn.

"Morning," he said.

She shifted onto her back and stretched before rolling to face him again. "Good morning. How long have you been awake?"

"Just a few minutes."

"How's your hip?"

She shifted her legs and shrugged one shoulder. "A little sore, but that's all."

She pushed up on one hand and crossed her legs under her. Her hair draped around her shoulders, long waves falling around the curves of her breasts, which were inconveniently on display in her fitted tank top. She leaned over and dug around in her backpack, tugging out a flannel button-down shirt, which she threw over her shoulders. He watched as she shimmied into a pair of fleece leggings. She glanced over her shoulder as she slid her feet into a pair of lightweight boots. "Don't suppose you'll be making coffee this morning?"

He grinned. "No need to ask."

She returned his grin and unzipped the tent flap, disappearing through it. He dug through his own backpack and tugged out another set of clothes. Moments later, he was lacing up his boots when he heard a shuffling sound and then a thump. Lacey's sharp cry was distinct. He scrambled out of the tent to find her on the ground by the blackened fire circle.

Peter and Chad, two of the photographers on the trip with them, were nearby. Chad was kneeling beside Lacey. "You okay?" he asked.

Quinn raced to Lacey's side, kneeling down. "What happened?"

Lacey had fallen in a tangle, her legs crossed at the ankles. She started to move, all but swatting Chad and Quinn away, but her hand flopped on the ground. Quinn eased an arm around her back, propping her weight against him. "Easy. Tell me what happened."

Lacey shook her head. "I can't see well. Everything's all blurry."

Chad caught his eyes. "She said a minute ago that her legs felt tired and then all of a sudden she collapsed."

Quinn's doctor brain switched on and he started rifling through possibilities right away. Given her slip yesterday, it could be related solely to that, or it could be something else. Right now, he just needed to get her comfortable.

"Let's get you over to one of the chairs." He and Chad slowly eased her up.

He could sense her irritation. The fact she didn't shove them away and stand on her own concerned him. Once she was seated in a camp chair, he stood and glanced around. "Can you grab me that water bottle?" he asked, gesturing to Peter who'd been waiting nearby while he and Chad had helped Lacey to the chair.

Peter snagged the water bottle in question and strode in his direction. Quinn met him on the way. "Notice anything before she fell?" he asked, his voice low.

"Not much more than what Chad said. She mentioned her legs felt tired. Before that, she seemed, I don't know, kind of out of it. Just for a minute or so and then she fell."

Quinn nodded as he took the proffered water bottle

from Peter. "Thanks. We'll give her a few to see if she's feeling better. Hope you guys don't mind."

Peter's eyes widened. "Of course not! You've already given us the best trip we've ever had. We're happy to sit tight as long as we need. Don't even worry about it."

"Good to know. Let me see how she's doing."

Quinn headed back to Lacey's side, hooking his hand around a camp chair on the way over and setting it down beside her. "Have some water," he said, handing her the bottle.

She accepted it from him and took a long swallow. After she lowered it, he noticed her grip was shaky, so he reached over and took it from her. "How you feeling now?"

She canted her eyes to his and he saw fear in their depths, such an unusual feeling for Lacey, it worried him. "Weird. I feel weird," she finally said. "After I came out of the tent, I just started to feel funny. One of my legs felt numb and both of them felt weak. For a second, I couldn't see right and then I just fell. That blurry thing is gone and my legs are starting to feel more normal, but it's just weird. What the hell happened?"

Quinn's mind flipped through possibilities, but he didn't want to go there right now with her. "Maybe your fall was a little harder than you thought. Let's see how you feel after a little bit. You still up for coffee?"

She grinned and nodded emphatically. "That might be just what I need."

* * *

TWO DAYS LATER, Lacey made her way along the gravel path leading to the airstrip that would fly them out of Katmai and back to Diamond Creek. After her odd episode the other morning, she'd had some of Quinn's coffee and felt like herself after that. The rest of the trip had been uneventful. Well, they'd had a close encounter with a brown bear and breathed a sigh of relief after they avoided two mama moose and their calves. Quinn was taking up the rear as they made their way to the airstrip. She could hear the whirr of the plane's prop in the distance. She glanced skyward and suddenly her vision blurred again. She stopped right where she was and shook her head. Just like the other day, her legs felt weak and one of them started tingling. "No, no, no, no," she mumbled to herself. She must have looked up too quickly. That's probably what happened the other morning. She ignored the weakness and tingling and started walking again. Her right leg wouldn't cooperate. She felt as if she was dragging it behind her. On sheer will alone, she kept trudging along the path.

Before she knew it, Quinn was at her side, catching her as she fell. His hold was so strong, steady and sure. She just let go because she couldn't hold herself up anymore. The last thing she remembered were Quinn's amber eyes locking onto hers. "You're okay. I've got you."

AVAILABLE NOW!

When We Fall

Go here to sign up for information on new releases: http://jhcroixauthor.com/subscribe/

Thank you for reading Stay With Me! I hope you enjoyed the story. If so, you can help other readers find my books in a variety of ways.

1) Write a review!

2) Sign up for my newsletter, so you can receive information about upcoming new releases & receive a FREE copy of one of my books: http://jhcroixauthor.com/subscribe/

3) Like and follow my Amazon Author page at https://amazon.com/author/jhcroix

4) Follow me on Bookbub at https://www.bookbub.com/authors/j-h-croix

5) Follow me on Twitter at https://twitter.com/JHCroix

6) Like my Facebook page at https://www.facebook.com/jhcroix

* * *

Last Frontier Lodge Novels
Christmas on the Last Frontier

Love at Last
Just This Once
Falling Fast
Stay With Me
When We Fall
Hold Me Close
Crazy For You
Into The Fire Series
Burn For Me
Slow Burn
Burn So Bad
Hot Mess
Burn So Good
Sweet Fire
Play With Fire
Melt With You
Burn For You
Crash & Burn
Swoon Series
This Crazy Love
Wait For Me
Break My Fall
Brit Boys Sports Romance
The Play
Big Win
Out Of Bounds
Play Me
Naughty Wish
Diamond Creek Alaska Novels
When Love Comes
Follow Love
Love Unbroken
Love Untamed
Tumble Into Love
Christmas Nights

Catamount Lion Shifters
Protected Mate
Chosen Mate
Fated Mate
Destined Mate
A Catamount Christmas
Ghost Cat Shifters
The Lion Within
Lion Lost & Found

ACKNOWLEDGMENTS

To my dogs who make life fun, to my hubby who keeps inspiring me, and to some feathered friends who have kept me laughing this summer. Always: my readers. Hugs and gracious thanks for your support!

xoxo

J.H. Croix

ABOUT THE AUTHOR

USA Today Bestselling Author J. H. Croix lives in a small town in the historical farmlands of Maine with her husband and two spoiled dogs. Croix writes contemporary romance with sassy women and alpha men who aren't afraid to show some emotion. Her love for quirky small-towns and the characters that inhabit them shines through in her writing. Take a walk on the wild side of romance with her best-selling novels!

Places you can find me:
jhcroixauthor.com
jhcroix@jhcroix.com

www.ingramcontent.com/pod-product-compliance
Lightning Source LLC
Chambersburg PA
CBHW050507190726
48284CB00003B/717